MY STORM

TIFFANY PATTERSON

PROLOGUE

asha
2006

"You better not say anything." The bulky prison guard sneers at me, gripping my arm.

I flinch at the pain, but I don't even look up at him to give him the satisfaction of knowing that he's hurting me. *Fuck him,* I think as I cut my eyes in the direction we're walking. We continue down the long hallway, my over-sized orange jumpsuit dragging against the linoleum floor. A ray of sunshine catches my eye, and I realize we're heading toward the front of the corrections facility. I haven't seen the front of the building since I first arrived about a month or two ago. Easy to lose track of time in a place like this. My curiosity finally takes over and I wonder out loud. "Where are we going?"

"You're leaving," he says matter-of-factly, pulling me toward the metal doors.

I squint in confusion. *"Leaving?"*

"That's what I said, ain't it? Or you could stay here. It's not like you won't wind up right back in this shithole. Your kind always do," he says sharply and then mumbles under his breath about what a waste all the girls in this place are. He presses the buzzer and waves to the

1

overhead camera to have the security guard in the control room release the door.

We pass through one sliding metal door and have to wait until the one behind us closes before the one in front of us opens. I swear, even though this is just a juvenile facility, they are clearly preparing inmates for life in an adult prison. The guard next to me remains silent, eyes on the door in front of us. My mind begins wandering.

Why am I being released? I couldn't afford bail. And there's no one I can think of who cares enough about me to post it. Where am I supposed to go? I can't go back to what I was doing before. I'll die before I do that shit again; a promise that I made to myself while I was in here.

The clicking of the door in front of us as it opens draws my attention and my heart begins palpitating. The guard roughly grabs my arm again and begins to pull me down another long hallway. I'm inclined to snatch it back, but I control my temper.

"You need to get your shit. You ain't have much on you besides some trampy clothing, a beat-up wallet, and a ratty notebook anyway."

"LaTasha Jenine Edwards," the guard behind the front counter reads my full name from an old school ID.

My eyes widen, hoping no one has touched my notebook. It's not worth much to others, but it's my prized possession. I open the envelope holding my meager belongings. The wallet is empty except for my ID. I know I had a twenty in here too, but I assume some guard took that because I don't see it. I hate that the money is gone. I flip through the pages of my notebook, happy to see it looks like it's still intact. Two photos spill out. The small piece of me that isn't numb inside blossoms with happiness. I look into the chocolate face of the woman, her skin wrinkled from time and life, but her eyes shine bright as she looks down at five-year-old me sitting on her lap. The picture behind it is one of me when I was a few years older, maybe around nine. It's me in a pair of pigtails. There's an older girl around sixteen with me. She has her arm protectively draped my shoulders. Her all-seeing eyes are a mixture of protectiveness and sadness. These two—the older woman and the younger one—are the only two people I know who've ever loved me. My grandmother and my older sister. The last one was a secret that I wasn't supposed to know about. One is dead now. The other... Well, I don't know where she is. She probably forgot all about me. But I'll never forget how she protected me as a kid. I swallow a lump in my throat as I wish she were here to help me now.

"Let's go." The guard gruffly pulls me out of my reverie and toward the entrance area to another door. Again, we wait for one door to close before the next one opens.

I work hard to shove the emotions that had just bubbled to the surface back down where they belong. The door in front of us slowly creeps open, and I am caught between wanting to sprint out of this hellhole or turning the other way to run back inside because I don't know what lies on the other side for me.

"Why the hell hasn't anyone tried to contact her family?!" a familiar, demanding voice inquires.

My heartbeat quickens, and the small vessel of hope I thought had been all but extinguished begins to grow in my chest. *It can't be.* We round the corner and I see her. She looks more mature than the last time I saw her, but those hazel eyes are still the same ones from the picture.

"Ma'am, we're going to need you to calm down," a male guard replies.

"The fact that you're still standing on two feet and not laid out is indication that I'm calm right now," she quips back with snarl. "She's been here six weeks and no one has tried to contact anyone for her? What was she arrested for?"

"Prostitution."

"*What?!*" she asks incredulously.

I close my eyes at the shame of that one word.

"Yup, girlie."

"Lieutenant," she cuts the smug guard off. "Lieutenant Coral Coleman of the United States Army, not girlie." She takes a step toward the guard, and I notice a man behind her move to intervene.

He's not a guard. The way he hovers protectively over Coral, I assume he's with her.

"Well, *Lieutenant*, the inmate whose release you're demanding was arrested for prostitution."

Another pang of guilt seizes my chest. The guard nor Coral have noticed us yet.

"She's fucking seventeen years old. You find a seventeen year old out on the street…" She pauses as if her next words are hard to say. "If she was *prostituting*, was locking her up your only solution?! Where's my sister?" she demands.

At this point, it looks as if Coral is ready to tear this place down brick by brick. And the tall, good-looking man with the green eyes behind her looks like he'd help her.

"C-Coral," I call out shakily, still shocked she is actually here.

She turns those intense hazel eyes on me, and I see something I haven't seen in a long time from anyone. Concern. If I could still feel my heart, I think it'd be breaking right now.

"Tasha," she whispers as she comes toward me.

It's the first time I've heard someone call my name with any type of emotion besides disdain in a long time. Within seconds, I am enveloped in strong arms. Although I haven't felt them in years, her arms are just as comforting as they were when I was seven years old and she hugged me after beating up a couple kids who were bullying me. My first reaction is to pull away, feeling dirty, shame, and then anger.

A frown forms on her face when I push out of her embrace. I avoid her gaze, looking over her shoulder at the man who obviously came with her.

"What happened to her?" she asks as she pulls back and stares at the ugly bruise around my right eye. I look back at her to see she's still looking at me, but the question is directed at the guard behind me.

He shrugs his shoulders. "Fight."

I roll my eyes at his lie, but I remain silent.

Coral looks up and her eyes narrow as if she can tell he's lying. She's always been good at reading others. She turns her eyes back on me. "Let's go. You won't ever be back here again." She gives the guard behind me another hard glare before tapping me on the shoulder and jutting her head toward the door, signaling that it's time to go. The man who is with her comes over to us.

"Tasha, this is my friend Liam. Liam, this is Tasha, my sister," she introduces.

"Nice to meet you, Tasha," he greets me friendly. The hard stare he gave the guards has transformed into a friendly smile when he looks at me. He's handsome and by the grin he gives me, I can tell he's a charmer. But still, I don't know this guy, and very few men have been nice to me without wanting something in return. So I hesitate to return his greeting.

"Hey," I say as I give him a small wave.

"Come on," Coral encourages me, and we walk toward the door. "It's a few hours drive back to the city. Do you want to get something to eat before we head out?"

"Back to the city?" I pull up short. My eyebrows almost touch my forehead. That is the last place I want to return to.

Coral must see the terror in my eyes. She steps in front of me, gripping my shoulders. "I've rented a hotel suite for the next couple of days. We're not going back to the Bronx. It'll be okay," she reassures.

I begin to wonder if she knows the whole story about how I ended up here. "I-I thought you forgot about me," I confess out of nowhere, biting my tongue so I don't spill anymore of my fears.

She begins massaging my shoulders consolingly. This time I don't recoil from her touch. It's the first one in years that doesn't send a wave a nausea through me.

"I've looked for you for a long time. I could never forget about you. I made you a promise. I failed at keeping it, but now that I've found you I won't let anything happen to you. Okay?"

Her words hit me dead center and all my emotions come rushing to the surface at once. I look up at her through watery eyes and nod, unable to form words. It takes a moment but I manage to swallow them down, regaining my composure. We catch up with Liam who is waiting beside a white Mercedes. I've only seen cars this nice from afar. I'm shocked when Coral presses the button to unlock the doors.

She must notice the surprise on my face and tosses me a half smile. "It was a graduation gift," she says, tilting her head toward Liam who is on the passenger side.

"Maybe she'll let you drive it." He grins.

"Not until she gets her license. Get in." Coral holds the back door open for me.

I climb in the backseat. As we pull off, the sense of relief I feel magnifies the further we get from that awful facility. I gaze up at the sky and wonder what happens next, but I'm too tired to think for too long. I can't remember the last time I'd felt safe enough to sleep more than a few hours at a time. Soon, I relax and rest my head on the back seat and drift off into a deep sleep, feeling safer than I had in a long time. My big sis has come for me.

* * *

I STEP out of the bathroom of the luxurious hotel suite with the softest towel I have ever felt wrapped around my body. Another one is on my head, absorbing the water from my wet hair. It's been a long time since I've had a decent shower. I'm pretty sure I stayed under the hot water spray for over an hour.

"Tasha," Coral calls through the closed bedroom door. "I have a change of clothes for you."

I pad over to the door and open it ever so slightly.

She holds up the clothes for me to see. "Can I come in?"

I nod and open the door a little wider, allowing Coral entrance. I look over her shoulder for her friend, Liam, who's here with us, but I don't see him.

"Li picked these up from the store and went to go get something to eat. It's late and room service is closed for the night," she explains.

I take the pair of sweatpants, T-shirt, and panties from her hand, embarrassed to think that her friend even bought me a pack of underwear. Coral turns her back to me, giving me some privacy to dress. Once I'm done, I sit on the bed.

Coral walks over to me and points to the towel on my head. "Can I?" she asks.

I notice the hairbrush and comb along with other hair products. I nod, grateful for her consideration in asking. I'm pretty sure she can tell I'm squeamish about being touched. In spite of my usual displeasure of being touched by others, I sigh at the comforting feel of my sister's fingers in my hair.

"I've missed you, Tash. Where were you living?"

I lower my head and shrug. "Mama moved us to Virginia for a while after Nana died. From there we moved to Atlanta and then back to Virginia before she disappeared."

"How long has she been gone?"

I shrug again. "Close to four years, I guess."

"You've been on your own this whole time?"

I remain silent, not wanting to admit everything that's happened to me in the last four years. Just thinking about it makes me want to climb right back in the shower and scrub my skin until it's raw.

"We have a few more days to talk. You don't have to tell me everything now. But..." She pauses uncharacteristically, seemingly unsure of her next words. "I think you should let me tell my aunt and uncle about you. That way you can stay with them—"

"No!" I yell, standing. "I don't want them to know about me. They're not even my relatives. They're *yours*."

"I know, but they're really good people and I know they wouldn't mind taking you in. You can't be on your own again, Tasha," she states emphatically.

"Fine. But why can't I stay with *you*? You came back for me, so why can't I just come live with you?"

My sister sighs heavily before answering, "Tash, I'm only in the States for a few more days."

"Why?" I croak, feeling a band of cold seize my chest. I thought I had found some type of solace. I should've known it wouldn't last.

"I'm only on a two-week leave. I've spent seven of those days looking for you. Exactly six days from today I'll be on a plane back to Iraq."

"*Iraq?*" I ask astonished and frightened.

Coral rises from the bed to stand in front of me. "Yes. I'm in the middle of a twelve-month tour."

This time I don't even bother to stop the rush of tears that springs from my eyes. I can't believe it. Just when I thought I would be okay, my one lifeline is telling me she has to leave again and go back to a war zone no less. While I was in juvie I watched the news a lot whenever they let us. Every other day it seemed like they were reporting on a new bombing or more U.S. soldiers that were killed in the line of duty.

"It's dangerous over there. Do you have to go back?" I question, knowing the answer but hoping against hope she'd tell me she'd stay with me.

"Tash, I have to go back. Otherwise, I'll be AWOL and eventually, arrested. Plus I promised—"

"You made a promise to me too!" I spit out angrily. "You said you'd always look out for me, but you've been gone! I was all alone." My whole body begins to vibrate with anger and fear.

"I know, sis. I'm sorry. I never stopped looking for you, though. Not once," she adds, squeezing my shoulder.

I stare up into her hazel eyes and the tense set of her jaw. I know she is telling the truth.

"That's why I want you to live with my aunt and uncle. They'd be there for you in my absence. And we could tell Stacey. You don't have to be alone."

"I don't want them to know," I say shakily, wiping a few tears from my eyes and snot from my nose. I can't think of anyone who'd want me. I'm tainted. My own mother and father didn't want me. Of course, no one else would either.

"I thought you might say that." She pauses. "I've done some research on a place. They take in young girls who've been in your situation."

"You mean like a foster home or something?" I question skeptically.

"No. It's nothing like a foster home. This place is based in Central Massachusetts and it's run by a couple of nuns. They have counselors, job training, and a place where you can finish school. You didn't graduate, right?"

I shake my head. "No. Mama pulled me out of school to move. Then we kept moving so much that I fell so far behind until I just stopped even trying."

"Do you still write and draw?"

I nod and motion to the notebook that I took out of the envelope that contained my belongings at the facility.

Coral looks at the notebook and turns back to me, grinning. "See, at this place you could take classes on creative writing, earn your diploma, and maybe go on to get your degree if you want. I've already checked it out. They take in about five girls a year, but you get your own room with a lock and key. Meals are served family style, and most of all, you don't have to be afraid. I'll call every week when I can and I've already created an email account for you, so you can email me whenever you want once I leave." She pulls out a small business card.

Haven House, I read silently from the card scripted with big, purple letters. The address, phone number, and website address are listed on it as well. I flip the card over, and the insignia is of two hands holding a smaller one. *Put your hand in ours and we'll never let it go*, again I read the back of the card in silence.

Coral hands me another piece of paper with the email address she's created for me. For the first time in a long time, a hint of a smile appears on my face. The paper reads BXGirl1988. The BX is for the Bronx, the New York borough we were born and raised in, and 1988 is the year of my birth. I think of all the planning it took not only for her to find me, but to set me up with all of this.

"You never forgot about me?" I croak, still looking at the card in my hand.

"Not once," she states adamantly.

9

"Tell me more about this place," I whisper.

"Let me finish your hair as I tell you."

I nod, sitting back down on the huge bed facing the mirror. Coral sits behind me, legs splayed apart, so I can fit between them for her to do my hair. This position reminds me of so many girls I remember sitting between their mother's legs getting their hair done. My mother never took that kind of time with me. My nana took care of all my grooming needs as a child. I look over Coral's mocha skin and slim yet toned physique, comparing it to my dark chocolate skin and plump body. I was teased as a child because of my complexion and body. I enjoy the gentle way Coral massages my scalp, moisturizing it and my hair before combing out the knots from the ends to the roots. It eliminates some of the pain and soothes me. As she does my hair, she continues to tell me about Haven House. It's far enough from the city, out in a rural area surrounded by lots of nature. They specialize in treating adolescent girls and young women who've endured past trauma. The facility is funded by a federal grant.

I remain silent, listening to everything she says and I come to realize this is my chance for a better future. I know going to Haven House is the next step in moving past these last horrific four years and the pretty shitty thirteen years prior to it. With that realization, I take a deep breath and close my eyes, reveling in the knowledge that this might be the start of a whole new life.

"Okay, I'll go," I say, cutting her off after making my decision. Through the mirror I see the relief on her face. It matches my own feelings.

CHAPTER 1

*J*eremy

"Get on your knees," I command in a low but sharp voice. I watch as the dark blue laced bodysuit that barely encases her full-figured body stretches and moves as her knees sink to the carpet. She peers up at me with those golden eyes, and my heart begins to beat erratically. I've been in this position many times before and have never felt the rush of energy I'm feeling now.

"You know you disobeyed me, right?" I question, making sure my voice is leveled and controlled.

"Yes, sir."

"And what happens when you disobey?"

"Punishment, sir."

I nod. "That's right. Subs who disobey are punished. Eyes on the floor. Don't look at me and don't move."

She complies instantly. Her submission causes a stir in my groin. I move around her, walking over to my closet filled with toys; many of which are meant for occasions such as this.

"Let's see. I would normally use my hand for punishment, but I think you need a little more stimulation tonight." I run my fingers over my leather flogger before grabbing it off the hook. "This will do." I stroll back over to the

woman with the killer curves and skin the color of midnight. I lick my lips, wanting desperately to taste every inch of that skin, but first she must learn her lesson.

"I never understood why parents tell their children that physical punishment will hurt them more than it will hurt the child before they inflict pain. Now, I know. Present yourself like I taught you," I instruct.

At my words, she bends over onto all fours, presenting her plump bottom to me. I am so tempted to reach out and grip it intimately. But not this time. My sub is still in training. If I falter now, she will never learn the rules.

"You will count each strike of the flogger out loud. Do you hear me?"

"Y-yes, sir."

"Begin counting."

Beep! Beep! Beep!

The loud noise pierce through the scene, shattering the silence.

"What the fuck?!" I groan, groggily, rubbing my eyes awake. I open my eyes to look over at the nightstand where my cell phone is beeping due to my early morning six o'clock alarm. "Shit!" I reach over, realizing it was just another dream. Another restless night dreaming about *her*. Shit has been this way for months.

"Good morning, lover," a soft feminine voice behind me purrs as I turn off my alarm.

I turn my gaze over my shoulder to see Stephanie's brown eyes and smiling face. Her caramel complexion is glowing even after all the activity we did last night. I kept her up half the night. *And I still can't stop dreaming about someone else,* I admonish myself as I push the sheets off me and rise to sit on the edge of the bed.

"Morning," I return.

"You're an early riser. *He* must be ready for another round," Stephanie says, reaching around to grab my stiff cock that is indeed already awake. Too bad it's this way for a woman who's not currently here in my bed. I grab her hand, halting her movement.

"Not now," I say, standing.

"Jeremy, you're obviously in need of a release. I can help with that," she says, coming to stand in front of me. "Let me make you feel good before your workout."

Before I can react, she's on her knees, pulling down my boxer briefs. Ordinarily, I would stop her for disobeying me, but she's not one of my subs and I do need a release after the dream I've just had. I wind my hand into her hair and tug as she begins bobbing up and down on my cock. I close my eyes and envision another woman on her knees in front of me doing this very act. I tighten my grip on her hair and give myself over to the pleasure of her warm mouth on me. Within minutes I cum and I release into her mouth. Opening my eyes, I'm disappointed to not see the woman in my imagination in front of me.

Stephanie stands, completely nude in front of me. Her smooth skin, perky breasts and flat tummy would turn any man on. "Let's finish this in the shower," she purrs, stepping around me. I turn to watch her sashay toward the bathroom. I shrug and follow her, knowing I still need more of a release after yet another night of dreaming about a woman I can't have.

"Will I see you at the club this weekend?" she asks, once we finish showering and she begins dressing in the clothes she wore over the night before.

I remember the club she's referring to. It's not my usual scene, but this weekend is a special night. "Maybe. I'm going out of town this week." I give her a hard stare when I see she's about to pout.

"Okay. Maybe I'll see you there."

"Maybe." I nod. "Let's go."

* * *

A FEW HOURS LATER, after a workout and yet another shower, I'm on my way from the downtown hotel where I entertain overnight guests, heading to the outskirts of the city. It takes about forty minutes to get to my destination in rush hour traffic, but my aggravation is worth the drive this morning. I need my cousin, Liam, and the CEO of our company, Bennett Industries, to sign some documents before I can leave for my trip this afternoon. When I pull up to the wrought iron gate, I roll my window down so the scanner can scan my face. Once

I'm recognized, the gate automatically unlocks and allows my entrance. I drive up toward the huge mansion Liam had built especially for the love of his life. I smirk as I remember him painstakingly going over all the details with his architect long before he even knew how his situation with Coral would work out.

I park in front of the door and climb out to ring the bell. But before my finger reaches it, the door opens. I frown at the man who greets me.

"You can't put a goddamn shirt on before answering the door?" I ask Liam.

"It's *my* damn house. I'll answer the door naked if I damn well please. Shit, you're lucky I put sweatpants on. CeCe and I just finished a yoga session," he says, wiggling his eyebrows.

I grunt and step inside as I get the meaning behind his words. "Anyway, I need you to sign these before I head out to Arizona," I inform him, slapping the folder stuffed with papers against his bare chest. "What you got to eat around here?" I push through the door, strolling down the hallway toward the kitchen. My nostrils are hit by the smell of bacon, eggs, and toast.

"Good morning, Ms. Mary," I greet, pressing a kiss to her dark, soft cheek.

The older woman is Liam's former nanny who now works part-time for him even though she's supposed to be retired.

"Good morning, Jeremy. Long time no see. Work keeping you busy?" she asks, preparing a plate for me.

"Yes, ma'am. Liam is working me to death."

"Shut up, you bum," Liam says as he enters the kitchen.

"Have a seat," Ms. Mary demands, setting my plate down on the counter.

Before I can sit down, Liam's four-year-old daughter rounds the corner, sees me, and yells, "Uncle Jeremy!" Then she sprints over to me.

I pick her up and place a big kiss on her cheek.

"Hey, don't kiss my daughter first thing in the morning. Who the hell knows where those lips were last night."

"Or this morning," I retort, winking.

Liam glares at me, and I laugh as I pick up a toothpick from the counter and place it in the side of my mouth. I carry Laura over to her chair where Ms. Mary has already put her plate on the placemat.

"I could tell you all about the woman I had last night," I say low in Liam's ear before I strut back to the counter. "I mean, now that you're a married man and all you might want a few pointers on how to keep your woman satisfied," I continue.

"I've got that covered, you jackass. Otherwise, she wouldn't be walking around here with her belly full of—"

"Good morning."

Liam's tirade is interrupted by his wife's greeting.

I turn to stare at Coral. Her mocha skin is glowing against her yellow sundress. Her short cropped hairstyle, with an auburn-tinted top, shows off her high cheek bones. Her baby bump is evident underneath the dress.

"Hey, Jer. How're you this morning?" she asks.

"I'm good, but apparently not as good as you and your husband. He was just informing me how he keeps you satisfied as evident by your expanding belly." I smirk.

Coral's eyes narrow as she glares back and forth between her husband and me. Liam simply shrugs and pulls her in for a kiss.

"Get off me." She pushes him away lightly. "Anyway, what are you doing here this morning?" she asks, moving away from Liam and goes over to Laura who is thoroughly enjoying her pancakes. Coral begins putting two braids in Laura's hair, preparing her to be picked up by her nanny.

"Liam needs to sign some papers on the Tucson project. I'm heading out there today."

Coral nods with her back to me. I pick up a glass of fresh squeezed orange juice that Ms. Mary placed by my plate.

"How's it going out there?" Liam questions.

"We're a little behind schedule, which is why I'm heading out there earlier than expected. I need to speak with the head designer. I have a feeling he's trying to cut costs on some shit, but I've got it handled. I just need you to sign those damn papers so I can do what I need to." I point at Liam.

He nods. "We'll need to—"

"Ugh! I suck. Everything I write is awful!" A feminine, exasperated voice shrieks and the back kitchen door that leads outside is suddenly opens, cutting Liam off.

Every inch of my body comes alive in a way it hadn't been just a few seconds ago. I only see her from behind as she immediately goes over to stand in front of Coral. I take in the baggy T-shirt that's unable to hide the luscious curves of her backside covered in a pair of black leggings. The same backside I envisioned bent over ready to receive the thrashes from my flogger as I'd dreamt just this morning. I'm surprised to see her feet are bare.

"I wrote 5,000 words yesterday and deleted them all this morning because they were terrible. How could I even think I could be a writer?" The strain and doubt in her voice makes me want to reach out and comfort her.

"Tasha," Coral begins calmly. "You're a phenomenal writer. I'm sure whatever you wrote wasn't terrible. You should've let Laura and me take a look at it before you deleted it." Coral looks down at Laura.

"Yeah, Aunt Tasha, I wanna see what Danica is going to do next!" Laura agrees excitedly.

"So do I, sweetie, but I suck!" she retorts.

Coral frowns. "Tasha, stop. You don't want to teach Laura that type of language."

"I'm sorry. I'm just so frustrated. Freaking months of writer's block is killing me!" She waves her hands in the air and turns, finally seeing me staring at her intently.

Her demeanor immediately changes. She lowers her hands, cupping them in front of her. "Oh, I'm sorry. I didn't know we had company," She pauses her rant. "Good morning, Liam. Jeremy." She nods at me before her eyes dart back over to Coral and then back on me.

Something happens in my chest when she says my name and I

have to fight to keep my eyes on her face and not scan the rest of her body. "Good morning, LaTasha."

I see her inhale when I greet her by her full name. I've done that ever since I found out Tasha was just a short name for LaTasha.

"How about this?" Coral interrupts our stare off. "Why don't you come with me to the community center for the day? You've been cooped up inside for weeks trying to write. Some fresh air would do you some good. The children love gardening with you."

Tasha peels her eyes from me. "I-I think that would be good. I do miss them," she admits on a sigh. "Let me go change," she says, scurrying toward the door while avoiding eye contact with me.

I notice Coral glare at me before she turns to Laura. "Come on, princess. Let's go get your stuff for your swim lesson today. Afterwards, your nanny will drop you off at the community center where you can spend the rest of the day with me and Aunt Tasha."

"Yay!" Laura says, clapping. "Bye, Daddy," she cheers, running over to Liam to place a kiss on his cheek when he picks her up.

"Bye, princess."

"Bye, Li." Coral kisses Liam.

He wraps his arms around her waist before she can pull back. "Bye, Cece. Be good for Mommy," he says to the baby inside her belly.

"Yeah right... This kid acts like he can't sit still." Corals grins.

"*He?*" I question once Coral leaves the room.

Liam nods like the proud dad he is. "We found out awhile ago, but you've been um, *traveling* a lot for work lately."

I can hear the skepticism in his tone, and as if that wasn't enough, the damn smirk on his face tells me he's pulling my damn leg. I hate that shit.

"Care to tell me what's been so important that it's kept you away for the last five months or so?"

I narrow my gaze at him. "The same thing that's always been up —*work.*"

That goofy grin on his face grows even wider as he looks at something over my shoulder. "Yeah, work...or some*thing* else," he suggests pointedly, his eyes continuing to follow whatever it is behind me.

I don't even have to look to know *who* he's referring to. *I don't have to look*, I silently tell myself even has my head turns on its own volition to watch LaTasha make her way from the guesthouse down the trail that sidesteps the back entrance to the kitchen. She winds around the entire exterior of the house, heading toward the front. She has changed into a pair of jean shorts, another T-shirt, and tennis shoes. Her kinky tresses are thrown up in a messy bun. The sun hits her perfectly smooth, dark skin beautifully at every angle. I watch her as she passes by the kitchen windows until she is no longer in sight. That's when my eyes collide with a pair of green eyes that look just like mine except they contain a hint of mirth.

"You know Coral's going to kick your ass, right?" Liam asks with a warning.

I grin at him to cover my agitation. "Why would she do that? She figured out she married the wrong Bennett?"

"You fucking wish," he retorts defensively.

Nothing gets Liam more pissed than the thought of his wife not being with him.

"CeCe is very protective of Tasha."

"And?"

"And I'm ready to watch the fireworks when you finally decide to make your move. It's gonna be better than any 4th of July show I've ever been to."

"There won't be a show because I'm not going to make any moves. LaTasha is off-limits," I state sternly.

"Why is that?"

"Why is what?" I pretend to not know where this line of questioning is going.

"Don't play stupid. Why is she off limits?"

"She's practically family. Plus she couldn't handle...me," I explain.

I'll admit I've had this attraction for LaTasha ever since the first time I laid eyes on her. I've spent many nights dreaming about her and waking up with a stiff cock, tortured by the memory of holding her in my arms the one time we danced at Liam and Coral's wedding. But there is something about her. I can tell she's been hurt in the past and well, I'm not an easy lover. Being with me the way I would want her would push her past her limits. So I hold back. I do my best to avoid her and I spend my time with other women who aren't what I really want just to get a small bit of relief.

Liam looks at me seriously. "Tasha's no shrinking violet. She's been through a lot, but she's tough." He pauses and then that goofy grin returns. "Plus I doubt either one of you will have a choice. Sometimes the inevitable is just *inevitable.*"

I roll my eyes at Liam's cheesy bullshit. "You know you were more tolerable when you didn't have Coral and you were a lot more cynical about life. I'm starting to regret the part I played in helping you get her back."

Liam throws his head back and laughs at my comment before standing and coming over to me. He places his hand on my shoulder. "Oh, there's going to be fireworks indeed." He chuckles some more. "Let me shower and get dressed and then we'll discuss these documents. You should heat up your breakfast. It's cold by now." He gestures toward my now cold plate of food.

I shake my head as he leaves and I rise to reheat my food in the microwave. Liam may be smart, but he's wrong about this. LaTasha and I aren't meant to be. *I just need to find a way to keep her out of my dreams at night and I'll be fine,* I think as I sit down at the table with my warmed up breakfast and begin eating.

CHAPTER 2

*T*asha

I look over at the dark blue Lexus SUV parked in front of the door and immediately, thoughts of the owner of the vehicle float to mind. Those sparkling green eyes that are often laced with humor but belie a dark intensity that rattles me deep inside. This morning I had no idea he was here when I burst into the kitchen on what has become a usual tirade complaining about the writer's block that has gripped me as of late. When I finally noticed him staring at me so intently, I was sure he was thinking I was crazy. It took all my willpower not to turn and run out of the door and hide in the guesthouse. Well, I should probably stop calling it the guesthouse seeing as how it became my *permanent* residence when I moved from Vermont down to Dallas to be closer to Coral while she's expecting.

"You ready?" Coral startles me out of my thoughts.

I jump hearing her voice behind me. "Yeah." I clear my throat. "Yup, I'm ready."

"You sure you're okay?" she asks curiously.

"I'm fine."

She stares at me for awhile, trying to read me.

I hate when she does that. "Don't do that."

"*What?*"

"You know what. You're treating me like I'm one of your suspects or something; trying to read me for any trace of deception."

"Trace of deception?" Coral raises an eyebrow, smirking.

I lower my head and grin. "Yeah. I've been doing research for a character. One who reads people's body language and that term comes up frequently."

"Listen to you sounding like Harriet the Spy," she teases.

"Shut up," I retort.

"Let's go. Mitch is meeting us at the front gate," she grumbles as we both climb into her Mercedes.

It's not the same Mercedes she had ten years ago. This one is a newer version of the car Liam bought her as a graduation gift. Mitch is Coral's security guard anytime she leaves home. It's been months, but she's still pissed that Liam is forcing her to travel everywhere with security.

"How's it going with Mitch these days?" I question, knowing it will lead to a rant.

She snorts. "I can't believe Li is still doing this. Don't get me wrong. Mitch is a good guy and all, but I can take care of myself."

That's what she always says. And I'm sure there isn't a person alive who has met Coral and doesn't realize she's capable of handling herself. I've no doubt that the very car we're riding in has no less than two weapons at her immediate disposal. But I am grateful my brother-in-law takes such good care of her even if it ruffles her feathers a little bit.

"Everyone knows you can take care of yourself, but you also deserve to be taken care of. No one does that better than Liam Bennett."

"Whatever," she says, rolling her eyes as we turn onto the highway that will lead us to the community center where she's the director. Mitch is right behind us in his dark SUV.

Although, I'm looking out the window, I can feel Coral's eyes on me.

"What?"

"That was an unexpected surprise this morning," she says, catching me off guard.

"What was?"

"Don't play dumb. I know you didn't burst in the kitchen expecting to see *Jeremy*."

I shrug nonchalantly. "No, he's not there most mornings. Why would I have expected him to be there today?"

"No reason. Just making conversation. That was the first time you've seen him in how long?"

One month, two weeks, and three days. "I don't know. Maybe it's been a few weeks, I guess."

I can tell Coral knows I'm lying, but being the dutiful sister she is, she doesn't call me on it. The truth is I have every encounter with Jeremy committed to memory. From the first time I saw him standing next to Liam as they waited for Coral to walk down the aisle they'd set up in their backyard for the second wedding ceremony in the presence of all their family and friends. I remember the way the sun glinted off his dark brown hair that he let flow freely. Even today I recall the way his jaw moved as he worked the ever-present toothpick on the side of his mouth. I remember later that day how I felt like I was falling into an abyss as he held me the one time we danced together. Strangely, the usual recoil I have when meeting someone new, especially a *man*, wasn't there. His embrace felt *natural*. I can even recollect the sadness I felt when I saw him a month later, and he'd cut his hair so that it only fell to his chin.

"Earth to Tasha," Coral interrupts my fantasizing. "You in there?"

"Y-yeah. What were you saying?"

"I was saying we're here." She frowns at me.

I turn and indeed, we're parked in front of the community center. "Oh." I avoid eye contact with Coral, unfasten my seatbelt, and get out of the car.

She is still frowning at me even as Mitch opens her door for her and helps her out of the car. "Thank you," she says.

"Hey, Ms. Coral and Ms. Tasha," a couple of the younger kids greet us when we first enter.

It's the beginning of July, so the kids are all out of school for the summer and many of them love nothing more than spending their days here for our day camp.

"Good morning, Jayshawn and Michael," Coral and I greet the boys.

Once they leave, I follow Coral to her office. When she turns the lights on, the first thing I see on her wall is a huge poster of the cover of my first book, "Danica's Odyssey." Right next to it is a poster of the second book cover, "Danica's Quest" and then the cover for "Danica's Conquest", my third book. I knew the posters were there because I've been to Coral's office a number of times in the last few months. But seeing them always startles me. I stare at the posters for a few seconds, my pride turning into a somber feeling as I think about the writer's block I've been experiencing over the last few months. I've been writing and making up stories since I first learned to write at the age of five and I've never experienced anything like this. I have no idea how to handle it.

"Hey, you're not supposed to be thinking about writing right now. You're here to help out with the kids," Coral reminds me.

"I know, but it just sucks. I hate this," I say, feeling like a failure.

"I know, but it'll work out. You just moved across the country not too long ago. Maybe you just need time to adjust to your new surroundings."

I shrug. "Maybe that's it. I doubt it, though." I don't tell Coral that I suspect there's another reason behind my writer's block.

"How about you do the reader's circle this afternoon? They're almost finished "Danica's Odyssey" and they absolutely can't get enough of it."

I smirk at that. The reader's circle is for the kids ages nine to about twelve years old and it takes place in the midafternoon right before they're picked up to go home. I've read from my book for them before. The interesting part is no one here except Coral actually knows I'm the author of the Danica series. I write under a pen name and I've made it clear to my agent and publisher that I wish to remain anonymous. I haven't done the usual promotional tours, bookstore signings, or anything else that requires face-to-face interaction. Still, even with my reluctance to get out there in person, Danica's book series has sold like hotcakes. Despite the great sales, I've been getting even more of a push from my agent to step out from behind the books and show my face.

"Earth to Tasha," Coral summons again.

"Sorry. I did it again." I grin. I have a tendency to get lost in my own thoughts even while in mid conversation. I think it's the writer in me. I spend so much time in my head that it becomes habitual to forget others are around.

"I'm used to it. Let's go. I've got to stop by the classrooms and different groups before I get a swim in with the older kids."

I nod and follow Coral out. I watch her do her thing, conferring with the teachers and staff who work there during the summer, before she heads off to her office to change into her bathing suit and shorts to swim with the older kids. I watch her retreating back. This is a huge difference from her previous job of running all over the world trying to save it, but she's taken to it like a fish to water. I have to confess I'm so relieved too. I hated the thought of Coral being in such danger at all times. Life's not guaranteed to any of us, but at least she's safer now, and I know Liam will do his best to protect her at all times. I smile at that thought just as I spot Mitch following Coral toward the pool.

* * *

"Are you going to read to us now, Ms. Tasha?" Lucy, one of the children asks as we finish up our lunch.

I grin at the bit of ranch dressing she has on her cheek from the salad she just scarfed down. "Yes, Lucy." I laugh, handing her a napkin to wipe her face. I turn the lights in the lunchroom down low and take my seat toward the front while the children move closer.

I pick up the book to see where they have left off in the story. Each day a different counselor or teacher reads to them a bit after lunch to calm them down before their parents pick them up.

"Oh, this is one of my favorite parts. Danica's in big trouble since the wizard has stolen her ability to see into the future," I say out loud.

"But you haven't been here in forever, Ms. Tasha. How do you know what happened to Danica?" one of the children asks, catching me off guard.

"Are you kidding me? I've been reading on my own. I love reading about Danica," I explain, covering the fact that I'm the one who actually wrote the book. The name of the author on the cover reads "L.T. Jones." L.T. is for LaTasha, but Jones is my grandmother's last name. I chose it to pay homage to the woman who first encouraged my love of reading and writing. "Okay, let's get started. I'm excited to see how she's going to fix this."

I begin reading, getting lost in the world of science fiction, featuring a young girl with afro puffs and skin the color of a dark chocolate Hershey's bar just like mine. I begin reading, remembering the different stages I went through when I first started writing this book. I laugh at some of the funny parts right along with the children and get sucked into the sad parts like when Danica finally remembers the night her parents were killed. I lose all track of time, and when I look up from the book, I notice that most of the older children are watching me just as enthralled as the younger students. It's not just them either. Most of the teachers and counselors are standing around the lunch room watching and listening attentively as well. Even Coral is amongst them. I give her a half grin before lowering my head. I may hate the idea of being publicly known as the author, but I'll never get over the feeling of pure joy at seeing people enjoy the words I've written.

"Okay, guys that's where we'll leave it today," I say, sticking the bookmark inside and closing the book. *My book.*

"Awwww," the children whine.

"Will you be back tomorrow to read to us? We love it when you read to us, Ms. Tasha?" Jayshawn asks excitedly.

I give Coral a look before turning back to him. "Sure, I'll be back tomorrow," I agree. *It's not like I've been able to write.*

I might as well spend my time here. I spend twenty-minutes

helping the children pack up all their stuff and prepare themselves to leave for the day. When there are only a handful of children left, most of whom are with their parents talking to their counselors, I notice a girl, who looks to be about twelve years old, waiting by herself. I've seen her here on occasion before. Out of the corner of my eye, I see Coral talking to a group of her staff, so instead of asking her about the girl, I wander over to her. I don't know what has drawn me to her nor do I question it.

"Hi," I greet her.

Dark brown eyes peer up at me suspiciously. Her golden-brown skin looks a little flushed from the summer heat. "Hey," she returns and then looks off.

"It's hot out here. Do you want to sit inside in the air conditioner while you wait?"

"No. I'm fine."

"Okay. Well, here's a bottle of water to help. I just got it from inside and brought it out for me, but it looks like you could use it. It's unopened. See, the seal hasn't been broken." I show her that the seal is indeed still intact.

She eyes me and then eyes the bottle for a moment. I wonder how long she's been out here waiting to be picked up. Finally, she grabs the bottle and opens it after some effort. She gulps half the bottle down in a few swallows. For some reason, I start to feel an ache in my chest for the little girl who I've suddenly become drawn to. She reminds me of someone...someone who used to wait outside of school sometimes for hours because their mother had forgotten about them.

"I'm Ms. Tasha. I don't think we've met. I'm Ms. Coral's sis... uh... *friend*," I introduce. "What's your name?"

"Trudy," she answers before taking another sip of water.

"Do you want another bottle of water?" I ask as she finishes the first one.

Trudy looks at the empty bottle as if she's just realized the water is all gone. Then she looks back at me and nods.

"Okay. Hang on." I dash inside to the kitchen and grab two more bottles of water, an apple, and an orange from the fridge. "Here," I say, passing the water and fruit to Trudy, while keeping one of the bottles for myself. "Did you enjoy story time today?" I attempt to make conversation as we wait.

"It was cool." She shrugs.

"Have you read any of Danica's stories before?"

"Nah. I just heard them here. I liked the part where she tricked the wizard into thinking she was bigger than she was and was able to stop him," she says, becoming excited. But before she gets too wrapped up in her excitement, she deflates. "It's cool." She shrugs.

I nod. "I liked that part too. Will you be back tomorrow? I'll be reading again."

"I dunno. If my mama can bring me, I guess I will."

"Well, I hope you'll be here. I think we might finish the book."

Her eyes widen just a bit, and I can tell she's interested, but she quickly recovers. Before I can get another word out, a honking horn grabs her attention and mine.

"Trudy! Come on, girl. I ain't got all day!" a woman in the passenger's seat yells out.

Trudy quickly grabs her belongings along with the water and fruit. "Bye." She waves.

"Bye, Trudy. I'll see you tomorrow."

She looks at me and gives the faintest smile before turning and running to the dark red vehicle. She climbs in the back seat and before she's even had time to fasten her seatbelt, the car pulls off. I watch as the car heads down the street and rounds the corner, a sad feeling growing in my chest.

"Hey. I've got some paperwork to do in my office for a little while and then Laura's nanny will drop her off here. We'll probably go to the children's museum for a little bit. You cool with hanging out or I can take you home?" Coral asks, coming up behind me.

"I'll hang out with you guys for the day. Laura's lucky to have a mom like you," I say, remembering how the woman I suspect was Trudy's mother had treated her just a few minutes earlier.

"I'm not her mother. I'm just..." Coral trails off.

"Yeah, yeah..."

We've had this discussion before when Coral told me that Liam had brought up the issue of her possibly adopting Laura.

"I'll read on my tablet while you work and wait for Laura out here. Oh, before I forget, Stacey is coming next week for a visit," Coral informs me.

My eyes widen as I look at my sister. "For what?"

Stacey is Coral's younger sister and my other older sister; only she doesn't know about me.

"She has a work conference to attend here in Dallas and she'll extend her trip a few days to visit." She shrugs as if it's no big deal. "Maybe this time you can actually talk with her and you know...tell her the *truth*." She gives me an expectant look as if waiting for me to say something.

For months, Coral has been trying to get me to reveal the truth to Stacey.

"Tash, I know you're scared and nervous, but Stacey is the least judgmental person you'll come across. She's a social worker for God's sake. And you don't have to tell her everything all at once."

I wince at the word *everything*. Naturally, I don't want to tell Stacey or anyone else about my tragic past. But looking at my sister whose eyes now shine with empathy, I remember she's the only living person in my life who I've trusted since I was a child.

"Alright, Coral, let me think about it." I grin when her expression turns hopeful. I even laugh, realizing how much more expressive with her emotions she's become since marrying Liam. Then again, it might just be pregnancy hormones. "I'm not making any guarantees," I hedge. "I'm just *thinking* about it."

"That's more than you've offered to do in the past, so I'll take it. Alright. Let me go get some work done, so when Laura gets here we can head out."

CHAPTER 3

Tasha

"Dammit!" I yell as I toss yet another shitty sketch of a scene I've been trying to work out in my head. I've found that it sometimes helps to try and draw out a scene when I'm having trouble writing it. Second to writing, I love drawing. It usually helps, but not this time. Frustrated, I stand from my chair and head to my bedroom, pushing my recently laundered load of clothes to the far side of my bed so I can sit down. I take a seat with my laptop perched on my lap. I don't even know what I'm doing until I pull up a website for an event I saw happening tonight at a club not too far outside of the Dallas area.

"Wearing leather is highly encouraged," I read out loud. For months I've been reading about different "scenes" in the BDSM community since I discovered a certain someone with green eyes was into it. I wonder if he's going to be at this club tonight. "I doubt it," I say to myself, recognizing this event was mostly for people who lightly played around and weren't serious players. And according to a conversation I'd overhead—okay, okay more like *eavesdropped* on between Coral and Liam, Jeremy more than dabbles in this community. I've spent many nights wondering what it would be like to be tied up or to feel the sting of his hand or flogger against my skin as he peers down at me through those long dark lashes. *Damn!* Just thinking about it causes a tingling sensation between my —thighs, which is something no one has ever caused to happen to me before.

Before I know it, I'm up looking through my closet for an appropriate outfit. I sort through tons of leggings, T-shirts, and baggy jeans before I come to the conclusion that I have nothing to wear to an event such as the one I want to attend tonight. The only nice outfit I have is the midnight blue dress I wore to Coral and Liam's wedding a few months ago. It's a nice bodycon dress that hugs all of my curves to perfection. Needless to say, I wasn't the one who picked it out as my fashion sense is more on par with asking myself which pair of leggings is most comfortable to sit around and write in for the day. Poor choice in fashion aside, I decide to go with the dress, but I definitely need some new shoes. All I have are flats and that's not going to work. I would ask Coral to go with me, but I don't plan on telling her where I'm going tonight. I check the clock on my laptop to see it's five after eight, which means I have less than an hour to shower, get dressed, and head to a shoe store before it closes at nine o'clock.

"Ouch!" I yell, tripping over another pile of clothes that lay next to my bed. I lose my balance and my hip makes contact with the side of my dresser. I rub the tender spot and grumble to myself on how I need to be more organized. I walk into the bathroom to shower, apply the little bit of makeup I'm capable of applying successfully, get dressed, and head to the shoe store before it closes.

* * *

Jeremy

"YOU MADE IT!" Maritza, another fling of mine, calls out as I enter the VIP section of Club Paradise.

Normally, this club wouldn't be my type of scene. It's for newbies and those who want to pretend they're in "the life." I don't pretend shit. But I'd just landed back in Dallas a few hours ago after having to fire our designer for dragging his ass. So now I need something to help me relax. I knew a few of my old flames would be here, so why not give it a whirl? Maybe I could persuade a couple of them to join me back at the hotel for the rest of the night. Hopefully, that'll prevent me from dreaming about the woman I promised myself I'd stay away from.

"What you got for me?" I look over at the ebony beauty with brown eyes and dark skin so smooth it looks like it's glowing. *Her skin's got nothing on LaTasha's, though.*

"It's been a long time, sir," Maritza purrs in a way that used to get my cock's attention. Tonight I don't feel much for the woman in front of me. I find myself comparing the sharp planes of her petite figure to the rounded curves of another woman.

"Yes, it has," I respond.

"Would you like a drink, sir?" Maritza questions, falling back into her submissive role as she always does in my presence.

I nod. "You know what I like," I tell her before sitting on the large round sofa that's especially for VIP's.

"Here you are, sir." Maritza returns with my scotch on the rocks.

"Thank you," I say as she scoots in next to me on the sofa.

She's wearing a tight leather dress that's so short that it barely covers her ass. I half wonder how she was able to make it from the car into the club without giving everyone a peep show. I shrug internally, remembering she is no longer my submissive so she is free to wear whatever she likes. I feel her hand wrap around my upper arm just as Stephanie walks up to us.

She smiles widely. "So you decided to join us after all. I wasn't sure this scene was interesting enough for you," she comments.

"I'm here." I shrug, looking her up and down. I take it her tight leather skirt, off the shoulder, shimmering top and thigh high leather boots. "Sit down." I motion for her to take a seat on the side of me opposite Maritza.

"This should be an interesting night." She giggles, looking over at Maritza.

The two women nod at one another. I look between them,

contemplating bringing both of them back to my place for the night, before looking out and surveilling the rest of the club. Most women are dressed in either leather skirts or dresses, and the men are rocking leather pants, some in leather vests. The only leather I'm wearing tonight are the cuffs I usually wear out. Otherwise, I'm dressed in a white button up and a pair tailored dress pants. I can tell most of the men here are pretending to be Doms looking for a sub for the evening. A lot of these men couldn't be trusted in a real Dom role. I secretly hope none of the women here fall for the bullshit act they're putting on. An unskilled and unlearned Dom can be dangerous.

The strobe lights make it difficult to make out faces, but I am able to make out a few I recognize. I raise my glass at a couple of subs I know before taking a sip. I let the liquid burn its way down my throat as I sit back, cross my right ankle over my left knee, and throw my arm atop the back of the couch, making myself more comfortable. Stephanie, still seated on my right takes this as a signal to squeeze in closer to me. Although it wasn't my intention to have my personal space invaded, I don't move her away. I need the distraction. I smirk at Maritza to my left when I feel her fingers run through my some-what long hair.

I continue surveying the patrons at the club when the backside of a woman catches my eye. My heart rate quickens slightly, my body telling me what my mind is still trying to figure out. "The hell?" I question, under my breath, waiting for the woman to turn around so I can confirm her identity. The dim lighting in the club make the dress she's wearing appear black, but I know it's navy blue. It stops just above her knees and holds the twists and turns of her luscious body the way I want my hands to. I manage to hold myself together until I see a male patron eyeing her like a piece of meat. I don't give a shit that I too am salivating over her like she's a perfectly seared, medium-well sirloin. That's between me, my cock, and that damn dress she's wearing.

"Would you like another one?"

I completely ignore the question coming from my left as I continue to scope out the scene ahead of me.

"I'll get you another."

My brain registers Maritza's comment, but I make no outward indication of it. I'm too busy trying to tamp down the rising heat in my stomach from seeing *her* in that dress again. I let my eyes travel down the length of her five-foot-four frame. "Fuck," I whisper when I see the four inch, black, spiked heels on her feet. My eyelids lower a fraction of an inch when I notice her unsteadiness in those heels as she walks toward the bar. Her awkwardness in those shoes makes me want her even more. Still, I use every bit of resolve I've built over the years to remain in my seat. That is, until some wanna-be Dom moves in behind her, feeling on her ass prior to even saying anything to her. That's mistake *number one*. You never touch without permission. As soon as I see the uncomfortable look on her face as she turns her head, I'm out of my seat.

* * *

Tasha

MAYBE THIS WAS A MISTAKE, I think as feel a stranger's hand on my ass. I immediately grab for my purse, which contains the mace I carry with me all the time. I turn to the offender behind me, uncomfortable yet ready to use my mace in this club if need be.

"Excuse me, Miss," says a man who is about two inches taller than me in these heels. He's got brown eyes and dark blond hair and he's giving me a hard glare with his hand still on my waist.

I push out of his embrace, but instead of freeing myself, I stumble a bit because I'm not used to wearing heels. This encourages Mr. Stranger Danger to grip one side of my waist and my opposite arm with his other hand to steady me. He also pulls himself in closer.

"Look a bit unsteady in those heels," he says, looking down at my new shoes—shoes I now regret ever buying.

"I'm fine. Thank you," I say, keeping my face neutral.

"You definitely are fine. Your Dom let you out of the house in those shoes? He should be shot or better yet, dumped *for me*," he says, licking his lips.

I can feel the bile as it begins to creep up my throat. I may not know everything about this lifestyle, but my instincts and research alerts me that this dude is some type of fake Dom. He's someone who's watched one too many pornos featuring ropes and floggers and now thinks he's an expert.

"Why don't you try it?" I hear behind Mr. Stranger Danger and I look over his shoulder.

My breath catches. I can't believe *he* is here. Even in the darkened club, I can make out those green eyes with a fire blazing behind them; the usual toothpick tucked into the right side of his mouth.

"Try what?" Mr. Stranger Danger, startled, turns from me. He looks Jeremy over, sizing him up.

"Dumping her Dom," Jeremy says, placing his hands in his pants pockets. I get the feeling it's a move meant to maintain his control. "You told her she should dump her Dom for you. But any *real* fucking Dom would know never to approach a sub to undermine their Dom. By the way, take your fucking hands off of her," he asserts, stepping closer to the man.

Thankfully, Mr. Stranger Danger's hands immediately drop from my waist and arm. A sense of relief floods my bloodstream and I take a step back. Jeremy looks me over carefully, from head to toe. Then pins the fake Dom with his glare.

"It's your lucky night. I'm going to give you some advice since it's clear you have no clue what you're doing. First, don't ever try to undermine another Dom's territory. Secondly, if you ever touch *her* again without permission, the very last thing I'll be doing is talking. We clear?"

Jeremy's hands are still in his pockets. His demeanor suggests that he could be having a regular conversation with the guy, but it's his *eyes*. They tell the real story. In this moment, I realize that the eyes are truly the windows to the soul. According to Jeremy's *window*, his soul is saying he is not the one to mess with. Mr. Stranger Danger must also pick up on the message. He tosses up his hands in a surrendering motion.

"Hey, man, I didn't know."

"I know you didn't. You can go now," Jeremy returns.

I'm pretty sure Mr. Stranger Danger nearly sprains an ankle trying to move quickly out of Jeremy's line of vision. I watch as he disappears into the crowd, hoping he doesn't try that same act on some other woman. I turn back to Jeremy, embarrassed but wanting to thank him for getting rid of that guy before I had to pull out my mace. "Thank—"

"Let's go," Jeremy demands, staring straight ahead at the exit. My apology is cut short as he grips my arm and pulls me toward the door. His grip isn't overly restraining, but it's tight enough for me to know he's serious.

"Go? Wait. What?" I ask, trying to keep up with his long strides. However, I find it difficult to do in my new heels. I tug at my arm, trying to free myself. I don't know what he thinks this is, but I don't appreciate being manhandled. I open my mouth to tell him exactly this, but his words cut me off.

"Where are your keys?" he asks, still not looking at me.

We make it past the entrance door.

"Wait!" I say, finally pulling away from his grasp. "Where are we going?"

"*We* aren't going anywhere. *You're* going home," he says coolly.

"But—"

"But *nothing*... You have no idea about this lifestyle. You saw that creep in there? He's far from the only one willing try to get over on a naïve newcomer."

"How do you know I'm a newcomer?" I question, feeling insulted. Yes, it's true, but he didn't have to pull my card like that.

He simply frowns as he looks me over. Then he turns his eyes on me as if he has answered my question. "Let's go. Where's your car?" He grips my arm again, pulling me toward the parking lot.

Despite my embarrassment of his obvious dismissal, I feel my heartbeat quicken from the warmth of his hand against my skin. I peer out of the corner of my eye to see if he feels what I'm feeling, but I only see the hard set of his jaw as he scans the parking lot for my silver Corolla. When he spots it, he picks up his pace toward the car.

"Take out your keys," he requests once we reach my car.

I squint at his staunch dismissal of me. "I'm not ready to leave. Answer my question. How do you know I'm a newcomer?" I become satisfied by the look of surprise on his face by my act of boldness.

His eyes scan over me from head to toe. "I just know," he half growls and a half whispers.

I shiver at the glazed, intense look in his eyes, which have darkened slightly.

"Then show me." I surprise my own self with that comment. I don't know what the heck just came over me, but I know that the only interest I have in this lifestyle is the man standing in front of him. And I'm tired of denying my attraction to him. I need *something* in my life to change or get me excited since my writing has sucked as of late.

"What did you just say?"

"You heard me. Show me."

"Fuck," he curses under his breath, hand still gripping my arm. "You don't even know what the hell you're asking." He lowers his forehead to mine, running his finger along my jawline.

My eyelids flutter shut due to touch on my skin. I swallow, licking my lips. "Y-you're right, I don't. But I know you wouldn't hurt me." I don't know how I know that, but I do.

"LaTasha," his voice is strained.

"If you're too scared to teach me..." *Holy shit!* I have zero idea where my boldness is coming from, but I know being this close to him makes me want more.

"You don't need someone like me. I'm not an easy or traditional lover. I don't do candy and roses and shit. Do you get what I'm saying?" he pauses.

I simply stare at him, growing more intrigued.

"I do paddles nipple clamps and floggers. Red marks and bruises turn me on," he's damn near growling, his finger stroking down the side of my neck. "I'm not scared to teach you. I'm scared of breaking you," he admits.

Why does that admission warrant a gush of wetness in my panties?

"I've been through worse. I haven't broken yet," I purr.

Jeremy's jaw tightens. He's struggling with something. He pulls back and grips my chin between his thumb and forefinger, tilting my head up to look at him. His lips are so close to mine, I'm too tempted to reach up and press my lips to them. But I won't go that far.

He's glaring into my eyes, searching for something. "Meet me at Al Biernat's next Friday night. I'll give you some time to think about it. I'm no half-ass Dom, LaTasha. If you want this with me, there's no half stepping allowed. I will demand *everything* of you," he warns.

Why do his words both frighten and excite me at the same damn time?

"Seven o'clock sharp. I don't tolerate tardiness," he informs, releasing his grip on me.

I mourn the loss of his touch just that quickly. "O-okay, Al Biernat's next Friday, seven o'clock."

"I'll have my security escort you home. Get in your car."

There's a slight tremor in my hands as I dig through my bag for my keys. When I find them, I open the car door and hear a car pull up behind us. Jeremy looks over and nods toward whoever's in the dark car with tinted windows.

"They'll call me to let me know you got home safely."

I don't even comment about not needing someone to follow me home. I simply nod and get in. Jeremy pushes my door closed and watches me as I start my car and pull off. Even in the darkness of the parking lot, I can feel his gaze on my car. I shiver at the thought of him watching me.

CHAPTER 4

Tasha

I sigh, rubbing my temples in frustration. It's been a few days since my encounter with Jeremy at the club, and if I thought going out that night would help my writer's block, I was sorely mistaken. If anything, it has only gotten worse. At least before, I was writing *something*. It may have been crap, but at least I was writing. But since that night, all I can think about are those damn green eyes. They hold so many questions, intentions, and mysteries. All I want to know is what's behind them. *Jesus*! I sound like a sap. That's not my usual MO. Most of the time, I'm actually repelled by men I don't know that well. That's *so* not the case with this man.

I'm also feeling anxious about my lunch date with Coral and Stacey this afternoon. Stacey got in last night, but she's staying in the hotel where her conference is being held. She, Coral, and I are having lunch today here at the house. To say I'm nervous would be an understatement. I feel the urge to cook, which usually happens whenever I'm nervous. Since it's extremely early, I figure I'll prepare breakfast before everyone at the main house wakes up. A few minutes later, I use my key to enter the dark kitchen of the main house, turning on lights as I move toward the refrigerator. I'm in the mood to make a big meal, so I begin pulling out eggs and flour to prepare blueberry waffles. They are Laura's favorite.

"Another big breakfast today, huh?"

"Shit!" I'm startled, turning to Liam. I had been so enthralled in meal prepping, I hadn't heard him enter the kitchen behind me.

"Sorry." He chuckles. "Didn't mean to scare you."

I toss him a half smile. "Don't be sorry. I probably shouldn't be wandering around someone else's house without being cognizant of my surroundings."

At that Liam frowns. "This is *your* home too. You should know that by now."

I nod. "I know. I just meant that my home is the guest house and this..." I say waving around, gesturing to the main house. "This is where you, Coral, and Laura live," I explain, avoiding eye contact because his eyes look so much like Jeremy's.

"You know this is your home. Every part of this property," he says reassuringly, pulling out a stool from the counter and sitting.

"Thank you," I say before moving to the sink to wash my hands to begin cooking. "Is Coral still asleep?" I ask, looking over my shoulder.

Liam gives me a warm smile, nodding. "Mmmhum... She rarely wakes before seven these days, which is late for her." He laughs.

"Don't I know it? She used to call me at five in the morning, sounding like she'd been up for hours already." I got many 5am calls from my sister when she was out trying to save the world.

"Yeah, Laura usually crawls in the bed with us sometime around five, and they end up sleeping in for a few hours." He smiles reverently while looking down at his phone. His background photo displays one of those occasions of Laura and Coral sleeping in bed.

"I always knew you two would end up together. Even when you... uh...*left*," I say hesitantly, knowing that Liam's decision to leave Coral years ago wasn't one he'd made of his own free will.

He looks up at me. "I always knew too since we were eighteen years old."

"*That long?*" I question.

He nods. "Yup. I was young, but from the moment she first told me to get lost, I knew she was the one for me."

We both laugh at that recollection. Coral and Liam have given me their versions of how they first met during their first semester in college.

"So what about you?" he asks after we both sober.

I raise my eyebrows, surprised. "Me?"

"No, the other *you* in the room."

I roll my eyes. *Smartass.*

It's funny the somewhat brother-sister relationship Liam and I have formed over the years. I haven't told Coral this, but even when they weren't speaking all those years, he still kept in touch with me every now and again. He'd check in on me to make sure I was okay when Coral was out of the country. It was then that I realized how much he loved my sister.

"I don't know." I shrug. "I'm just trying to finish the fourth installment of Danica's series."

"That's not what I'm talking about." He stares at me, giving me a serious expression.

His eyes remind me so much of Jeremy's that I have to look away. I turn toward the counter and pull out a mixing bowl to make the batter for the blueberry waffles.

I can still feel Liam's eyes on me, so I turn back to him. "I don't know what you're talking about," I lie.

"Oh really?"

He eyes me and I roll my eyes again.

"Fine. I'm nervous as hell about meeting Stacey and..."*I want to screw the hell out of your gorgeous cousin and that terrifies me.* I decide to leave that last part out.

"Telling her you're her sister?"

"That and her finding out the rest." I avoid looking at him, busying myself with the food on the stove. "I know Coral says she won't judge me, but still, telling someone about my past..." I stop, shaking my head.

"We all have a past," Liam clarifies.

"Yeah, but not everyone's past is as fucked up as mine."

"You mean that everyone isn't a *survivor* like you." He pats my shoulder, comfortingly.

My eyes water as I turn to see his genuine expression.

"I know someone else with a past who I know wouldn't be intimidated by what you've been through."

I give him a perplexed look. "Who?"

"Jeremy," he states.

My eyes widen. Have I been that damn obvious in my attraction to him? Did Jeremy tell him about the other night?

"No, he hasn't told me anything about you two. But... Well, I have eyes. He's good people. And I'm not just saying that because he's my family and best friend."

"I don't know for sure what or *if* there's anything going on between Jeremy and me," I admit.

Liam nods as he grabs an apple from the fruit bowl on the counter. "Don't rush it. He's not going anywhere. Trust me on that." He tosses me a knowing smirk before exiting the kitchen to head down the hall.

I'm left standing there, wondering what he'd meant. Is Jeremy really attracted to me? I'd begun to convince myself that he had only invited me to dinner out of pity. I guess I would find out in a few days.

* * *

"I STILL CAN'T BELIEVE you're going to be a mom soon." Stacey laughs across the table as we sit outside eating lunch.

I look over at her, noticing her warm brown skin tone, honey eyes, and head full of natural coils and curls that she has styled in a high puff. Her long limbs and neck move with the grace of the dancer she once was. Well, actually, she still is. As a matter of fact, she dances burlesque at a popular club in Atlanta.

"Tasha, can you believe it? I mean, I know you haven't known Coral as long as I have, but could you imagine her being a mother?" she questions me.

I swallow deeply and force a smile. "No, I can't imagine it.

Although she has incredible protective instincts," I state, remembering how much my sister has taken care of me over the years.

Coral rolls her eyes and waves her hand dismissively. "Whatever. Don't get all emotional, you two. Butterball here has already turned me into a sap. And as the aunties of this kid, I expect you both not to spoil him rotten like you do with Laura already." She points and glares at both of us.

Stacey holds up her hands defensively. "I make no promises."

"Nor do I," I concur, laughing.

"Stace, how's the conference going?" Coral asks.

Stacey's eyes widen in excitement. "Oh, it's going well. I'm learning so much. This conference is on how family dynamics affect people with eating disorders and their recovery. Very interesting stuff."

"Family dynamics isn't that interesting." Coral tilts her head, looking at me.

For my part, I stuff another one of the crab puffs we'd ordered in my mouth, squinting at Coral.

Stacey being the rather intelligent person she is, looks between Coral and me. "I'm not a body language expert like some people, but even I can tell there was some sort of hidden meaning in that comment," she concludes, eyeing Coral.

Coral's eyes shift over to me as if to say, *spit it out!*

I stuff another crab puff in my mouth.

"Tasha," Coral implores. "Just say it."

"*Somebody*, say it," Stacey adds, sounding nervous.

I close my eyes tightly, remaining silent.

"Look, Tash, if there's one thing I've come to realize, especially in the last few months, is that *family* is the most important thing in the world. I'd never want Laura or Butterball to feel like they couldn't tell me anything or like they were alone in this world." She looks directly at me now with what looked strangely enough like tears in her eyes. I don't ever think I can recall a time when I saw Coral cry. "Tasha, it's okay. Just tell her," Coral urged.

Despite the tenseness of the situation, I smirk at the nickname Coral's given the baby in her womb. Last time she was at the doctor, he told her the baby was in the ninetieth percentile in size and weight. Ever since then, Coral's taken to calling him Butterball.

I looked at Stacey and then down at my now empty plate. I had no idea how she would take this, but if Coral believed it was okay, then so would I. "I'm your sister," I finally admit.

Stacey's eyes widen as she stares at me before looking over at Coral for the truth.

Out of the corner of my eye I see Coral nod. "It's true."

"What? But how? That doesn't make any sense."

"I was a secret...*our father's* dirty little secret." I can't help the bitterness in voice.

"*Our father*? Wait, you mean..." Stacey trails, off trying to put the pieces together in her head.

"Yes, our father," Coral begins. "He had an affair while Mom was sick. Tasha's mother lived upstairs in our apartment building. They had it off and on for years as Mom's disease progressed. Eventually, Tasha was born."

"But that was *years* ago. How long have you known about Tasha?" Stacey's voice rises.

Coral doesn't look perturbed in the least by Stacey's questions. "I found out when I was about twelve. You were seven and Tasha was five. I overheard him on the phone one day with Tasha's mom who was threatening to take him to court for child support. Mom had passed recently and his drinking had gotten out of control. After that, I realized he had another daughter, but he wasn't taking care of her. So I made it a point to befriend the child and look out for her," she states, rubbing her belly.

"Just like a big sister. But why didn't you tell me?"

"That was my doing," I interrupt Coral. "I didn't want anyone to know. I was ashamed."

"*Ashamed*? It wasn't your fault the adults in our lives had lied and cheated. You were innocent."

I grin at Stacey, seeing the social worker in her now. "I know that, but..." I pause, not wanting to go into the totality of my history and my *real* shame. I'd long ago stopped blaming myself for my parents'

43

actions, but there are things in my life I'd yet to completely let go of. I look to Coral, remembering that day a decade ago when she came and found me in juvenile prison. No, I didn't want to go into detail about that yet.

"But nothing," Stacey persisted. "It's terrible what our father and your mother did to you...to *us*. And I guess I can understand you not wanting anyone to know until you were ready, but I just wish you would've told me. What if something had happened to you while you were away at war or trying to save the world? We could have lost contact and I would—"

"That wouldn't have happened," Coral interrupts.

"Why couldn't it have possibly happened? Tasha didn't know where I was—"

"Quincy knew and our aunt and uncle did too."

"*What?!*" I shriek, pinning Coral with a glare.

She pauses, looking back and forth between Stacey and me. "I told Quincy after I found you in New York."

"What?" I ask again, rising from my seat. "How the hell? No! *Why*? Why would you tell them?" I was angry and afraid. I was afraid because I wondered what Coral had told her about my life when she'd found me in New York.

Coral pivots to me, looking me right in the eye. "I told them because like it or not, the reality was I was going back to a warzone, and the possibility that I would never return was very real. And if that would've happened, I knew Quincy wouldn't have hesitated to carry out my wishes to protect you and look after you. I knew Aunt Ruth and Uncle Gerry would have welcomed you into the family, and you wouldn't have had to be alone. I had made a promise to look after you when we were kid, and I broke it once. I wasn't about to let that happen again."

I was left speechless at Coral's words. My vision blurred as my eyes became watery. She had looked out for me in ways I never even knew nor could I imagine. I feared daily that she wouldn't come home when she was on deployment. "Dammit! How the hell am I supposed to be pissed at you when you put it like that?" I whine, wiping my eyes.

"Yeah, she has a way of doing that," Stacey chimes in.

I turn away from Coral, grinning at Stacey. "She's a damn piece of work."

"And probably has more secrets than we can even fathom."

I nod in agreement as Coral chuckles.

"Stacey, I'm so—"

"Don't be." She holds up her hand. "You had your reasons for keeping me in the dark. Hopefully, one day you'll trust me enough to tell me the full story," she states as she grips my hand. "For now, I'll settle for getting to know my sister." She looks at me expectantly.

"I'd like that," I agree.

"Welcome to the family, little sis, as fucked up as it is." She laughs.

I laugh at that too. I sigh releasing a weight I hadn't even known was there. I'm starting to feel like I actually have two sisters.

Tasha

"ARE you having dinner with us tonight?" Coral asks over the phone.

I bite my lower lip as I stare at myself through the full-length mirror, twisting and turning. I'm trying to figure out if this is the right outfit for tonight. It'd been a few days since the big reveal with Stacey, and she'd gone home to Atlanta the day before, but not without giving me her contact information to keep in touch. She'd already texted me a few messages. Although I was hesitant to return them, I started to feel a little more comfortable letting my guard down.

"Tasha? Hello?" Coral's voice breaks through my concentration.

"Oh, sorry, Coral. What did you say?"

There's a pause before she asks, "I said are you coming to the main house to have dinner with us tonight?"

My chest caves in as I let out the breath I'd been holding, hoping she didn't pick up on anything. "No, not tonight. I'm actually going to go to a local Starbucks to see if I have any luck writing in a different environment." I'm proud of how even my voice sounds as the lie slips out.

"You're still experiencing writer's block, huh?"

I nod, avoiding looking at myself in the mirror, ashamed of lying to Coral. The truth is I haven't even ventured to pick up my laptop in about a week. "Yeah," I reply to her question.

"Well, you're the writer, so if you think writing in a different space will be helpful, I guess it's worth a try. I've gotta go, Princess and Butterball are getting hungry."

"Alright. Go feed my niece and nephew."

"Yeah, yeah... Later."

"Bye."

Once I hang up, I go back to assessing myself in the mirror. The dress I just purchased has short sleeves and it's fuchsia. The hemline stops just above the knee and the bodice cinches in a little at the waist. I actually smile a little bit, liking the fit and the way the color of the dress looks against my skin. For years, I avoided wearing anything that brought more attention to me. As a child I was taught that because of my dark skin, bright color fabrics weren't appealing on me. It's taken years in therapy and encouragement from my sister to move past that lie. Even now as I look at myself, a small part of me wonders if the dress is too much.

You're too dark. That's why ya daddy don't want nothing to do with you. If you were prettier, he'd claim you like he do those other two!

I shut my eyes, remembering the hurtful taunts my mother spewed at me when I was just six or seven years old. It was always her excuse why my father wouldn't even acknowledge my presence when he did come over to our apartment. He'd head straight to her bedroom, barely paying me a backwards glance. An hour later, he'd be gone, leaving my mother to yell and rant her frustrations out on me.

"Shake it off, Tasha. They're gone. You're still here," I whisper to myself. I move away from the mirror, finally deciding to wear the dress. I remove it to take a quick shower and moisturize, before applying a little bit of makeup. I opt to wear a pair of nude pantyhose and black peep-toe, shoes with a medium block heel. After one final look in the mirror, I feel confident. "Good enough, I guess," I say, shrugging before I turn to grab my keys and purse from the living room. I decide to take the long route to the garage where my car is parked so I don't have to pass by the main house on my way out. Coral will know something is up if she sees me in a dress. I'm more of a leggings and T-shirt kind of girl. Within minutes, I'm in my car and passing through the gate to make my way to Al Biernat's. I try to ignore the little shiver of anticipation that passes through me as a vision of Jeremy's sharp gaze from the other day flashes in my mind. Those eyes have me both excited and fearful of what's in store for me this evening.

* * *

Jeremy

"What the hell am I doing?" It's a question I've asked myself multiple times in the fifteen minutes I've been sitting across from the restaurant.

I look down at my dashboard clock. It's 6:50. Without thinking, I reach down to retrieve a toothpick from where I keep my stash between the seats. I'd love to say this act isn't a result of my nervous anticipation of the evening ahead, but that would be a lie. When I take another look at the clock and see that only two minutes have passed, I readily admit the knot in my stomach is a result of disappointment rising up. Maybe she's decided not to come after all.

"Shit!" I curse to myself, frustrated with all the damn ministrations going on in my damn head right now. This is the goddamn reason why I'd never approached Latasha in the first place. She's usually guarded and cagey around me. Since the first time meeting her at Coral and Liam's wedding, I've felt the urge to reach out and protect her and put her over me knee. For months now, I've worked hard to keep my distance, thinking what I have to offer her would be too much. Obviously, from where I'm sitting right now, that plan has been shot to hell.

Grunting at my lack of willpower and what it could possibly mean, I look up and the first thing I notice is a pair of dark chocolate legs mired by nylon stockings. My lips turn down into a deep frown that only lasts for a half a second when I move my gaze up the rest of her body. She's covered in a fuchsia dress that accentuates the glow of her skin. Her hair is pulled back in a tight bun her nape. I take a moment to watch as she is greeted by the hostess who's standing at her booth outside the door of the restaurant. With concentrated effort, I peel my eyes away from her to check the time. 6:56.

"Good girl," I mumble. I abhor lateness. I've given the restaurant specific instructions not to show her to the table until after I arrive. Finally moving, I turn my ignition off, and step out of my Lexus SUV. I button my suit jacket and make my way to the door.

As I approach, I take in the curves that even the relatively, loose-fitting dress she's wearing can't hide. I grin, thinking of all the things I could do with those curves.

"Good evening, LaTasha," I say just above a whisper, leaning in behind her. I notice a small shiver as my breath grazes across her nape.

She turns, wide-eyed, but quickly recovers. She clears her throat before speaking. "Hi, I thought you'd be inside already."

"I've been waiting on your arrival."

She nods. "That makes sense, I guess." Her eyes dart from one place to another as if she's trying to avoid eye contact.

"Let's go inside, shall we?" I suggest. "Darlin', reservation for Bennett," I say to the young, blond hostess.

"Yes, right this way," she announces cheerfully, grabbing a couple of menus and motioning for us to follow her.

Instinctively, I place my hand at the small of LaTasha's back and wave my other hand for her to walk ahead of me. Of course it's the gentlemanly thing to do, but more than that, I want to take in her backside as we pass through the restaurant. The sway of her dress around her plump backside and thick legs keep me transfixed so much so that I have to pull up short once we reach the private dining space I'd requested for the evening. *Pull it together, Bennett.*

"A private room?" Latasha asks, an eyebrow raised.

"We have some things to discuss and I assume you wouldn't want others to overhear this particular conversation," I answer, looking down into her face.

She looks down, and if she were a few shades lighter, I swear she'd be blushing. "No, I guess not," she responds.

"I didn't think so." I usher her toward our private table for two, pull out her chair, and wait for her to sit before addressing the hostess.

"Your server tonight will be Ally. She'll be with you shortly. Enjoy your dinner."

"Thank you, darlin'," I state before she bounces off.

"Thank you for being early."

Latasha smiles. "No problem. I'm kinda a stickler for time myself."

I notice her wiggle in her chair a subtly. "You're nervous. Why?"

"Why?" she asks, repeating my question to her.

"Yes, why?"

"Well, umm... This isn't exactly a normal conversation or relationship thing we're about to discuss."

I grin and lean forward, elbows on the table. "Whose definition of normal?"

At that question, she stares at me, contemplatively and shrugs. "I don't know. Society's, I guess."

I frown. "The same society that allows women and children to live in poverty? Or the society that allows the people meant to protect us to shoot unarmed citizens? That's the society with such high moral standing you want to uphold?" I reach across the table to squeeze her hand briefly as she smiles bashfully. Pulling back, I remove my hand and sit back in my seat.

She considers that for a minute. "You're right. It's just this is my first time venturing out into 'the life.' That's what it's called. Right? The Life? I mean, I wonder why it's called that. It's an interesting term, I guess. But how many people actually incorporate this into their life? I mean, you'd think..." She stops when I reach across the table once again, clasping her hand.

49

"You ramble when you're nervous."

"Not usually, but you..." She pauses.

"I what?" I prod.

"You take me out of my comfort zone."

"That's the duty of any good Dom," I explain.

"I can't believe I'm actually having this conversation," she mumbles.

I decide to ask her a question I've been wondering. "Why did you come to the club that night?"

Her face takes on a contemplative expression. "Well..." She sighs, smoothing her hand over her hair. "I...um...had some trouble with work and I thought getting out would help take my mind off it."

"But you knew it was BDSM night. Why did you choose *that* night?" I question, not letting her off the hook so easily.

She pulls her hand from my loose grip. "Well, I'd seen some stuff on the life online and it—"

"It *excited* you," I say, finishing her statement for her.

"Yes."

"Did you wonder if I'd be there?"

"Yes," she answers, her eyes skirting away from me.

"Okay."

"Okay?"

"Yeah, okay. My other questions can wait for a little longer. Right now, it's time to order our meals." As soon as I finish my sentence, our server appears with glasses of water along with a bottle of the red wine I'd ordered in advance on a tray. We put in our orders, and just a few minutes later, our salads are served. We eat for a few minutes in silence. I wonder what Latasha is thinking. I can see the wheels turning in her mind, but I opt to wait her out.

"Can I ask you a question?"

"Go ahead."

"How come you always call me LaTasha?"

I raise my eyebrow. "That is your name, right?"

She grins. "Liam said you were a smart ass."

I chuckle before I wipe my mouth.

"Yes, it is," she answers. "I just mean, you refer to other women as darlin' and everyone else calls me *Tasha*. But you don't. How come?"

"I like being the only one to call you by your full name."

"My grandmother was the only person to call me by my full name." Abruptly she pulls her lips in as if she hadn't meant for that comment to slip out. "I like when you call me LaTasha." She smiles, looking me directly in the eye.

My chest fills up with some emotion I can't identify and I find myself having to fight not to look away from her gaze. I'm not used to this scenario. I've never had a problem maintaining eye contact with anyone whether it's friend or foe. Yet this woman...

"So, how does this work?" she asks, totally unaware of the effect she's having on me.

"It'll work however we want it to work," I state nonchalantly.

She tilts her head, looking at me.

I smirk. "A Dom-sub relationship is an exchange. It's not about violence or pain for the sake of violence or pain. It's reciprocal. You may experience periods of being uncomfortable, but you push through it because you know you will receive pleasure unlike anything you've experienced before. Now, that isn't to say you must endure anything. If you're really uncomfortable or if you're being triggered by something, then we can stop or slowdown. That's why safe words and sometimes safe signals or gestures are used."

"*Gestures?*" she interrupts.

I frown. "Love, one thing you'll learn about me is that I don't like being interrupted. But to answer your question, gestures or signals are sometimes necessary if say, you're gagged or your mouth is otherwise, *occupied.*"

I notice LaTasha squirm a bit in her seat, and it sends a sensation directly to my cock. Lucky for both of us, our server chooses that moment to bring our meals. I watch as LaTasha takes her first forkful of her crab cakes. When she closes her eyes, savoring the taste, it takes every bit of willpower in my body not to reach across the table and crush her lips to mine.

"Soon."

"What did you say?"

At that moment, I realize I said that I've spoken out loud. "Tell me something about yourself no one else knows."

Her eyes widen in shock. She wipes her mouth with her napkin before placing it back on her lap. "Really?" she asks.

I nod, completely serious. "A Dom-sub relationship is about *trust*. If you don't trust me, you'll never be able to submit fully. If I can't trust you, I could never bring either of us the type of pleasure that comes with your full submission." I look her straight in the eye.

Her lids flutter, but her eyes remain open as she turns her head, avoiding eye contact. "I've never had an orgasm," she nearly whispers.

"Why not?"

Her eyes shift back to me and she shrugs.

"I need a verbal response to my question," I admonish.

She sighs, brushing a stray hair behind her ear. "I...uh... It just never happened."

I know the answer is more complicated than that. "As I said, the basis of any fulfilling Dom-sub relationship is trust. There is no trust without communication. There is no relationship without those two things. You don't have to tell me everything that happened in your past right now, but at some point, I'd like you to open up."

She shakes her head and opens her mouth.

"One day," I insist although I don't even know why. I've never demanded past subs to open up and share their entire histories with me.

"One day," she says skeptically. "Now, you tell me something that no one knows about you."

I really should've expected that. I stare at this gorgeous woman in front of me and wonder if she knows how appealing she is. Actually, I don't have to wonder because I know she doesn't know. "My mother dumped me at a group home when I was ten years old."

Her mouth drops open. "You're telling the truth aren't you?"

I nod. "Yup. I told you—"

"Trust," she interrupts.

"Love," I growl lowly.

"I'm sorry. No interruptions. Got it. Please continue."

I half shrug. "Not much more to tell. She was tired of being a mother. It's not like she was a particularly good one anyway. Anyway, she dropped me off at a group home, and I wound up in foster care. A few years later, I was reunited with my biological father, who took me in and loved me like a real father should until the day he died." I've never revealed so much about myself to any of my subs. I can't figure out why it was so easy to do with LaTasha. There's a long pause as she takes in what I've just revealed. She stares at me observantly.

"I'm sorry you went through that. I know what it's like to be treated like a throwaway by your own parent." Her voice is somber, but her words provide some sort of balm to a deep wound. Although her sentiment is comforting, I silently hope she doesn't ask more questions about my history.

"May I ask another question?" Her voice has taken on a more upbeat tone.

I release a breath, realizing she's attempting to change the subject. I tilt my head. "You may."

"What do you get out of it? I've read articles and books on this, and different people receive various benefits from it. I mean, what do you get out of it beyond just orgasms?"

I smile inside, happy to hear that she has been doing her own research. I usually don't work with first-time subs anymore. I no longer wanted to be someone's introduction to the life. But again, *LaTasha* is different. The thought of another Dom teaching her the world and pleasures I wish to teach her unsettles me.

I push my plate to the side and lean onto the table for emphasis. I stare directly into her eyes. "I get to know that your every pleasure is in my hands. I'll have the joy of seeing your body tremble in anticipation of what I'm going to do next. I get off on knowing that my subs entrust me with their very well-being, both inside and outside of the bedroom. I like control." Truth is that last part is a lie. I don't just like control. I *crave* it. "Does that answer your question?"

I lean back in my chair as Tasha stares at me with a lowered gaze. I watch as she reaches for her glass of water.

"Why?" she asks, surprising me.

"Why what?"

"Why do you crave control?"

I clench the cloth napkin in my hand reflexively, remembering parts of my childhood I wish I could've long forgotten. "Growing up in foster homes tends to make one feel out of control a lot," I shrug, casually. "I guess now as an adult, a part of me needs to reclaim that control I lost early on."

Her mouth forms into a perfect "O" as she absorbs my honesty. "I can definitely understand that," she finally sighs.

"Since we're being so honest," she says after clearing her throat. "How do you know it will work?"

"*Work?*"

"Yes. I mean, how do you know it will work for *me?*" Her voice is bashful almost.

I nod in understanding. I reach across the table and use my index finger to make small circles on the outside of LaTasha's wrist. I feel her tremble from that small amount of stimuli and smile smugly. "You feel that?" My eyes move to my hand on her wrist and back to her eyes.

"Yes." Her voice has taken on an airiness.

"The shiver you give just from my hand on your wrist is how I know we'll be great together. *If* you can handle it," I challenge.

An arched eyebrow raises. "*If* I can handle it? What's that supposed to mean?"

"Exactly what I said. I'm not an easy lover and I've done everything to stay away from you since you've moved here. I sensed your hesitation from the moment I asked you to dance at Coral's wedding. I can feel it now. I hear it in your voice when you admit to never having had an orgasm. As a Dom it's in my nature to take from you what you want to hold back. Can you handle that?"

Her gaze lowers, the challenging look of moments ago disappearing. "I think so," she finally answers.

"We'll see," I retort. It's time to switch to something less heavy.

"Now, I have a question for you. Why are you having difficulty writing?"

"*Writing?*"

"Yes, I'm looking forward to Danica's next adventure and how she'll get out of the mess she's in."

"You read my books? Wait. How did you know *I* was the author? Did Coral tell you?"

I force myself not to laugh at her bemused expression. "Yes, I've read them. And no, Coral isn't the one who told me you're the author. I have my own *resources*." I refuse to tell her that once I met her at Coral and Liam's wedding I did a little background research on her. That's when I found out she was the author of one of the most popular series on the New York Times' list. I became intrigued and actually began reading the series in my spare time.

"Oh...okay. Well, I don't know why I'm having trouble writing. It sucks too because I've never experienced writer's block. Usually, I have to force my brain to shut down so I can do normal things like sleep. But now, it's just... I go to my laptop to write and everything that comes out is a garbled mess. Words and creating alternative or fictional realities have always been my thing, you know? Ever since I saw the image of Storm on the first Marvel cover I was ever given, I've had no problem imagining and writing about new worlds. And now..."

"Did you say Storm and Marvel?"

She nods. "Yes, I know comics are usually thought of as being for boys, but I devoured them as a kid. Storm being my favorite, of course. She's just so strong and such a mystery. You know, because she was born in Kenya and was an orphan. Well, maybe you don't know. It's pretty nerdy stuff. I'm sure you didn't really—"

"Didn't really what?"

"Nothing."

"I for one always adored Storm. Or should I say *Ororo*? For years I hoped she and Wolverine would get together. I think they would've played off well on each other's strengths and weaknesses."

"You're a comic nerd too!" LaTasha's expression was wide-eyed.

55

"You thought you were the only one who read comic books to escape a shitty childhood? Who else could enjoy Danica's quests as much as I do? I see a lot of Storm's traits in Danica. I suspected you were a Marvel fan."

What feels like only minutes later, I look at my watch and realize we'd spent an hour and a half talking about our mutual admiration for comic books. After spending so much of my time having discussions and meetings about work, this is one of the best conversations I can remember having in a very long time. I'm reluctant to say the next words, but I have an early morning meeting the following day. "We should get going." I motion for our server to retrieve the bill.

"Thank you for tonight," LaTasha says as I stand behind her, pulling out her chair.

"The pleasure was all mine."

"Where're you parked or did you valet?" I ask once the check has been handled.

"I'm parked in the side parking lot."

"I'm right out front. We can go to my car and I'll drive you to yours so I can follow you home to make sure you get in safely."

"That won't be necessary. I know how to get home from here."

I abruptly stop walking toward the door to turn and look down at LaTasha, frowning. "It's not about whether or not you know how to get home from here. Anyone you go out with should care enough to make sure you get home safely. And if I'm going to be your Dom, it's my job to make your safety a priority in *every* aspect and not just while we're playing. Alright?"

LaTasha's face scrunches up. "But you haven't agreed to be my Dom yet," she retorts.

"We're working on it and that means I need you to understand that your safety is my priority. Okay?"

She pauses, staring at me. Slowly she answers, "Yes."

"Good." I replace my hand around her lower waist, escorting her to the exit. We remain silent as we reach my car and I open the door for her. I help her into the passenger's seat.

"Thank you."

Once at her car, I make sure she's in and wait for her to pull out of her space to follow her for the nearly thirty minute trip back to Liam and Coral's sprawling home. At the gate, she lowers the window to have her face scanned and then drives through to the driveway closest to the guesthouse. I park behind her and get out and walk her to her door.

"Thank you again for tonight," she says, opening her door.

I remain in the doorway, leaning against it. I tuck my hands inside my pockets. I stare down into LaTasha's eyes. There's so much emotion in their depths, but I'm sure she's not even aware of it. I saw it the first time I laid eyes on her and it's still there.

"Go ahead," I urge.

"How did you know? Never mind. Coral does that all the time too. Anyway, how do you know there's any chemistry between us?"

I raise my eyebrows. "*Seriously?*"

"Yeah, what if we begin this relationship or whatever we'll call it, and then there's no spark?"

You've gotta be kidding me. I stare at her and realize she's serious. Without thinking, I take a step forward, kicking the door closed behind me and wrap one hand her throat. My grip is loose and I allow my thumb to trail over the vein that pulses in her neck. At first the look she gives me is alarmed. I continue to press her back against the wall, pressing my body into hers.

"What're you—"

"Don't speak," I order before crushing my lips to hers. At first, I can feel her shock. Then her body trembles as she tries to figure out what to do until finally, she relaxes and allows me to take the lead. After that, my body relaxes as my tongue swipes over her entire mouth. I move my hand from her neck to the back of her head, pulling her hair. Her nipples pebble beneath the fabric of her dress. I know I should stop, but when she moans at the back of her throat, I step even closer into her. My other hand reaches up her thighs, under her dress and winds its way into her panties. Her moistness evident. Reluctantly, I pull back and bite her lower lip just hard enough to cause a slight amount of pain before releasing her completely.

I hold my wet fingers up to her dazed face. We're both panting, staring at one another. Even my damn legs are shaky. If I wasn't in as good shape as I am, I'm sure I would've fallen from the force of that damn kiss.

"This is what chemistry looks like?" I growl. "It'll be much better when you're cumming all over my cock."

With heavy lids she looks completely lost. "Shit," she whispers.

I nod. "Indeed." I knew it would be like this with her.

"I'm going now." I step back, feeling the loss of her body heat. Just before I grab the doorknob my brain starts up and I remember something. "I have an assignment for you."

"An *assignment?*"

I grin, looking down at her. It appears that she's struggling to remember her own name right now.

"Yes, I want you to try and remember the last time you felt physical pleasure."

"About five seconds ago," she quickly responds.

I let out a chuckle. "Before then."

"I told you I've never—"

"I know," I say, holding up my hand. "It doesn't have to be *sexual*. Not all physical pleasure is a result of sexual activity. Just try and remember when something made you feel good even if it wasn't to the point of orgasm, okay?"

She hesitates and then nods.

I raise my eyebrow. "I need a verbal response."

"I mean *yes*. Okay."

"Good. Go inside and don't forget to lock your door. Get some rest."

"Goodnight," she responds before turning and closing her door.

I wait to make sure I hear the lock engage before I return to my car. Halfway to my car, I can feel another presence behind me. I stop, every muscle in my body flexes with tension until I hear the stalker speak.

"You know you're going to have one angry scorpion to deal with if you hurt her sister."

"Have you ever known me to hurt a woman?" I turn and look my cousin in the eyes.

"I've seen you leave more than your fair share of broken hearts once you get bored," Liam responds.

"All those subs knew their time with me was limited."

"Does Tasha?"

"She will."

"You sure about that?"

"What is that supposed to mean?" I ask, becoming annoyed.

"Nothing." Liam looks toward the guesthouse and then back at me. "Just know CeCe's gonna be pissed if Tasha gets hurt and so will I."

"Aren't you the one who told me she's tougher than I thought?"

"Sure am. I'm also telling you to be careful or you'll have not only Coral to answer to if she gets hurt." The hard set of his jaw and arms braced across his chest indicate he's not joking.

"Noted," I say, nodding as I pick up on Liam's warning. "But remember that LaTasha and I are two consenting adults. Whatever happens between us is just that—between us. Got it?"

"We'll see."

Strange as it may be, I'm glad Liam is looking out for LaTasha. I don't have any intentions of hurting her, but knowing that Coral and Liam have her back makes me feel better for some odd reason. As I drive back home, I find my mind drifting off thinking about the enigma that is LaTasha and my insane reaction to her. My natural protective instincts rev into high gear whenever I'm around her.

"I might be in trouble," I mumble to myself as I reach my house and climb out of my car.

Needless to say, I spend the rest of the night tossing and turning with another one of my dreams starring a woman with dark chocolate skin, thick thighs, and a quivering lip right before she yells out my name.

CHAPTER 5

asha
     I close my laptop and leave it in Coral's office before I exit after exchanging goodbyes with the guys. A few of the center's tutors and counselors are setting up chairs to prepare for breakfast. I begin unfolding chairs at the tables and laying out forks and milk boxes for the breakfast we're about to serve. I hear the door creak open behind me and turn to see Trudy entering. I look at the clock, noting she's ten minutes early. She hasn't been around in about a week or so, and I've been worried about her.

"Hey, Trudy, how are you?" I greet.

"Hi, Ms. Tasha. I'm good. Look!" she announces happily, holding up a book.

I immediately smile at the excitement in her voice before I notice she's holding up my book. She has the first in the series of *Danica's Travels.* My chest rises with a sense of pride as I watch the sparkle in her eyes as she admires the book.

"My mama let me go to the library the other day. Well, I kinda sneaked off from where I was supposed to have been to go to the library," she admits.

At that I frown.

"Don't get mad. I couldn't convince my mama to take me to the library for nothin' and I really wanted to check out this book."

How could I be upset with her after that? Still I have to give her a little grief about sneaking off away from her mother. "Trudy, I'm glad you wanted to read, but you still shouldn't have sneaked away from your mother like that. What if something had happened to you?"

Trudy shrugs. "She wouldn't have cared."

"What?"

"Nothing, Ms. Tasha. But I've been reading and I really love Danica's story. She's so brave."

I nod. "She is. Here, let's sit down and we can talk for a few minutes about Danica."

We sit down and I let Trudy talk about how she's already finished the book, she is currently re-reading it. The only time I see her face sadden is when she talks about having to return the book to the library the next day.

"Hold on, Trudy," I say, standing and rushing to my bag on the other side of the room. I pull out my copy of *Danica's Travels* and bring it back to Trudy. "You can keep this one."

"*Really?*" she questions excitedly, yet unsure as if I'm going to take away the gift I just gave her. I see the look of a girl who's had things taken away from her before.

"Yes, really. It's yours. I've got more than one copy," I assure. "Now, I need you to help me put out the rest of these chairs and finish setting up for breakfast. Alright?"

"Yes, ma'am."

As more children emerge through the doors and Coral rounds the corner from her office, I feel a vibration in my pocket. After pulling out my phone and viewing my text message, a tingle shoots down my spine. My phone screen is filled with a profile image of Jeremy. It's a picture I sneaked a shot of on Liam and Coral's wedding day when he wasn't looking. Opening the message, I can't help but smile.

Jeremy: LaTasha, I'll be back in town later this afternoon. I'll be over at 6:30. I'm bringing dinner. Anything you don't eat? Have you been wearing my gift?

My heartbeat quickens after reading his text. It's been more than a week since our dinner and Jeremy has been out of town for work. Two days after our date, I got a delivery in the mail. I opened the box to find what looked like a jewelry box. I opened it to find two large glass balls connected by a string. They're called Ben Wa balls. Inside the box read Jeremy's instructions to wear them for at least an hour a day along with the benefits of them, which included longer, more intense orgasms.

Tasha: Yes, I've been wearing them. And have you seen me?

Jeremy: What's that supposed to mean?

I suddenly feel like my response wasn't the right one.

Tasha: Nothing. I just meant that there isn't anything I don't eat.

I add an emoji smiley face to try and make light of my comment.

Jeremy: I told you I don't like it when you're self-deprecating. We'll have to discuss punishments tonight at dinner. 6:30. See you then.

A tingle in my belly begins as I read the word "punishments."

"What are you grinning at?"

Oh shit. "Nothing," I lie, quickly putting my phone in my pocket.

Coral looks at me speculatively. "Uh, huh, well, Denise is doing the morning reading and Princess is going to be dropped off in a half an hour. We're spending most of the day in the pool today with the kids. Are you joining us or do you want to work in the garden?"

"The garden," I say without hesitation. Although I'm still consumed with writer's block, I think doing some weeding and vegetable picking will help me to zone out for a bit and get some more ideas. Also, it'll help expend some of this nervous energy before my date tonight.

"Okay. It's an early day today since we close at noon, so I'll see you in a few hours. I have to go do my rounds first," Coral says before taking one last look at me and turning to head outside.

I know she's thinking something is up with me, but surprisingly, she hasn't said anything. I wonder if she knows about Jeremy and me. I've had a little pep in my step for the last week since our date. Every morning I wake up to a "good morning" text and every night at nine o'clock sharp, my phone rings. As per one of his rules, I've exactly three rings before he hangs up. And if I don't answer, he'll be pissed. Tonight will likely be the real discussion on boundaries and the assignment he gave me a week ago.

About thirty minutes later, I have the kids help me haul the vegetables to the kitchen so the staff can prepare them for lunch. Just then, my phone buzzes again with another text message.

Jeremy: I have to change our dinner from 6:30 to 8. I'll pick up Thai on the way over.

Tasha: Thai is perfect. See you at 8.

"Ms. Tasha."

I hear someone behind me call my name. I turn to see it's Trudy. "Yes, sweetie?"

"Umm, I just wanted to say thank you for the book. I love Danica's stories. I'm gonna go to the library to get the second and third books. Do you know if there's a fourth book in the series?"

A pang of sadness hits my chest as she asks about the fourth installment in Danica's series. That's the book I'm supposed to be working on, but this darn writer's block is not letting up.

"Not yet, Trudy, but I'm sure one is on the way," I manage to say, hoping beyond hope that is the actual truth. To be honest, I've been somewhat fearful that the words will never come to me and my writing days are over. The thought of that scares me more than I can even comprehend. I've always had my writing and creative thoughts to get me through even the darkest times in my life. Now, when things are going well for me, the words seem to have stopped.

"Okay, I'll try to come back later this week. Will you be here?" Trudy asks, interrupting my pity party.

"Yes, I'll be here, but why later in the week? You can't make it tomorrow?"

"Nah, my mama says she's too busy to bring me tomorrow, and I don't got money for the bus." She shrugs, but I can see the disappointment in her eyes.

"Hang on a sec," I say, pushing my earlier thoughts aside and digging in my pocket for a ten dollar bill. "Here. You can use this for the bus to get here and back home. Is it enough?" I ask, wanting to make sure she has enough money to be able to make it to the community center for the rest of the week if need be.

Trudy's brown eyes widen in shock. "Yes, it is, but I can't take it."

"Why not?"

"Cause I can't pay you back."

I smile. "Trudy, it's okay. You don't have to pay me back. I just want to make sure you have enough money to be able to get here the rest of the week. You're sure that's enough? I have more in my wallet, but it's in the office."

"Yeah, this is enough, Ms. Tasha. Thank you!" she exclaims, obviously excited she doesn't have to miss the rest of the week.

"Alright, let's go help fold up the chairs. I'm sure your mama will be here within the hour."

Trudy nods, stuffing the money in her pocket and begins helping me put the chairs away. Forty-five minutes later, we are done and all the kids have been picked up. I see Trudy as she heads toward a beat-up, red Buick. The woman, whom I assume is her mother in the passenger's seat, barely looks at Trudy as she climbs in the back seat. As the car squeals off, I get that same gut feeling as the first time I saw Trudy's mother. I watch the car all the way until it turns the corner, disappearing from my line of vision.

"Ready to go?" Coral asks from behind me.

Shaking off that odd feeling, I nod my head. "Yup."

"Hi, Aunt Tasha!" Laura waves excitedly as she stands by Coral, holding her hand.

"Hey, Princess. Did you have a good day?"

She nods with the excitement only four year olds can muster. "Yeah!"

I listen attentively to Laura while she recounts her day in an animated voice. She continues to talk the entire time we drive home. After a while, my mind drifts to my date tonight. The butterflies begin fluttering in my belly with anticipation. As we pull up to the front gate, I'm still wondering how tonight will go.

* * *

"CAN I ASK YOU SOMETHING?" I say to Stacey over the phone.

"Uh, sure," she answers. "Go ahead."

I exhale. "It's about our father. Do you remember anything about him?" It's a question I've been wondering about a lot lately.

"Oh, wow! I wasn't expecting that."

"I know. It's just that I don't know much about him. And I never felt right asking Coral."

"No, no, I get it." She sighs. "Let me see. He wasn't particularly affectionate or attentive even when he was sober. He did get worse after Mom died, from what I remember. I was so young, though."

"Did you ever hear him mention anything about me even in passing?" I hate how much I want to know the answer to this question.

"No, Tasha. I'm sorry. I never heard him mention you, but he never really talked to us outside of yelling anyway."

"Did you ever hear him mention anything about... I don't know, hating having a dark-skinned child?"

"*What?* Who told you that?"

"My mother. She would say the reason he didn't acknowledge me is because of how dark I was."

"Damn!" She blurts out. "That's so fucked up."

I snort. "Tell me about it."

"Tasha, I'm sorry you had to endure that as a kid, but from what I know, Dad never mentioned anything about skin tone. He was a bastard for sure, but I never heard the other stuff."

I nod even though Stacey can't see me. "For some reason I've been wondering that lately. I've done quite a bit of personal work to let that go, but uh, I'm kind of seeing someone new, and I'm sure you understand how that could trigger old insecurities."

"Tuh, don't I know it? Meeting Andre conjured up all my past insecurities. But I knew he was really the one when I felt comfortable enough to reveal my eating disorder to him and he kissed the scars on my fingers that were a result of it," she explains, reminiscing.

Stacey and I have slowly been getting to know each other. We speak once or twice a week since she left Dallas. It's been easy getting to know her up close, from her own mouth, instead of Coral's. We spend another fifteen minutes talking, Stacey asking me about the new man in my life. It feels good to be having girl talk. I open up to Stacey about this new relationship with Jeremy, not revealing too much but just enough.

I hear some muffled sounds in the background. A deep male voice I recognized as Stacey's husband, Andre. I pull the phone away from my ear when I hear what sounds like smacking lips.

"Sorry about that," Stacey apologizes breathily. "Andre just got home."

I smirk at that. I could tell from past interactions that her husband could be highly possessive of his wife's time.

"Babe, say hi to Tasha," Stacey calls.

"Hey, Tasha," he calls.

"Hey, Andre. How are you?"

"I'm tired, but my wife is forcing me to cook every night." The laughter is evident in his voice.

"Don't believe him. This man loves to cook."

"Bullshit. I just love how you show your gratitude after I cook."

"Andre!" Stacey gasps and I giggle at his antics.

"Anyway, Tash. I gotta go. Talk to you later this week."

"Bye, Tasha," Andre interjects.

I hear Stacey yelling her husband's name over my laughter as I hang up the phone. It's really great to know that both of my sisters ended up with good men in spite of the terrible example my father set for all of us. An inkling of hope begins to stir in my belly, wondering if the same is possible for me. At the same time my phone buzzes.

Jeremy: Be there in fifteen minutes.

I smile as those butterflies start moving in my stomach.

CHAPTER 6

*J*eremy

I slam my car door after getting in, rubbing my hand through my hair. I can't believe how the last few hours unfolded after getting back from my work trip. I tilt my head against the headrest, hands gripping the steering wheel, and close my eyes as the events of earlier this evening replay in my mind.

"Welcome back, Mr. Bennett. How was Tucson?" my assistant, Cynthia asks as I enter my office.

"It went well, Cynthia. The way things are progressing, the spa should be ready by the fall." I strut over to my desk, picking up the phone messages that have been left for me while I've been gone. I was in Phoenix checking on one of our spas for two days before heading to Tucson for the last five days to meet with contractors. Liam joined us the last two days. He headed straight home from the airport, but I needed to stop in the office to go over some details for my other hotels in addition to making a few phone calls. Even though it's after five in the evening, my assistant stayed after to catch me up on the happenings in the office over the last week.

"Thank you for staying late. I'm just going to catch up on some work and head out in a little bit. You don't need to stay any later."

When I don't hear a response, I look up and see her normally unflappable demeanor has morphed into uncertainty. Immediately, the hairs on the back of my neck stand up. I'm not going to enjoy whatever she's preparing to say.

"Just spit it out, Cynthia," I say in an impatient voice. I sit back in my chair, stretch my legs under my desk, and fold my arms across my chest.

"Well, as you see you have quite a few phone messages," she states, nodding at the stack of message notes she's left on my desk.

My eyes flick over to the stack of messages. "I see."

"Most of those messages are from one person. A woman."

At that, I raise my eyebrow. It isn't the norm for women to leave messages for me at work, but it certainly isn't unusual enough to have Cynthia as flustered as she is at the present moment. My mind wonders what woman it could be. I've cut off contact with most of my past lovers, seeing as how when I'm done with a woman, I'm done. The only woman I've had on my mind lately is LaTasha and I know she wouldn't leave any messages on my work phone. Besides, we talked almost daily while I was away. If she needed to contact me regarding something urgent, she had plenty of chances to do so.

"Does this woman have a name?" I ask, growing impatient.

"Y-yes, but she's also..." Cynthia drifts off.

"Cynthia, I've been gone a week and I only came in the office to check a few things before I leave. Please say whatever it is you need to say about this woman so we both can get on with our day."

"Well, she says she's your mother and she's in town. She came in the office. She wouldn't leave and insisted on seeing you when she knew you were coming back today."

Everything after the words your mother goes right over my head. I can still see Cynthia's lips moving, but for the life of me, I can't figure out what she's saying. My mind is reeling. My mother...That can't be.

"I...um..." I pause, clearing my throat. "I'm sorry. Did you say my mother?" I hate the fucking tone my voice has taken on, sounding like that scared ten-year-old kid, entering his first foster home. By now, my previously relaxed seated position has changed into a completely upright one. My back is ramrod straight, hands tightly gripping the edge of my desk.

"Yes, s-sir...uh, Mr. Bennett."

I barely notice Cynthia almost slipping and referring to me as sir. That's against one of my office rules. No one employed here is allowed to call me sir

—ever. I save that moniker for more private affairs. "What name did this woman give you?"

"She said her name was—"

"Marilyn Aries." A woman's voice sounds from behind Cynthia, finishing the statement.

It sends a chill down my spine. It's been more than twenty years since I've heard that voice, but I already know who it belongs to. The last name is different, but the first name is the same. Cynthia steps aside, and for the first time since I was ten years old, I lay eyes on the woman who birthed me and left me.

I remain paralyzed; too caught up in a time warp to say anything. I simply stare at her, taking in the dark brown hair that has begun to grey at the roots, her thin five-foot-nine frame, and olive skin. Her complexion nearly mirrors mine. Lastly, we make eye contact. Looking into the dark brown irises of hers, I know this is indeed the same woman I had lived with for the first ten years of my life. The same cold look I always remember her giving me is staring back at me now, assessing me.

"I see you've done well with the business your father left you," she says, haughtily as she steps around Cynthia to glide toward my desk. She looks around the huge corner office. No doubt, she's taking in the modern décor and view of downtown Dallas that can be seen from the huge floor-to-ceiling windows.

"I'm sorry, Mr. Bennett, but she wouldn't leave. I can have security—"

I hold up my hand to silence my nervous assistant. "You may leave for the evening, Cynthia. Thank you," I say curtly, never taking my eyes off of Marilyn. I hear Cynthia's movements as she reluctantly exits my office. A few seconds later, the outer office door closes.

"What the hell are you doing here, Marilyn?" I bark between gritted teeth, seething.

"Marilyn? What happened to Mother or at least Mama? You used to like to call me Mama when you were younger."

I stare at her for a few more moments, barely able to believe this bit-woman's audacity. "You told me not to refer to you as anything other than Marilyn, especially in front of your male suitors. Remember, Marilyn?" I say her name again, reminding her that there is no love lost between the two of us. "What do you want? I'm busy," I assert, retaking my seat and picking up papers from my desk. I refuse to give her any more than minimal attention.

"I see someone has learned to perfect the cold shoulder." She sounds almost shocked at my reaction.

"I learned from the best," I respond without looking up at her. Continuing to look at my files, I hear her take a seat in the chair facing my desk. Her movement causes her perfume to waft in the air around me. White Diamonds. The same scent I remember her wearing when I was a child.

"Don't be like that, Jer-Jer."

My face immediately scrunches up at the old, stupid-ass nickname she used to call me as a child. "Jeremy," I correct her.

"Okay, Jeremy. Anyway, I see you are doing well these days."

No thanks to you.

"What do you mean no thanks to me? If it wasn't for me, you wouldn't have any of this." Her voice takes on a shrill tone.

I hadn't even realized I said those words out loud, but I refuse to take them back. "If it wasn't for you?" I repeat, making sure I wasn't hearing things.

"Yes! I chose your father and if it hadn't been for me, you wouldn't have had the opportunities you had."

"Lady, have you lost your goddamn mind?!" I can tolerate a lot of bullshit, but this damn woman coming in here and telling me I should be grateful to her is not one of them. "You dropped me off at social services when I was ten years old like I was a goddamn lump of coal. If I owe anything to anyone, it sure as shit ain't you!" I drop the papers on my desk and point angrily at her.

"Jer—" She stops when she notices the expression on my face. "Jeremy, I didn't come here to upset you. I just thought it would be...nice if we got to know each other as adults."

I squint at her, letting her know I am not buying her bullshit. "After twenty-three years, you want us to get to know each other? You know when a mother and son usually get to know one another? When that mother is raising her son; when that son grows and matures into an adult and that mother has been there every step of the way. But that was not the case for you and me. I stopped wanting to get to know you the day you dropped me off with one suitcase and never looked back. You and I have nothing to discuss," I *say, curtly standing. "Now, you can go on back to whatever corner of the world you reside in, living off your fourth or fifth rich husband's wealth. Then we both can pretend that this little reunion never happened." I begin placing the papers on my desk back in their folders and gathering my belongings to leave.*

Marilyn stands. "Jeremy, please. We need to talk."

"I already told you we have nothing to—"

"I'm dying!" she declares loudly, cutting me off.

My whole body freezes up and I probably could've been knocked over by a feather. The logical part of my brain is telling me I shouldn't give a fuck. This is the woman who abandoned me, but the part of me who is still that little ten-year-old kid, takes over. I turn back to my desk, sit down, and stare at Marilyn. "Talk."

I LIFT my head from the steering wheel, shaking off those thoughts. I look over at the dashboard clock. It's 7:45. I just texted Tasha to let her know I'm on my way. I refuse to cancel. I'll just have to deal with that other shit later. My stomach growls as I inhale the aroma of the Thai food I picked up, reminding me that I haven't eaten since this morning. I was supposed to have landed much earlier than I actually did, but I got caught up with some work matters. And then of course, once I got to the office, I got surprised by Marilyn, which was an entire shit show. Despite my weariness, the idea of seeing LaTasha sends a rush of warmth through me. I wish I could figure out what's drawing me to her, but I can't. Now, tonight despite the magnitude of what walked through my door earlier today, I find my nerves calming down with the knowledge that I'm only a few minutes away from seeing her face. I don't remember the last time I had this type of reaction to any woman.

"Get a grip, Bennett," I grumble to myself at the same time I pull up to mansion gate. I lower my window for the security camera to scan my face and open the gate. I'm the only person who does not live on this property but has this type of access. Liam doesn't play about his home's security, which is likely a smart move due to the fact that his wife is a trained spy with lots of enemies. His own father had tried to kill her once. But that's a different story for a different time. Right now, I'm focused on my own wo...err...*sub*. Right. My sub. Not my woman. I don't make any woman mine.

After parking, I stroll down the walkway toward the door. Before I even lift my arm to knock, it opens. My breath catches at sight of LaTasha for the time in the flesh in more than a week. She's wearing a simple pair of skinny jeans and an off-the-shoulder, purple T-shirt. My insides settle in relief. That's never happened to me before and it feels good. I instantly decide purple is her color and make a mental note to tell her to wear it more often for our dates. Despite the simplicity of the outfit, it hugs her curves just enough to give a full outline of the plush body that lies underneath. I raise my eyes, taking in the swell of her breasts and curvature of her shoulder to her neck. I admire her smooth, dark skin that glows with health. For a heartbeat, I wonder if she'll shiver if I were to lick or better yet, *bite* the space right where her neck meets her shoulder. I have to stop myself from taking a step forward and finding out. Everything I've taken in so far is no match for the moment our eyes collide. Those damn eyes are filled with undeniable anticipation and hesitance.

"Hell—"

Her greeting is cut off by my lips against hers. It'd been days since I felt those soft cushions underneath mine, so I decided to take liberties. I kiss her, biting and nibbling on her bottom lip. I press my tongue into her mouth once I feel her give in to the kiss. Her hand comes up to cup the side of my face.

"Now, that's the proper way to greet me." I say against her lips. I needed that little taste after the evening I've had.

"C-come in. Do you need me to take that?" She gestures toward my hand holding our dinner.

"No. Just lead me to the dining area."

"It's right this way," she says, walking ahead of me.

We walk through her living room and I smile at the eclectic décor of her home. The furniture is all bright colors, and although I don't notice any clothes strewn about, I get the impression she's recently cleaned up on my behalf.

"You can put it here. I'll get the plates and forks. Would you like water, wine, juice or soda to drink with dinner?" She turns her head to look at me over her shoulder.

"Coke is fine," I respond, making no secret that I'm eyeing her backside.

"Umm..." She pauses and fully turns to face me with her eyebrows crinkled. "I don't have Coke. I only have Sprite and Ginger Ale."

I nod. "Sprite is fine." I grin watching her walk away. This is the first time I see her in skinny jeans, and she looks damn good in them.

"Thank you," I comment as she returns. I remove the plates and forks from her hand, while she places the two cans of sprite on the table with her other. "I got chicken and shrimp pad Thai and spring rolls. Any preference for chicken or shrimp?"

"I'll have shrimp please."

I scoop a hefty amount of shrimp pad Thai and a couple of spring rolls onto her plate before placing it in front of her.

"Wait. Shouldn't this be reverse?" she asks, standing.

"Reversed?" I ask as I fill my plate with chicken pad Thai. I inhale deeply as the aromas of the food fill the dining area. My stomach grumbles even louder than it had earlier in the car.

"Yes, I should be serving you. Right? Isn't that a sub's job?"

I nod, finally realizing what she was getting at. "If that's one of the terms we agree on. But we'll get there. Sit and let's enjoy our meal before talking."

"Okay," she agrees, falling back into her seat.

"Mmm..."

I look up to see LaTasha's eyes closed as she chews slowly. The look on her face reminds me of a woman in ecstasy.

"You can't moan like that unless you're ready for me to do something about it," I say, looking directly at her.

Her eyes pop open. Immediately, the way she licks her bottom lip makes me grip my fork harder.

"Oh..." she replies bashfully.

73

"Yeah, *oh.*" I resume eating my food. It is delicious and I understand the pleasure she receives from eating. Still those sounds emanating from her mouth are a little too much for my already frayed nerves right now.

I raise an eyebrow when LaTasha clears her throat after a few minutes of silence, only marked by the sounds of forks hitting the plate and chewing. "How was your work trip?"

I sit back in my chair, wiping my mouth with a napkin before speaking. "Work was a little hectic. We've had some problems at this site, so we had to get new contractors awhile back. But things are running much more smoothly now. I had to be down there to sign some contracts and look over the shoulders of the new contractors to make sure the work is actually being done. These new guys are good."

"Good. I'm glad it's going well." She smiles.

A warmth spreads throughout my chest at her smile, and I instantly decide to change the subject.

"How's the book coming along?"

The forlorn expression that forms on her face answers the question. She blows out an exasperated breath and shakes her head. "Not well at all. Still stuck in this damn writer's block. It's actually starting to scare me. What if I'm never able to write again? How many fans of this series will be disappointed? Almost daily I go to the community center with Coral and I hear some of the kids excited to read about Danica and her next adventure and triumph but then all I feel is guilt. Guilt I might not be able to deliver it to them. Of course they don't know I'm the writer, but they do ask me sometimes if I know when the next book is coming out. I just give them some lame excuse that I've heard the author was hard at work or something. Then I come home and *nothing.* The words aren't flowing. I can't remember a time in my life when escaping into the fantasy world created by my imagination wasn't a savior for me. And now? It may be gone."

The desperation that begins to peek through in her voice grips my chest. I know the feeling of being abandoned, but to think it's your own brain that is abandoning you has got to be the worst possible feeling. Nevertheless, I've picked up on something LaTasha likely hasn't and I want to investigate it further. For a few seconds I just stare at her without blinking. My face doesn't give anything away as I pick up my glass of soda and bring it to my lips. I take a few sips and wipe my mouth before asking my next question.

"When you wrote your first few books, you were living in Vermont on your own, right?"

Her face wrinkles in confusion for a nanosecond, obviously trying to figure out what my question has to do with what she's just said. However, that's for me to know.

"Yes, well, sort of. I actually wrote my first book years ago and quickly followed it with my second book. It wasn't until about three years ago after I got my publishing deal that I wrote my third. I was in a little bubble almost. Didn't really talk to anyone besides Coral while I was writing the first three."

I nod, realizing my assessment of her problem was spot on. "I see." I take another sip of my drink and push my plate away from me, finished with my meal. "Come here," I say, tapping my thigh for her to sit on my lap.

She hesitates at first, but eventually rises slowly and walks toward me. I grab her hand, pulling her to my lap and begin massaging her lower back. Her sigh reveals she's relaxing into my embrace.

"I gave you an assignments on our last date. Did you remember?" I purposely didn't discuss the assignments in our other conversations throughout the week because I'd told her it was something we would discuss in person. Also, I needed to see how well she would follow instructions after they're given once. I don't like repeating myself. That's something my subs have to learn right away.

She lowers her lids. "Yes."

"Love, when I ask a question, I need you to look at me unless directed otherwise. Alright?"

"Yes," she answers, raising her gaze to meet mine.

"Do you remember your assignments?"

She starts to nod, but then she answers, "Yes. It was to remember the last time I'd experienced pleasure of any kind in my body. Then came the uh...balls."

I smirk at her awkwardness discussing the Ben Wa balls.

"First things first. Were you able to remember a pleasurable time?"

"Mmmhum," she answers.

"What does *mmm hum* mean? I need actual words."

The edges of her eyes tighten as she squints at me, frustrated. However, she continues. "I mean *yes*. I remember a time."

"Go on," I prod.

"About three months ago, Coral made a spa appointment for us. We did massages, manis, and pedis. The whole works. Anyway, the most enjoyable part of the day for me was the massage. It was my first massage ever. I usually don't like being..." She pauses to clear her throat, shifting in her seat. "I don't like being touched, but the masseuse was professional, so after a while I felt more comfortable. I decided to tell her to apply more pressure. She was being too light at first, but when she began to press harder on my muscles, euphoria overcame me. Well, maybe not *that* extreme, but it felt good. The harder she pressed, the more I liked it."

I nod, satisfied at her answer. "Is that the only time you can remember pain bringing you some type of pleasure?"

Her head tilts, thinking over my question when I see the light bulb go off. Her eyes grow wide as she looks at me, astonished. "No, it isn't."

I don't say anything put pull her in closer on my lap.

"My mama wasn't the nicest person to me," she says explains, rolling her eyes. "Anyway, when I was young and she got angry at me, she would pinch me. She wasn't overly physically abusive or anything, but pinching was her way of letting me know she was displeased about something. I remember one time I spilled a glass of Kool-Aid on her bed while watching TV. She was pissed when she came home and saw the stain. She grabbed my arm and pinched the skin on my forearm hard. At first, it hurt like hell, but then... I don't know. It kind of tickled. The longer she held on, the more intense the prickles of pleasure became. I know she was yelling or saying something, but all I could concentrate on was how much I felt that pinch. I'd forgotten all about that." She looks as if she's just unlocked a long-lost secret. And she has. "Is that *normal?*"

"For people in this life it is. Many of us, subs especially, recall discovering at a young age, the link between pleasure and pain."

"I do remember reading that in my research." She nods. She blows out a breath as if she had been worried about her thoughts. "Are you full or do you have room for dessert?"

"What'd you have in mind?" I ask nipping her earlobe and enjoying the shudder I feel in her body.

"I-I made pecan pie and bought vanilla bean ice cream to go with it," she purrs.

"You cook?"

"Y-yes."

"I'm definitely looking forward to dessert." I grin, moving my hand up her thigh and tightening my other arm around her waist. I grip her chin with my thumb and index finger, pulling her face to meet mine. I hungrily take her mouth, exploring every inch of it. I swear I'm hearing and experiencing things with just a kiss from this woman until I realize that buzzing sound in the background is my phone. Angrily, I pull back and stare at her swollen lips for a second before pulling my phone out of my pocket. Rarely do I get calls this late at night unless they're important. When I see it's the number from the hospice, I grunt in disapproval.

"Everything okay?"

"Yes. Well...I don't know, but I've gotta go," I inform LaTasha when I read the text message from the hospice director.

"Oh... Are you sure?" she questions.

I take my attention off my phone and put it onto the woman on my lap. Damn if I didn't want to stay. I'd had some interesting plans for tonight, but they'll have to wait.

"I'm sure. Walk me to the door," I request, taking another nip of her bottom lip before standing and placing her on her feet.

Reluctantly, I let her leave my embrace to turn and lead the way to the door.

"I have another assignment for you. When you're in the writing, zone about how many words do you write per day?" I ask once we've reached the door.

She ponders. "Uh man, it feels like ages since I've been in the zone, but when I'm on, I can normally write anywhere from three thousand to five thousand words a day. Sometimes I get in ten thousand on a really good day. Why?"

"Because I want you to have written ten thousand words by our next date, which will be this coming Friday."

Her eyes bulge in disbelief. "Ten thousand words in less than a week?! Have you not been listening to me? I've barely been able to write 3,000 words over the last three months!"

I frown. "Love, I don't like the tone you're using." My voice is calm and even.

"Well, I don't like this assignment."

My head tilts. "Too damn bad."

"How am I supposed to come up with 10,000 words? I just don't think—"

"Don't think. Just write. I didn't say they had to be good. You don't even have to read them to me. Simply write." I pause, wanting very much to laugh when I notice her eyes clouding with anger. She keeps it in, though. "So we're clear, right? Keep wearing the Ben Wa balls and write ten thousand words. Those are your next two assignments."

LaTasha sighs audibly, visibly disgruntled.

"Love, I need an answer."

"Fine," she huffs.

I work hard to hold in my laughter at the grim expression on her face. I know she won't be able to complete one of the tasks I've given her, but I've made the demands for a good reason. One she'll have to wait to find out why. "I have a busy work week, but there's an exhibit I'd like to take you to see Friday," I say before I press a kiss to her cheek. Without even thinking, I lean down and bite her earlobe, loving the way she shivers at the contact. *Patience.* I have to remind myself. The last thing I want to do is rush this. I still have doubts as to whether or not she's ready for everything I have in store for her. But we'll find out sooner or later.

"This Friday. And wear something the same color as this shirt and show off your legs." I grin as she looks at me skeptically and down at her shirt.

"You like this color on me?"

"I do."

She gives a half grin, still angry but obviously please by my compliment.

The tightening in my chest is my cue to leave before I make this a much longer evening and do some things neither of us are prepared for right now. I lean over and press my lips to her warm cheek, reveling in the softness of her skin and her scent that is a mixture of vanilla and her natural essence.

"Thank you for dinner," she nearly whispers.

"Anytime, LaTasha. Make sure to lock the door behind me." I step outside, closing the door behind me. I wait until I hear the click of the lock engage before I walk to my car. I know even if her door were left wide open, save for a bird, there's nothing or no one who could get into her home. Security here is just that tight. Still I need the confirmation of hearing the lock to know she's safe. As I walk down the pathway toward my vehicle, I try to convince myself that my slight obsession with her safety is just me being my typical Dom, protective self. I almost believe the lie.

I look up at a window of the main house on the second floor. For a moment, I see the outline of a person standing in the window, before the light in the room disappears. From the layout of the house, I know that's Liam and Coral's bedroom. I grin and continue on to my car, knowing I'll be getting a visit soon. Unfortunately, right now I have to deal with another pressing matter.

CHAPTER 7

*T*asha

"Miss Tasha! I'm halfway finished with Danica's second book!" An excited Trudy runs up to me after lunch. We're getting ready to dismiss the kids at the community center. Since it's later in the summer, the center is now down to half days, so we end our day between noon and one o'clock.

I grin widely. "Really, Trudy? That's great."

"Yeah. Danica is so strong and fierce. I love her. Thank you for giving me the first book. I have to return the second book to the library this weekend, so I gotta hurry up and finish it."

"Oh, that reminds me. Stay right here," I say before hurrying off to Coral's office where I've left my belongings. I use the key she has given me to her office, opening the door. I go into my bag to pull out *Danica's Passage* and *Danica's Voyage*, the second and third books in the series. I have autographed both books. I leave the office and return to Trudy. "These are for you." I hand the books over to Trudy who now wears an awe-struck expression.

"*Really?!*"

"Yes. Open the front covers," I encourage.

When Trudy does, her eyes grow even bigger as she realizes what's inside.

Dear Trudy,

I heard you were a big fan of Danica's adventures, so I wanted to give you a few of my personal copies.

Sincerely,

L.T. Jones

The excited child looks up at me. "Oh my God! Is this for real?!"

I nod. "Yes, I have some connections, so I was able to get the author to autograph copies for you."

The excitement from Trudy's eyes helps me to not feel so bad about the lie. I still don't want anyone to find out I'm the author for more than one reason; one of which includes this damn writer's block that continues to take hold of my imagination like an iceberg. Thinking about my inability to write causes a knot of dread to rise in my belly. Unfortunately, it also means that I've failed to complete the assignment Jeremy gave me earlier in the week. Writing 10,000 words in a week has never fazed me before, but right now it feels impossible, I just couldn't get it done. I feel my anger surfacing the more I think about it. Jeremy knows I'm going through writer's block. Why the hell would he give me such an impossible task? Is this a typical Dom thing? I also hate to admit this, but the idea of disappointing him also doesn't sit too well with me.

"I won't let anything happen to these *ever.*"

Trudy's excited words pull me out of my own head and back to the present moment. "I know you won't," I assure her. "Is your mom picking you up today?"

Trudy's expression changes from excited to withdrawn in an instant. "Nah. She said she had something to do today. I think she's sending my aunt or someone to pick me up."

"Oh, do you need more money for the bus?" I ask as we head out the door to wait where parents pick up their kids.

"Nah, I think my auntie comin'."

"Alright. Do you mind if I wait with you? You can tell me what you think about Danica's adventures so far. I was thinking of starting a book club here in the fall for the after-school program. What do you think of that?"

"What's a book club?" she asks as she stuffs her newly acquired book into her book bag.

"It's a club wherein all the participants read the same book and then we come together once or twice a week to have discussions on what we think of the book."

"Will there be snacks?"

I laugh. "Of course! What good is a group discussion without good food?"

"Then I'm in!" Trudy agrees, grinning.

We talk for a few more minutes about book club ideas pertaining to the Danica books. We both feed off one another's excitement, talking up more and more ideas before I hear a male voice call Trudy's name.

She turns and her frown is instant. That look causes warning bells to go off in my head. On instinct, I move to stand in front of Trudy.

"Hello, sir. I'm Tasha, one of the volunteers here."

He glares at me. He's about 5'9" with almond skin. He dressed in a white T-shirt and baggy jeans. I wouldn't call him handsome by a long shot, especially now with the scrunched up face he's directing toward me.

"Yeah, I'm Trudy's step daddy," he returns.

"Oh... And your name is?"

"Gary," he says shortly. "Trudy, let's go."

"My auntie couldn't come and get me?" Trudy asks.

My worry grows when I notice she hasn't stepped from around me to greet this man who claims to be her stepfather.

"Nah. She ain't coming." He sucks his teeth. "Let's go, girl. Ya mama got shit to do."

I frown at the language he speaks to an eleven-year-old girl.

"O-okay."

"Trudy, you have a good weekend, sweetie. I'll see you here Monday morning at nine o'clock," I say, trying to reassure her.

"Whatever. Let's go, "Gary rushes to say before he turns and walks away, clearly expecting Trudy to follow.

"Trudy, are you okay?" I hurriedly ask.

"Yes, Miss Tasha. I gotta go. Thank you again. See ya," she says before rushing off behind him.

The sense of dread I feel watching her walk away doesn't ease up until the red beat-up Buick they get into is long out of my sight. I say a silent prayer for God to watch over Trudy as I turn and head back inside to collect my belongings. I plan on doing some more investigation into Trudy's home life. I know something isn't right there. For now, I turn my attention to gathering my things and heading home to prepare myself for the evening ahead.

* * *

"YOU LOOK BEAUTIFUL."

My belly warms at the deep rumble in his voice. I know he's telling the truth because the way his eyes rummage over my body in the deep purple romper agrees with his tone. The butterflies in my belly tell me just how happy it makes me that he's pleased with how I look.

I dip my head to get my thoughts together, still uncomfortable with the intensity of this attraction. "Thank you. You look great too," I finally answer, not blowing smoke at all. He looks great always. He's dressed in a pair of dark, tailored dress slacks and a white button up shirt with the sleeves rolled up to the elbow, displaying the array of tattoos on his arms. I plan on asking him about the tattoos in the future.

"Are you ready to go?" he asks, hooking his arm in an invitation for me to loop my arm around it.

I nod, but then remember his rule. "Yes, I am."

At that he grins, pleased. *And there goes those goddamn butterflies again.* I link my arm with his, and again that electrical current shoots through me as expected whenever we touch. I have to take a deep breath to actually move my feet. I have purchased a new pair of heels, and although they're a mere three inches, when you're used to walking in sneakers or flip flops daily, three inches is a lot.

"You okay?" Jeremy asks, sensing my nervousness.

"Yes, I'm fine. New shoes, that's all." I smile up at him.

He nods as I close and lock my door, retaking his arm as we walk to his car.

"Do you always have to call Liam to get in the front gate?" I ask as we pull off and out of the driveway. I know how tight security is on this property.

"No. I helped Liam design this property. I've been on the security list since he built it and was included in gate access for as long."

"He must really trust you."

"Of course. We're cousins, but he's the closest thing I've ever had to a brother."

"Is that why you helped him get back with Coral after all those years?"

Jeremy gives me a side eye before returning his attention to the road. "You know about that, huh?"

I laugh. "Coral mentioned you had something to do with getting them back in contact when you came to her security firm and asked for her help with a case."

Jeremy nods and grabs something from the console. I see it's a toothpick as he brings it to his lips. I stare at the way his jaw works as he chews. There really is something about a man with a chiseled jaw line that is utterly sexy.

"I did. It was time for them to get their shit together."

I giggle. "I agree. It took long enough. I guess I should thank you too."

He gives me an amused glance. "For what?"

"For two things actually. One, without you, Coral would still be off to God knows where trying to track down some terrorist or something instead of being seven months pregnant and running a community center. It means a lot to me that she's safe now. At least she's out of harm's way for the most part. Secondly, if Coral wasn't here in Dallas, I wouldn't be here either. I'm starting to really like this city. So, thanks." I shrug. I'd never had intentions of living anywhere besides Vermont before, but when Coral invited me to move in to be closer to her, I couldn't turn it down. Now, I've fallen in love with the city, the weather, the low-key nature, and most of all, being a part of what feels like a family.

I notice Jeremy's profile relax at my gratitude. "Coral and Liam would've eventually found their way back to one another. I just helped speed things along. As for the second part, I think your presence here is turning out to be more in my favor, so it's a win-win," he says, turning to fully look at me. It's only then I realize we've reached our destination.

"The Science Museum," I read the large marquee. And my eyes widen as I realize why he has chosen this place as our date. "There's an X-Men exhibit here!" I turn, looking at him excitedly.

His satisfied grin speaks volumes. "I've been meaning to come for the past month, but I haven't had time until now. I'm glad I didn't come alone, so now I get to enjoy it with you."

"I've wanted to come here too, but I thought it'd be too nerdy. I'm glad I waited too," I say, reaching for the door handle to get out. I'm anxious to see the exhibit. Before the door even releases, I feel a tight grip around my left arm. I look over stunned.

"Let me," he says sternly. He cuts off the car and gets out. Within seconds he is at my door, opening it and helping me out. "As long as I'm arounds you don't open car doors for yourself. Got it?"

"It's just a—"

He lowers his chin, his gaze leveling me.

"Alright. Got it." I nod. No need to put up a fight about someone wanting to behave like a gentleman.

"They also have hors d'oeuvres and drinks, so we can eat as we look around the exhibit. I thought that would be okay instead of going to dinner first."

"Yes, that's fine. Do they have a map or layout of the exhibit?" I question giddily.

"Of course." He smiles at me as we reach the entrance, obviously picking up on my excitement.

The nerd in me is in heaven as soon as Jeremy opens the door for me and I enter the museum. I'm in awe when I see a huge marquee featuring the famous metal claws of Wolverine from X-Men.

"The exhibit is up the stairs," Jeremy tells me, handing me a map.

I frown briefly, hating that I have to trek up a staircase in my new heels, but I quickly hide my displeasure and turn toward the stairs. I shiver as Jeremy places his hand at the small of my back. I do my best to keep my balance, but between these heels and Jeremy's closeness, it's difficult. He smells so damn good. Some sort of expensive cologne for sure, but underneath it is a scent I know is all him. I wish I could pocket his natural scent and carry it around with me all day. I to remind myself not to close my eyes and swoon over his scent as we continue to ascend the stairs.

"Oh, look! They have the original designs of the comics!" I say once we reach the top, pointing to one of the first glass cases.

For the next two hours, Jeremy and I are like kids in a candy store, moving from one exhibit to the next. The original comic drawings, the set designs, and costumes from the major motion pictures are all on display. Of course my attention is piqued even more once we reach Storm's costume and featured comics.

"You know, I hate that they had Halle Berry play her in the movies," I somewhat whisper to Jeremy as we make the final rounds of the exhibit some two hours later.

"Why?" he asks, wrapping his arm around my lower back.

I fall into his embrace, not even realizing how familiar his touch has become over the course of this date. I'm pretty sure a minute hasn't gone by that he hasn't had his hand on me in some way, whether it was a hand at my lower back, gripping my hand, or brushing a stray hair out of my face as I look over an exhibit. I've never had someone pay such close attention to me. Not this way, at least. It feels good.

"Because." I shrug, semi embarrassed at my reason. We begin to descend the stairs.

"Because is not an answer," he clarifies in an admonishing tone.

I sigh, unsure of how I want to answer his original question, but realizing I had opened myself up for it. "I don't think you'd understand."

"Try me."

I feel less reluctant to open up when I don't get the impression he's offended by my last remark. He appears more amused. I remain quiet for a few more seconds. Once we reach the museum's exit, I decide to go for it. Holding my head up to stare at Jeremy's penetrating gaze, I begin to explain. "I told you before that seeing Storm for the first time was somewhat life-changing for me. She was a beautiful and strong dark skin woman, but vulnerable at the same time because of her. Yeah, her eyes were blue and her hair grey, but she was undeniably a woman with a dark complexion. And for someone like me who didn't have many images of women who shared my skin tone, it meant a lot. So for Hollywood to cast Halle Berry, who is definitely does not have dark skin because she is bi-racial, it just—"

"Felt like a letdown," he states, finishing my thought.

I nod. "Yeah."

"You thought I wouldn't understand that?"

Feeling slightly chastised, I answer truthfully. "No."

"Because I'm *white*?"

I flinch at the honesty in his question, but to my surprise I don't see anger in his eyes. I see amusement. That makes giving him an answer a little easier. "Yes," I respond truthfully as we exit the museum. "Honestly, you have more representation in popular media than someone who looks like me, especially when I was growing up. So yeah, I wasn't sure if you'd get it or not."

He tilts his head upward as if he's considering my words. "I get it. Images like mine, the white male, are represented more prevalently in the media and in this society overall. I never had to worry about someone misrepresenting Wolverine's comic book with an actor who looks nothing like him. I remember my foster mom talking about representation when I was younger. She was a huge fan of Nichelle Nichols."

"*Uhura!*" I blurt out.

Instead of being annoyed by my interruption, he bursts out

laughing at my giddiness. The sound causes something in my chest to tighten.

"Yup." He opens the car door for me.

I climb inside. It takes me a second to even realize he'd said *foster mom*. It's the first time he's mentioned anything about his childhood to me aside from his mother's abandonment.

"Were you close to her?" I ask as he gets in the car.

He looks at me confused for a second. "My foster mom?"

I nod.

He pauses before answering. "Yes."

I decide to not question it further because I've picked up on his hesitance. "Are you taking me home?" I ask, changing the topic.

"Not yet. As I recall there were a couple of assignments I had for you that we need to discuss *in private*."

I clench my thighs together in anticipation and fear.

CHAPTER 8

*J*eremy

The motion sensor lights immediately turn on as I pull up in the driveway of my home. I turn to look at the expression of surprise mixed with hesitance on LaTasha's face. I press the button to raise the garage door and pull in. Wordlessly, I open the door, hop out, and go around to open LaTasha's door for her. I'm pleased when I see her wait for me to open the door instead of getting out on her own. It's a small gesture, but it shows she knows how to follow rules and I don't have to repeat myself. As for why I decided to bring LaTasha to my home instead of the usual hotel suite where I take my subs is an issue I choose not to entertain right now.

"You brought me to your home." If her face wasn't so expressive already, the surprise in her voice would definitely give her away.

"I said we needed to talk privately."

"Right. You did say that."

"Come on," I say, leading her through the door that enters the mudroom. Once there, I remove the suit jacket I'd been wearing and hang LaTasha's purse up on one of the wooden wall hangers. "Would you like anything to drink?" I ask as we enter the living room as the lights turn on automatically.

"Some water would be great."

"Coming right up. Have a seat." I gesture toward the large leather couch. "Make yourself comfortable."

I turn and retrieve two bottles of water from my refrigerator, returning in less than minute. I observe Tasha sitting, but she's noticeably uptight. I study her while she looks around the room, admiring the stone fireplace, huge saltwater fish tank, and the rest of the earth tone décor.

"Here's your water." I twist the cap off and hand it to her before placing my bottle on a coaster on the glass coffee table close to the couch. Coming to stand in front of her, I kneel on one knee. I hide my smirk when her eyes widen.

"W-what are doing?"

For a second, I fear she's going to choke on her water. "Hand me your foot."

"What?"

"Love, you know I don't like repeating myself and I know you heard me the first time."

She stares at me as if I've lost my mind for a few seconds before offering me her foot. I reach for it, removing her shoe I have no doubt she purchased especially for our date. I begin to rub her stocking-clad foot. A few seconds later, I reach for the other foot, which LaTasha offers up less reluctantly than the first one. Removing that shoe, I begin massaging both feet simultaneously. At first, she sighs lightly, but as I increase the pressure, soft moans emit from her throat. When my cock begins stirring in my pants because of those sounds, I know it's time to end this little massage.

"How did you know my feet were hurting like hell?"

I chuckle. "Lucky guess." I stand, moving toward the fireplace to light it before I join her on the couch. "Did you enjoy the museum?"

The slow grin that spreads over her beautiful face answers my question before her words do. "Are you kidding? Thank you for taking me."

"You're welcome. Let's discuss those assignments."

"Okay."

She begins nibbling on her lower lip. "LaTasha, I'm sure you don't know what you're doing to me every time you bite your lip. You're not ready for everything that lip is making me feel, so for both our sakes, I suggest you stop."

Her eyes bulge, and for a second and I think she's going to continue to challenge me. Oh, how I wish she would. It would make my plans for the night much easier. Unfortunately, she slowly releases her lip from her teeth's grips I must stand to put some distance between us.

I retrieve my water bottle to taka a sip as I stare off into the fire. I attempt to gather my thoughts for a minute. "Back to those assignments," I say, finally turning to her.

"Oh yeah..." She nods. "What do you want to know?" She's avoiding eye contact, which tells me she hasn't finished them. I'd already suspected as much.

"How were the Ben Wa balls?" I ask first, knowing that was the easier of the two assignments.

"Honestly, they were a little uncomfortable at first, but I wore them as you requested. I even did a little research on them and found there are exercises that go along with them. Did you know there're women who actually lift weights with their uh...*pelvic muscles?*"

I chuckle at the expression on her face.

"Anyway, they're getting better."

I incline my head towards her, pleased. "And the writing?"

That question causes her to break eye contact again, taking another sip of her water. "Um, well, I tried."

"*You tried?*" I raise an eyebrow.

She nods.

"Love," I warn.

"Yes, I tried," she immediately confirms. "But the words still wouldn't flow."

"So you didn't complete the assignment?" I replace my water bottle on the table and come to stand in front of her, towering over her.

"No."

"Stand up."

She hesitates and just as my irritation at her lack of compliance grows, she slowly rises, but bends down to grab her shoes first.

"Leave them. Follow me," I say, turning to suppress the urge to touch her. I walk down the hall and down the spiral staircase that leads to my playroom. I turn back once I reach the door to make sure she is behind me. I don't admit out loud that this is a momentous occasion. This will be the very first time that anyone besides me will enter this room. I've owned this house for five years and spent that same amount of time creating this room to fit the image in my mind. I never realized until this moment that I was waiting for the right sub to show it to. Turning the knob, I open the door and the light illuminates the space. I hear LaTasha's breath catch as I step aside to allow her entrance.

"This is my playroom. Well, it's *one* of them."

I watch as she steps inside, looking around at all the floggers, paddles, and collars hanging on the wall. Her hand grazes the steel pole that's erected in the center of the room. I can tell she's intrigued, which serves to heighten my own arousal. Seeing her in this space does something more to me than I'd ever imagined.

"We need to discuss punishments," I finally say, low.

"*Punishments?*" Those big, honey eyes look at me questioningly.

"Yes. I gave you an assignment and you failed to complete it. That cannot go unpunished." I run my finger along her jaw line, needing to touch her. "We've already talked about your hard lines and I've told you I'm not into sadomasochism. Punishments aren't meant to cause pain. Not always," I say that last part around a mischievous grin. "But failure to complete an assignment is an offense that can't be tolerated." I stroll over to the wall toward the hanging floggers. I've lost count of the total number I own. Each serves their own purpose. I pick up my red and black flogger with the leather one-inch wide falls. Perfect for this occasion.

"There are many ways I can punish you, but for this occasion, I think a flogger is the most fitting." I come to stand in front of her.

She continues to stare at me, anticipating my next move. When she doesn't run screaming, I take that as a positive sign.

"I'm going to bind your wrists with my silk scarf and turn you to face the wall." I pull one of my drawers open and remove a purple silk scarf I just purchased the week before when I realized I loved the look of purple against her skin. "Hold out your wrists."

Hesitantly, LaTasha obliges. I tie a double knot, securing her wrists together. Next, I lead her over to the large king size bed. "It's not too tight, is it?"

"N-no," she assures me.

"Tell me why you weren't able to complete the assignment I gave you?" I ask, turning her toward the wall. "Raise your arms and grab the bar above your head."

She raises her gaze to stare at the bar before raising bound hands to grip it. Her movements are stiff and hesitant, but her compliance speaks volumes regarding trust. "Writer's block," she answers.

"Okay, before we get started, you need to tell me your safe word."

"Safe word?"

"Yes. What is the word you want to use if I go too far or you become uncomfortable?"

"Wolverine."

My chest tightens. "Wolverine it is."

"Since this will be our first time, I'll allow you to keep your clothes on. And I'm going to use a less intense flogger. You will receive five lashes and you'll count out loud. Understand?"

She nods.

"Love," I growl.

"S-sorry. I mean, yes. Understood."

"Turn your head toward the wall, but keep your eyes open."

When she obeys, I take a step back, putting enough distance between us to allow the flogger to do its job. I lift my hand and send the flogger down in one swift swing, landing right across her buttocks. The sound reverberates around the room, and Tasha gasps.

"One," she sounds off.

I sigh in relief, a warm feeling overtaking me as I raise my hand again.

"T-two." Her voice has taken on a husky undertone.

My lower region reacts at her sensual tone.

"Threeee."

"Two more, doll," I say, angling my body a little different to ensure I hit a different spot on her plump buttocks.

"F-fourrr," she purrs after the fourth strike, her ass bouncing back as if begging for more.

My cock is rock hard just from the deep emotion—both pleasure and fear—I hear in her voice. Her body's reaction to this tells me she was made for what I'm doing to her. *Goddamn!*

"Fiiiive."

With my final swing, I drop the flogger at my side and reach up to untie her from the metal bar. Turning her to face me, I crush my lips to hers. She eagerly accepts my kiss, opening her mouth for me. I nibble and bite at her lips before I dive back in, consuming her whole. There is no half assing anything with this woman.

"Turn around," I order hoarsely after pulling back.

I reach for her zipper trying to ignore the trembling in my own fingers. Lowering the zipper, I push the sides of her romper down her arms. I bend down, biting the back of her shoulder, needing to see if she tastes as good as her skin promises. She's even better.

"Mmm..."

I grin at the pleasure she experiences from me gnawing on her flesh. I pull back, savoring the small imprint my bite has left on her shoulder. Without wasting much more time, I push the romper to the floor, bringing her panties and nude stockings down with it.

"I'm going to tie your wrists again once we're on the bed. Are your wrists okay? Not sore are they?" I already know I hadn't tied them tight enough to cause any real discomfort, but I still want to check in.

"They're fine," she answers as I turn her to face me again.

I lead her to the bed, lay her down, and use the silk scarf to bind her wrists to the metal headboard above her head. I take a step back to take in the sight before me. I've had this dream many times over the last few months, but none of them even compare to reality. I take in the uncertainty in LaTasha's eyes, and the way that bottom lip trembles with anticipation. The rise and fall of her breasts, tipped off by the hardened nipples barely able to be contained by the lacy bra that I haven't removed. Her belly is slightly rounded. I'm surprised when I see a small gold hoop attached to her belly button, but I make my face remain neutral as my eyes glide over the rest of her body. The buildup of tension in the room is apparent the longer I remain quiet, simply staring. I know her mind is conjuring up all types of fears and scenarios. I thrive on that feeling of uncertainty I feel emanating off her.

"Plant your feet on the bed and spread your legs," I finally tell her as I come to stand at the end of the bed.

Slowly, she opens her legs.

Goddamn. I can see the moisture pooled between her thighs. She was turned on from my flogger. I'm sure I've just been shown the gateway to heaven, I think as I take in her pretty pink pussy. My first instinct is to listen to my cock and find my way home deep inside her, but tonight isn't about me. Tonight, I want her to know what she can expect as my sub. She's already gotten a little taste of my flogger. That was as far as I had thought I'd go, but I need to have at least a taste of her. Again, I look over her entire body before my eyes settle on the wetness that is evident on the hairs that cover her mound.

"Wider."

She extends the gap, exposing more of herself to me.

"You are everything I thought you would be. How could you have ever doubted my attraction to you?" The reverence in my voice can't be mistaken. I remove my loafers and crawl on the bed toward her, settling my body between her legs. "Tonight, I finally get to taste exactly what I've been dreaming about for months." The words fall from my lips before I can stop them. Sitting back on my haunches, I reach to spread her wetness to her clit.

Another sharp intake of her breath sends a chill down my spine. I finally bend down, and tongue her bulging clit, circling it.

"Ahhhh," Tasha gasps and attempts to scoot back.

Pushing her legs further apart and encircling my arms around her upper thighs so she can't move away from me, I look up at her face. "Don't ever try to run from me." My tone is sharp. I lower my head again, circling her clit once more with my tongue before putting my entire mouth on her. When I do, I know there is no way I won't become addicted to her taste. The moans and sharp inhales sounding above me only intensify my efforts. I suck on her outer labia, making sure to touch every part of her delicious pussy with my mouth. It takes me a little while to realize that the moans I'm hearing are not only coming from LaTasha, but from me as well. I hear her straining against the restraint above her head, and now instead of running from the pleasure, she is pushing her clit against my face. When I feel her inner thighs begin to quiver, I know she is close.

"Cum for me, doll," I tell her.

Her body tightens up, her legs attempting to squeeze together, and I feel the flood of juices against my tongue. If all of that wasn't an indicator, the deep guttural groan I hear tells me she's just had the most satisfying orgasm of her life. Her *first* orgasm.

Satisfied, I release her thighs and sit back up on my haunches, looking down at her. Her chest is heaving as she struggles to catch her breath.

"Damn," she moans.

"That's just the beginning. But that's it for tonight." I say, reaching up to remove the scarf and massage her wrists. I lay down at her side, turning myself to stare at her and begin stroking her belly. "Do you need any water or anything?"

She begins to shake her head, but then she stops. "No, I-I'm better than I've ever been."

The smile she gives me wearing her post-orgasm glow satisfies me in ways I never thought possible. I fondle her belly-button ring. "This was a surprise."

She giggles. "I got it two and a half years ago after my first book was published."

"A gift to yourself?"

She nods. "And a reclaiming of my body, sort of." She shrugs.

I nod, wondering what that meant. "Do you have any questions for me? About what just happened or anything else?" I ask, continuing to play with her belly-button ring.

"Um, yeah, I do have a question."

"So ask."

"Can you tell me more about your foster mother?"

My head shoots back, surprised at this question. "Really?"

"Yes. I mean, I have questions about what just happened, but I need to let those play in my head a little more. In the meantime, I want to know more about you. I got the impression you didn't want to discuss your foster mother earlier, but I'm here practically naked, exposed to you after you've just spanked me. I think it's only fair that you expose yourself a little too."

I remain silent, contemplating what she's really asking me. It *is* only fair of me to share a piece of myself with her considering the circumstances. "You may have a point. What would you like to know?"

"Tell me how old you were when you went to live with her. What was she like? I sensed that you really love her when you mentioned her earlier."

I nod. "I did. Still do although she passed away many years ago." I lay back on the bed, pulling her into me. "She was the first person who showed me what love really is." I stroke the soft skin of her shoulder while staring up at the ceiling, my free arm perched behind me back. That's not an easy admission for me. For the rest of the evening, I spend our time together telling LaTasha about the first woman who ever showed me any real love. I was twelve when I went to live with Ms. Janice, whom I eventually started calling *Mama Janice*. Those were good memories to indulge in. Before I knew it, we'd both fallen asleep, smiling at the stories I'd told LaTasha about Mama Janice.

CHAPTER 9

Tasha

"Oh!" I yell out, surprised by my ringing cell phone. I look at the number and immediately answer. "Hey, Stacey!" There's more excitement in my voice than I can remember having in a very long time.

"Hey! How are you? How'd your date go last night?"

Stacey and I have continued to talk at least two to three times a week. So far, she's the only one I've discussed my budding whatever this is with Jeremy. She's just easy to talk to.

I sigh contently.

"Woah!" Stacey exclaims.

"What?" I question defensively.

"Nothing. It's just that sigh sounds like a good sign. Your date must've gone well."

"It did, but I-I don't even know how to describe what I experienced," I admit, biting my lower lip. I'm unable to explain what happened the previous night. Yes, I'd had my first orgasm, but it was so much more than that. Jeremy was so controlling and assertive, but at the same time so considerate. Yes, there was pain, but the pleasure far outweighed it.

"Goddamn, girl! That sounds like an out-of-body experience." She giggles and I join in.

"It sort of was. Can I ask you a question?" I hedge.

"Of course."

"Um..." I sigh, running my fingers through my hair. "Have you... uh...like... Has Andre ever spanked you?"

I pull the phone away from my ear when Stacey's boisterous laughter comes through. "Oh, that's what happened? Yeah, Andre can get a little possessive and dominating. He's not a full-on Dom, like Jeremy, but he definitely has tendencies. I'll have to tell you about this one time when we broke up while dating and he locked us in the bathroom at this gala. Whew!"

"Oh my God!" I laugh.

"Yeah. Shit, I'm getting hot just thinking about it. I need to send some pics to my husband. He loves when I do that in the middle of the work day."

"Yeah, I should probably get back to writing too."

"Ohhh, you're writing?" Stacey asks excitedly.

"Yup!" I happily answer that question for the first time in months.

"How's it going?"

"Great! My fingers can barely type as fast as the words come."

"That's great, Tash. Okay, I won't bother you any longer. But call me tomorrow so we can talk more."

"I will," I promise before hanging up.

I toss the phone on my bed, but not before turning off the sound to ensure I don't have any more interruptions. This is the first time in a very long while that I've been able to write for hours on end and I don't want any more unnecessary distractions. It's bad enough that my agent has been calling me nonstop over the past week asking me about how my latest manuscript was going. She also mentioned that damn event in New York this coming fall. I didn't have the heart to tell her I've barely written a thousand words over the last month. And I sure didn't feel like telling her there was no way I was going to that damn award ceremony. She could forget that. But all those thoughts scatter as soon as my fingertips touch my keyboard. I'm once again in the zone and it feels too good to get sidetracked thinking about award ceremonies and letting my agent down. Throughout the day, I only get up from my desk to go to the bathroom and refill my tea mug.

My thoughts remain intact and flowing until four o'clock when the alarm on my cell phone buzzes. It's the one setting I'd forgotten to turn off. I can hardly believe that nearly the whole day has passed while I was indulged in writing. I check my word count to see that I've written nearly fifteen thousand words today. Not only that, but I've edited and re-edited those words and they're actually good! I finally feel like I'm writing the book I started out writing months ago.

"What the hell happened?!" I ask out loud in my empty bedroom. As soon as the question comes out, an image of Jeremy comes to mind. I frown, confused as hell, but I needed to find out some answers. Without another thought, I pack up my laptop, notebook, and phone in my bag and grab my keys before I head to my car.

Within the half hour, I've reached my destination. I look up at the huge building in front of me. Bennett Industries. Jeremy's office is on the fifteenth floor. I show the ID Liam gave me when I first moved here just in case I ever needed entrance into the building at anytime. Passing the security desk, I head toward the elevator and press the up button. I haven't even thought about what I'm going to say when I see Jeremy face to face, but something is pushing me forward. I need to know what he did. I had been stuck in damn writer's block for months, but after one weekend with this man, it's gone. And there's no hint of it slowing down either. If my thoughts aren't filled with images of him, they're filled with more scenes to write, better ways to invoke context into my manuscript, and amazing storylines.

I take a deep breath as I exit the elevator, turning toward the glass doors that that bears the name *Bennett Hotels and Spas*. Opening the glass door, I'm surprised to see the front desk chair is empty. I look around I see Jeremy's door to the right. I know it's his office because his name is inscribed on the door plaque, which also indicates that he is CEO of the company. A feeling of pride warms me up when I read those words, but I suppress it as I move closer to the slightly ajar door.

"I said I'd be there when I can. I have a lot going on at work right now and that includes travel. My life doesn't just stop for you!"

I hear the agitation in Jeremy's voice although he's not yelling. I frown, wondering who he is talking to that has him upset. Jeremy isn't the type to get easily agitated. For some reason, I don't like to think of him being affected by anyone. The usual calm, unflappable, and even charming demeanor is what I'm used to.

"LaTasha."

I nearly jump when he says my name. I've forgotten that I'm standing in his opened doorway. "Hi. I'm sorry. I didn't mean to interrupt. I just, um…"

"I've gotta go," he says, hanging up his phone and standing.

"You didn't have to end your call for me. I wasn't eavesdropping. I came to see you and your assistant isn't out here," I say, pointing over my shoulder to the empty chair.

"She had the day off." He peruses my body up and down, his eyes lingering at the apex of my thighs before they move up.

I swear his gaze feels as if he's literally touching me.

"Come in," he says. The semi-amused grin already taking away the look of irritation that had been on his face just moments ago.

"No, really, I can wait out in the lobby." I move to back up and out of his office, but his voice stops me.

"Love," he admonishes.

The deepness of his tone sends an instant chill down my spine. I hate that I love the way he always calls me *Love* when he intends to scold me. "Right. You don't repeat yourself." I grin and turn, re-entering his office.

"To what do I owe the pleasure?" he asks, gesturing for me to take a seat in the chair facing his massive cherry wood desk.

I oblige. "Um, well, I've been writing all day. Like, *really* writing. Not just the one hundred or a few words here and there. And they're *good*. I've already read over all ten thousand of the words I wrote today."

"*Ten thousand?*"

I grin at the way his eyebrow shoots upwards, questioningly. "Yup.

I've been writing since six o'clock this morning. I only stopped for breakfast earlier and to go to the bathroom. Anyway, like I said, they're actually good. And I've made it to significant progress in my manuscript in just one day."

"Wait. Did you say, you haven't eaten since breakfast?"

I frown. "Yes, but..." I stop talking when Jeremy picks up his phone.

"Yes, John, order two turkey club sandwiches, fruit salads, a can of sprite, and bottle of water from Mike's deli. Have it delivered to my office, okay? Thanks."

I crinkle my brows in confusion.

"It's almost five o'clock and you haven't eaten all day. That's unacceptable." He shakes his head. "Our meal will be here in the next fifteen minutes."

"You didn't have to order me anything. I can just eat at home. I didn't come here to talk about food anyway."

"You need to eat," he says firmly.

I have to bite my inner lip to keep myself from rolling my eyes.

"So what *did* you come here for?"

"I wanted to ask you a question."

He merely looks at me and tilts his head to the side, encouraging me to continue.

"I want to know how you did it?"

"How I did *what*?"

I grin at the confused look on his handsome face. "I mean, before our weekend together, I could barely pull out a hundred decent words. Today I've written thousands, which typically isn't abnormal for me, but lately it had been. How'd you do it?"

His face morphs from one of confusion to understanding before a smirk emerges. He shrugs. "Alright, in the spirit of honesty, when I gave you that little assignment last week I knew you wouldn't be able to complete it."

"How'd you know?"

"Lucky guess." He grins.

I level a glare at him.

A deep throated chuckle emerges from him and I have to clench my legs together.

"Alright, on our date at your place you were talking about your writing and how your first three books were written more or less in isolation. Since moving down here and seeing others read your work and have growing anticipation of your next book, I could tell that was your roadblock."

My brows lower as I contemplate his words. "That makes a lot of sense and it's very perceptive of you. So..." I trail off hoping he'll answer my unfinished question.

"So Friday when you told me you had failed, I'd already decided your punishment, which was the little spanking I gave you. Sometimes a little maintenance spanking is necessary to loosen a sub up. It relieves their tension and anxiety. The session after the spanking wasn't planned, but..." He shrugs. "I couldn't resist." He licks his lips as if he's still savoring the taste of me.

I close my eyes and inhale deeply before opening them. "You knew that would break up my underlying tension and allow me to relax enough to write?"

"Yup."

"And you knew what I needed just from our conversations?"

"Mainly." He looks over my shoulder at the same time our meal arrives.

I don't even notice him move for the door because I'm too absorbed in my own thoughts. I've never had anyone outside of Coral and my grandmother pay such close attention to me. Someone who really *got* me. A strange feeling begins to rise in my stomach. It feel incredibly safe. I've only experienced this kind of security with three people in my life. One is dead, one is my sister, and the other is my therapist who's all the way in the Northeast.

"When it comes to our relationship, it's always my job to know what you need even before *you* know. Sometimes that's a spanking and others times it's a sandwich when you've been too busy writing all day to eat." His deep voice sounds off above me as he towers over me, offering me the sandwich and a bowl of mixed fruit.

"Thank you," I say at the same time my stomach growls from the aroma of the turkey club. "I guess I'm hungrier than I thought."

"Eat up. Then you can pull your laptop out and continue writing at the table," he says, gesturing to the large round table on the other side of the office. "I have a meeting to get to, but it shouldn't be longer than an hour or so."

"Oh, I can leave if—"

"Sit." His hand presses my shoulder down to keep me from rising. "I like to think of you in my office while I'm out handling business. I'll be back in an hour. You'll probably have another six thousand words by then."

I giggle. "I don't write that fast."

He grins. "I'll be back."

I watch as he grabs a few papers from his desk along with his phone and tablet before he heads toward the door. I turn, admiring his stature in the charcoal, tailored suit. I know the body underneath is very nicely sculpted. Unfortunately, I didn't get to see much of it this past weekend. After our very eventful Friday night, we ended up falling asleep as he told me stories about his foster mom. He had lived with her for three years and she'd even begun the adoption process, but then she became ill before it was completed, she had to stop. My heart ached at the sadness in his eyes when he talked about losing her. Soon afterwards, he was reunited with his biological father and went to live with him, although he didn't go into very many details about that relationship. The rest of the weekend, we watched movies and he told me more about the spa he's opening in Tucson. Although there wasn't much more physical contact besides what took place on Friday, it was still one of the best weekends I'd had in a very long time or maybe *ever*.

I grin as I carry my food and bag over to the table. I finish my sandwich, fruit and soda quickly because I wanting to resume writing as soon as possible. Jeremy was right. Judging by the way I feel, I probably could complete a couple of thousand words by the time he gets back from his meeting. Unfortunately, as soon as my fingers make contact with the keyboard, my phone rings.

I groan as I look at the name that pops up on my screen. Knowing I can't put her off for too much longer, I decide to press the answer button. "Hey, Camille."

"Damn, no need to be such a sourpuss. I haven't even called you at all over the weekend. Give me some credit."

I giggle. Camille is my bad-ass agent and the girl knows her shit. When she read my first manuscript she knew it would be a hit. I had doubts, assuming that a sci-fi series centering on a little black girl from the Bronx wouldn't be many people's cup of tea. But Camille knew what I didn't know or at least what I'd never thought of. The market was *hungry* for diversity. People, especially children, wanted to see characters that looked like them the same way I did all those years ago when I picked up my first comic featuring Storm.

"You're right. It has been more than forty-eight hours since you last harassed me."

"See? Recognize my growing patience. Anyway, how's the book coming along?"

That question actually made me smile. I finally had some good news on that subject. "It's going really well. Just today I wrote close to ten thousand words," I say, downplaying the actual amount I've written.

"Wow! That's great. So when should I expect a rough draft?"

"Patience, Grasshopper."

"Tasha!"

I bite my lip to hold in my laughter. "Soon."

"Alright. I'll accept that for now. Now, about that other thing," she says in a sing-song voice.

"Here we go."

"Yes, here we go. I've been trying to get you to agree on this New York appearance for months. Do you know what a huge honor it is to be a National Book Award finalist? It's especially an honor in the genre you write in. Come on! You *have* to attend the ceremony."

"I don't *have* to do anything but write these books, stay black, and die," I retort in my best Joe Clarke played by Morgan Freeman voice. I don't like doing public appearances. Camille knows this and has known it from day one. Yet here we are. Yes, being a National Book Award finalist is a huge honor. But I just can't embrace the idea of attending the ceremony in New York.

"Look, it's August and the ceremony isn't until late October. I still have a little more than two months to convince you. I'm not giving up on this," she says before abruptly hanging up.

I'm not surprised because that's how most of our conversations have ended lately. Camille is the high-strung type, which makes her a great agent, but it sucks for me when we bump heads.

"Whatever," I mumble as I get back to typing. I'm enjoying the high of being back in the writing zone too much to let anything else bother me right now.

* * *

Jeremy

STEPPING off the elevator into my luxury hotel suite in downtown Dallas, I feel the tension releasing from my shoulders. I've been booked solid with meetings and business appointments, leaving little time for anything else. Ordinarily, a busy work week is a good thing, but because I haven't seen LaTasha in nearly five days since she appeared unexpectedly at my office door, I'm beyond a little restless. We've communicated mainly through phone calls and text messages this week and she's been making great progress on her book. It's funny how I can hear the difference in her voice. The relief in her tone is evident and it makes me crave her even more. But work prevails. I'm due to leave Sunday afternoon for another trip to Tucson, leaving me with not nearly as much time as I'd like to spend with her. I grin as I run my hand down the side of my face, feeling the stubble that's starting to grow. I may not have as much time as I'd like to get even more acquainted with LaTasha's body, but I sure as hell will make use of the time I've got. Hence, the reason I'm here now.

I make my way through the huge living room space, removing my suit jacket and tossing it on the couch along the way. I only sleep here on really late work nights and when I'm entertaining women. However, I've never brought LaTasha here. When I entertained her in my home it felt most appropriate.

I enter the bedroom and head straight to the closet where I keep my toys. My hand barely makes contact with the doorknob before I can sense another person in the room. This hotel, *my* hotel, has the highest level of security possible, especially my suite. There's only one other person who has access to this suite when I'm not around, and *he* wouldn't be in here waiting for me in my bedroom. But his wife on the other hand...

"At close to eight months pregnant, you're still sneaking around like the damn spy you are. Does your husband know where you are?"

"I'm sure Mitch has told him by now," Coral retorts in an amused tone.

"I've been expecting you. What took so long?" I question, finally turning to face her.

She remains seated at a chair by the side of my bed. She'd obviously moved it from its original location to prevent me from seeing her when I first entered. She shrugs. "I've been a little preoccupied," she says, rubbing her belly.

I nod. "How is the little guy?"

The smile that spreads across her face tells it all. "He's great. Suddenly, her face turns serious. "But I didn't come here to talk about me."

"I figured as much," I state dryly, placing my hands in my pockets. I lean against the dresser behind me with my feet crossed at the ankle.

"Okay, smart ass. So you know if you hurt her, I will be making another unexpected visit. Only it will be in the middle of the night." Her narrowed eyes and flared nostrils demonstrate the seriousness of her words.

"I'm sure many men have been intimidated by that look. And I know you're not all talk. But save the tough-guy shit for someone else. You know me better than to think I'd hurt any woman."

"I just thought it was prudent to let you know in person where I stand."

"I know how deeply you take care of your family."

She raises a brow at me. "You know she's my sister?"

I remain silent staring at her.

"You had one of your guys do a background check on her?" she asks, standing. She approaches me head-on.

Again, I say nothing.

"What did you find out?"

"Enough to know her family background and that there's a gap in her teenage and early adult years. No records at all. *Someone* worked really hard to eliminate any records of LaTasha from ages thirteen until about twenty-one."

"Someone must have." She shrugs.

"Who hurt her?" It's a question I couldn't hold back.

Coral's face turns hard and angry. "They've been dealt with."

"*They?*"

Coral closes her eyes for a brief moment, a pained look of regret crossing her face before she quickly masks it. "This damn kid is making me soft," she states, rubbing her belly and taking a couple of steps back to sit on the edge of the king size bed.

"You've always been a big-ass softy."

"Fuck you. Bennett."

"*Language!* You know by now the baby can hear words in the womb." I chuckle.

"Yeah, well *this* baby's going to come out with quite the vocabulary already between Li's edgy vernacular and mine." She grins.

I laugh even harder at that. "I'm surprised you can still walk the way Li's been all over you."

Coral laughs out loud for the first time. "He loves this pregnant belly."

"It's not just the belly."

Another tender smile crosses her face as she falls silent. That smile makes me happy for my cousin and his growing family. He finally has the love he's waited a long time for.

"You know she's writing again." Coral's comment breaks the silence. "I know that's because of you."

"That's because of *her*," I correct. "She's meant to write."

"Yeah, but she's been stuck in that funk of a writer's block for a while. If I hadn't been so preoccupied with my own life, I would've realized that the move here combined with the pressure she placed on herself to please her readers were the causes. You helped her with that. How? I don't know nor do I *want* to know." She eyes the closet door a few feet from me, and I can see a number of thoughts running through those hazel eyes. I won't confirm or deny any of them.

"I'm just happy she's happy. Thank you for that. Just make sure she stays that way," Coral says before she stands.

"Save the threats for your husband. LaTasha and I will be fine." I grin.

"Good. As long as we have an understanding," she says over her shoulder as she walks past the bedroom door. A few seconds later, I hear the chime of the elevator button and the doors sliding open.

Grinning, I shake my head. I knew sooner or later that Coral would show up making threats about me possibly hurting her sister. I turn back to the closet, finally opening it and seeing my stash of accoutrements hanging on the wall. This is a much smaller version of the playroom I have in my home. It's always been useful for when I had my past subs stay overnight. I reach for one of my floggers made out of rabbit's fur, a paddle, and a pair of brand new diamond encrusted nipple clamps. A thrill shoots right to my groin when I imagine LaTasha's perky brown nipples being squeezed in this clamp. The vision nearly causes me to groan out loud. *Jesus, what the fuck is wrong with me?* I've never been this turned on by just the mere thought of a woman. Shaking the image from my mind, I grab a pair of special, unused razors. I smirk at the plans I have for these babies. Finally, deciding I have everything I came for, I send a text message to LaTasha telling her to be ready by seven o'clock tonight.

CHAPTER 10

Tasha

"Coming!" I yell from my bedroom to the front door. I assume it's Jeremy right on time for our seven o'clock date. Unfortunately, I'm running a little late, having gotten sidetracked at the community center. Then I came home and wrote for hours. I rush for the door and open it wide. "Hey, sorry, but I was helping Coral at the community center. She had to hire a temporary director because she's going on leave soon and I helped with organizing information for the new director. Then I came home and started writing. Then I got this really great inspiration from a scene for my cover, so I started sketching that out. And before I knew it, it you were knocking on the door. And I know—"

"LaTasha, take a breath." His facial expression is serious, but I detect laughter in his eyes.

Closing my eyes, I inhale deeply and exhale slowly. I blink and my eyes open. Now, I feel less unhinged by the warmth and laughter swimming in his eyes.

"Hello. How are you? May I come in?" He asks, but enters simultaneously, forcing me to take a few steps back. He closes the door behind him. "No need to fret. I'm a few minutes early."

I look at the clock hanging on my living room wall and realize it is still ten to seven. "Oh." I exhale, feeling slightly relieved that I wasn't as late as I thought I was.

"I was in the area already and thought I'd be a few minutes early picking you up. Go finish whatever you were working on and feel free to pack it up to bring for the weekend."

"Sure thing." I start to head off before I stop abruptly, remembering my manners. "Did you want anything to drink while you wait?"

"A bottle of water would be fine."

"Coming right up." I retrieved the bottle of water and take it to him, before heading back to my bedroom to shut down and pack up my laptop and drawings to bring with me this weekend along with my clothes of course. Since Jeremy already told me we'd be staying in tonight, I decided to wear a white flowing skirt that stops a couple of inches below my knees and a sky-blue button up top.

"Don't forget to pack the Ben Wa balls!"

I almost drop my laptop when I hear him yell from the living room. Covering my mouth with my hand, I giggle out loud at the same time I retrace my steps and open the drawer where I keep the Ben Wa balls. Grinning I neatly tuck the box holding the balls into my overnight bag before doing a mental check to make sure I have everything else I'll need over the next day and a half. Feeling satisfied, I turn off the light and exit my bedroom and re-enter the living room where Jeremy's back is turned to me. He looks hunched over as if he is reading something on the coffee table.

"What's this?" he asks as I step closer.

Shit! I mentally curse after I realize what he has in his hand. It's the invitation to the National Book Awards Ceremony I'd received today and carelessly tossed on the coffee table. I accidentally left it exposed for Jeremy to see.

"That's just some invitation to an awards ceremony. My agent constantly sends me those things." I roll my eyes as if it's no big deal.

"You're not attending?"

"No. It's not until late October, and by then, Coral would've had the baby. So I want to be around to help her. Camille is always sending me these things."

"*Camille?*"

"Yeah. She's my agent."

Jeremy finally looks up from the envelope with half of the letter sticking out. He stares at me. It may just be my imagination, but I could swear his eyes are a shade darker than normal. And it's not that sexy eye change in hue that happens whenever he's turned on. My heartbeat doubles and I hold my breath, wondering if he's seen through my lies. After a few seconds of just staring, he finally takes one last swig from his bottle of water.

"Is this everything?" he asks, as he grabs my overnight bag from my shoulder.

"Yup." I sigh in relief.

"Great. Let's go." He turns and heads toward the door, not bothering to wait for me.

I find that unusual as he's usually so touchy-feely, but I brush it off. It is Friday evening. It's probably been a long work week for him, I reason to myself. I shut the lights off and step out the door, making sure it's locked behind me. As I turn, Jeremy places his arm at the small of my back.

"I like this skirt," he says low in my ear, causing my panties to dampen.

See. He's not upset.

* * *

"You like Italian, right? I had one of my favorite spots deliver," he says as we enter his home.

My nose is immediately hit with the succulent smell of fresh basil, tomato sauce, and garlic bread. My stomach answers his question for me.

"I figured." He laughs.

"What'd you order?"

He places my bag down by the couch and directs me to the dining

112

room where the large table is covered with a delicious-looking spread of Italian food.

"I ordered the caprese salad, fried calamari, garlic bread, prosciutto wrapped melon, salad greens of course, and a few others."

My eyes roam over the spread after he lists the different items on the table. "I'm pretty sure this is enough food to feed an army."

"Army?" His voice takes on an offended tone as a crease appears in his forehead. "You meant a marine unit."

I giggle, remembering the banter that often goes on between him, Coral and Liam. They tease each other about their respective branches of the military. Liam and Coral served in the army, so they feel the need to deride Jeremy for being a marine.

"I'm sorry. I meant, this is enough food to feed the *marines*." I laugh as he pulls out a chair for me.

"How was your day?"

We settle in and I begin telling him about helping the new temporary director get acquainted with the rules and regulations of the community center. She's a part-time counselor, but she's been away completing graduate school, so she needed some training on the director's responsibilities.

"You didn't want to take over the director role when Coral is on maternity leave?"

I shake my head. "No because I much prefer hanging with the kids every now and again and getting my hands dirty in the garden or reading them stories. That's better than being the director. Plus since I've gotten my writing mojo back, I probably will only be there for about two to three days a week over the next few months. My agent has been hounding me to get this manuscript complete."

He peers at me over his glass and I see something flash in those green eyes, but he blinks and it's gone.

"How about *your* day?"

He wipes his mouth with his napkin, drawing my attention to those sensuous lips of his. The moment that napkin leaves his mouth, I'm sure he's saying something about work, but my attention is fully drawn to the movement of his lips. Absentmindedly, I lick my own lips, remembering the way his mouth made me feel just the previous week. I've never experienced anything like it before of course because it was my first orgasm. Unfortunately, it's been a week and because of Jeremy's strict rules about not touching myself when he isn't around, I haven't been able to even try to replicate it. Not that I'd even be able to replicate the feel of his lips on me. Nothing could copy that, I'm sure.

"Are you finished?" he asks, breaking my concentration.

I clear my throat and take a sip of red wine. "Yes, I am. It was delicious."

He gives me a panty-wetting grin before rising from his chair to take our plates. "No. Sit," he insists when I rise to help him.

Shrugging, I sit back down and popping one of the melon balls into my mouth. My eyelids flutter as the sweetness from the fruit melds with the saltiness of the prosciutto, causing a delicious firestorm in my mouth. "Mmm…" I moan out loud.

"I love that you enjoy your food with gusto."

I lower my head, embarrassed. I laugh. "I've always loved food. My grandmother used to pull me in the kitchen to be her little taste tester." I smile fondly at those memories.

"I know from experience a woman who is able to indulge in food and savor it is also able to experience pleasure in so many other ways." He leans down, trailing a finger along my jaw line, He stares deeply into my eyes.

I shiver from the sheer intensity of his gaze. I've always found Jeremy to be an extremely attractive man with an acute ability to convey a message with a single look. Right now, his look is suggesting that he's a predator and I'm his prey. That thought sends a warm chill down my spine, and I realize I don't mind being his prey. Leaning into his touch, I close my eyes and lick my lips again. Months ago, if someone would've told me I could feel this uninhibited and so close to such a virile man, I would've laughed in their face. But Jeremy makes it easy to just feel, be in the moment, less self-conscious and less fearful. I'm still trying to figure out what it is about him that makes me more inclined to put my fears aside.

"Stand up, LaTasha."

As if attached to his body instead of my own, my legs immediately move, doing as he asked.

Once I stand, he pulls me into his arms, never breaking eye contact with me. "Have you still been wearing the Ben Wa balls as instructed?"

I nod. "Of course."

"Of course, *what?*"

"Sir." It was my first time referring to him as sir and it felt good.

"I want you to go into the playroom and remove your clothes down to your panties and bra. Then wait for me on the bed while I finish clearing the table." It wasn't a question, but a commandment.

"Yes, sir." I can already feel the wetness pooling in my panties just from the deep rumble of his voice and that sharp look in his eyes. The way he can switch from friendly banter to Dom in seconds is thrilling and sure as hell keeps me on my toes, which I'm sure is his intention. With one last look in the deep pools he calls eyes; I pivot and head down the hall and down the steps to the playroom. As I step inside, I'm assaulted by memories of the last time I was in this room. My first orgasm had occurred right on that bed. I grin, running my hand along the silk sheets that now adorn the bed. The cool, smooth, and soft feel of the sheets beneath my fingers makes me anxious to feel them beneath the rest of my skin. I remove my skirt and shirt and fold them before placing them on top of the dresser. I turn toward the full-length mirror, looking at myself in my matching pink lace bra and panty set. I admire my appearance. I settle on the bed and tuck my legs underneath my butt, sitting up on my haunches to wait for Jeremy.

Seconds later, I hear his footsteps drawing closer to the room. I'd left the door open and soon he appears at the entranceway. I allow my eyes to rove over his entire body before finally lowering them toward the floor, per his rules. There's long stretch of silence as he simply stares at me. His gaze is so powerful that it feels as if he is touching me. My heartbeat quickens with anticipation as I wait for his next move. Finally, he steps fully inside the room and shuts the door behind him.

"Did you enjoy yourself the last time we were in here?"

"Yes, sir." *Damn, those words slip so easily from my mouth.*

"Good." The satisfaction in his voice sends a thrill of pride through me.

"Are these new?" he asks, running a finger along my bra strap, down my waist to the top of my panties.

"Yes, sir."

"I like them."

I smile at that, but remain silent. I'd bought these with him in mind.

"Stand up and take them off." He steps back from the bed, giving me space to step off.

I stand, my hands trembling from how turned on I've become just from his simple caresses and instructions. Carefully, I reach back and undo my bra, releasing it. I manage to stifle my grin when I hear Jeremy's muttered curse as my breasts spill out. With my bra in one hand, I manage to push down my panties with the other before I step out of them.

"Hand them to me."

I place them in his outstretched hand and keep my eyes cast downwards. I hear him walk over to the dresser and place something heavy on top of it.

"Look at me."

My eyes immediately shoot up to his, and for the first time, I see that he has removed his shirt. Now, he's only wearing a pair of dark slacks. I allow my eyes to roam over his masculine frame, taking in the sculpted muscles of his abdomen. Many of them are decorated with various tattoos. I lick my lips, wanting to taste his entire body. I stand taller, feeling the pull of my own desire toward him.

"Unfortunately, I have to leave town Sunday morning so I won't be able to spend as much time as I would like indulging in this body of yours." He moves closer to me. "But tonight I plan on giving you something that will help you remember who you belong to while I'm gone."

My mouth falls agape and heartbeat quickens at his words. *Who you belong to.* The words that'd never appealed to me before seem to be a boom to my arousal right now. "Stand with your legs apart and close your eyes," he says as he turns away from me.

Inhaling deeply, I do as he's requested. I hear a rustling noise and then I feel his presence once again in front of me. He wraps a silk tie around my eyes, rendering me temporarily blind. I feel goose bumps rise on my skin from his nearness as his breath kisses the skin of my shoulders.

"Oh!" I blurt out as I feel his hand caressing the hood of my pussy.

"You're wet already," he gloats as his fingers find their ways deeper into my folds.

I whimper at the feel of his fingers on the most intimate part of my body. I begin thrusting my hips into his hand.

"Not yet." He chuckles.

I frown at the loss of his touch. I sense him lowering himself in front of me and I wonder if he's going to put his mouth on me. But instead of the warmth of his mouth, I feel wetness as he rubs the curls on the hood of my pussy again. I feel some sort of lathering sensation and realize he has put shaving cream on me. I want to ask is he shaving me and tell him I could have done that at home, but I don't have permission to speak. Seconds later, I feel the stroke of a blade. It doesn't hurt. Quite the opposite actually. He is extremely adept at this, moving the razor so lightly yet efficiently that I know he's done this before. His movements are very measured and careful, ensuring that he doesn't cut me. Tingles begin rising all over my body at the intimacy of this moment. There is something intensely erotic about having someone shave my most intimate body part. Of course, it could just be the man doing it. The feeling of being so cared for overcomes me once again at his skillful hands. And yes, I become even wetter.

"Mmm, that looks good," he states, rising up. "Don't move yet," he instructs.

"Yes, sir."

I feel him rub the remaining shaving cream off of me.

"Alright," he says at the same time he pulls the blindfold off. "Open your eyes."

I blink a few times, allowing my gaze to readjust to the low lighting in the room.

"Look in the mirror," he says, pulling me to the full-length mirror.

I look at myself in the mirror, lowering my gaze to the area he has shaved and immediately I gasp. I gasp in shock. Staring at the mirror, I read his initials, JB, in calligraphy essentially engraved into the trimmed hairs of my pussy. *How in the hell?*

"Practice." He grins. "Now, even though I'll be gone for another week, you'll know this pussy belongs to me. Not even you are allowed to touch it without my permission. Is that clear?"

"Y-yes, sir," I absently state, while still staring at his handiwork in the mirror. He actually shaved his initials into my pussy hair. But damn if it doesn't feel good.

"Good. And right now, you have my permission to touch yourself. Lie on the bed, prop yourself up on your elbows, and spread your legs."

I look up at him, frowning. I'd much rather that *he* touch me. He simply stares back at me waiting for me to do as instructed. Walking to the bed, I lay as told. In this position I can see all of myself in the mirror and Jeremy standing right next to it has the same view. Even in the dimly-lit room, I can see his eyes have darkened in hue, alerting me that he is indeed as nearly as turned on as I am.

"Pinch your nipples."

I raise an eyebrow at him.

"Love..." The admonishment comes out as a low growl, and I know even that half second of hesitation is causing Jeremy to lose his patience.

I smirk with the realization that his desire for me is likely fueling his impatience. Finally, I reach up and pinch my nipple. "Ohhh," I moan as the painful yet pleasurable sensations shoots through my body, heightened by the way Jeremy's eyes become hooded as he stares at me.

"Again. The other one," he commands.

I can do nothing but his will in this moment. I gasp as I pinch my other nipple, purring as another powerful sensation rips through my body.

"Spread your legs wider and show me how wet you are."

I do so and he bites his lower lip.

"Lower your hand to my pussy. Show me how you want me to pleasure you."

At his words, I trail my fingers down my breasts, over my tummy, and to my sopping wet core.

"Move your finger to your clit," he instructs.

Doing so, I bite my lower lip at how sensitized that area already is.

"Now move lower, use your two fingers to spread your wetness to your clit."

I do, reveling in how wet I am already.

"Circle your clit with your two fingers and look in the mirror. Watch yourself as I watch you."

"Ohhh!" I moan as the intensity in my core builds up, heat spreading throughout my body. I look at myself in the mirror and I can see my sex juices glistening on my fingers.

"Taste yourself."

Shit. I raise my two fingers to my mouth, licking my juices.

"Now, dip your fingers to *my* pussy, insert your two fingers. Show me where you want my cock to go."

Goddamn. I don't know what is turning me on more—his words or staring at myself in the mirror as I get myself off. That's a lie because I know it's *him*. It's *all him.*

"Show me, LaTasha," he growls.

I begin pumping my fingers faster to mimic the movement I want Jeremy to do with his penis between my thighs instead of my fingers. The buildup begins to feel so good, I let my head drop back and my legs splay even wider. I can tell I'm getting close...so close. Just a few more pumps...

"Stop!"

What?! I want to defy him. It feels too good to stop, but something

119

inside of me won't let me dare disobey him. "Sir, please!" I try to beg, asking for just a few more seconds. I'm so close.

"Close your legs and sit up." His voice is filled with finality.

I sigh and reluctantly close my shaky legs and sit up, glaring at him.

He grins mischievously at me, knowing that now my impatience is growing. I want to finish what *he* started.

"It's been a long day and I need to get some rest. You will sleep down here tonight. You don't have permission to touch yourself. If you do, I *will* know."

"*What?*" I barely get the full word out before he turns and is out the door, shutting it behind him. "What the hell just happened?" I ask, looking around the room as if the walls can answer me. I don't even know how long I wait, sure that he is going to return and allow me to finish this. The throbbing between my thighs insists that I continue to completion. I continue to wait, staring at the door, willing it to open with Jeremy standing on the other side with that mannish grin on his face and hooded eyes. But it doesn't happen. There's *nothing*. My eyes well up with tears of frustration. I try to get my breathing under control and lay back on the bed. Unfortunately, the coolness of the silk sheets only heightens my arousal. That was Jeremy's intention, I'm sure. I stare up at the ceiling, still hoping he will return, but all that happens is the fire that was raging through my body begins to die down to embers, eventually extinguishing. I'm only left with is a deep sense of longing, loneliness, and confusion. Finally, realizing he has no intention of coming back tonight, I begin tossing and turning, trying to get comfortable enough to fall asleep. Needless to say, that was a fruitless endeavor.

CHAPTER 11

*J*eremy

"What?!" I yell into the phone at my assistant. It's seven-thirty in the morning on a damn Saturday. I know she's calling to remind me of my flight and itinerary information for the next day, but I'm already pissed off.

"Mr. Bennett, your pilot had to change the flight departure from eleven to ten tomorrow. Also, I left some papers on your desk that you need to sign before you leave. I can bring them to you or email them over, but then you'd have to email or fax them back."

"I'll be by the office tomorrow morning to sign them. Bye." I hang up rather rudely, but my assistant is used to it. I groan as I get out of bed, my damn cock rock hard from yet another damn dream starring the woman who is asleep downstairs. It was a rough night to say the least. The absolute last thing I wanted to do last night was leave her like that, but that's the thing about punishments. Sometimes they hurt you more than the person being punished.

I strip off the boxer briefs I wore to bed and turn on the shower to the coldest setting. This is my second cold shower in less than ten hours. I'm probably on the very edge of getting blue balls from that damn stunt last night. Yet as much as I want to jerk off to give myself some sort of relief, I know it would only make it worse. Cumming in the shower instead of in between those dark brown legs like I want to would just be torturous. Instead, I let the cold water cool off my fiery need. I must remain in the shower for at least thirty minutes. Finally, I step out, throwing on a T-shirt and sweatpants, opting to skip my workout for the day and go make breakfast.

As I descend the steps, I'm pleasantly surprised by the aroma of bacon, eggs and waffles. I follow the scent to the kitchen and I'm nearly blown over by the sight of LaTasha at the stove, her back slightly turned to me. Staring her up and down, I see she is covered in the black robe I'd left for her in the playroom. I let my eyes roam over the swell of her buttocks, wondering if she's wearing any panties underneath until I see a faint pantyline when she shifts her body.

"I don't like you wearing panties in the kitchen," I say, my eyes still on her ass. I grin when she jumps, startled by my presence.

"I didn't know you were up. I couldn't sleep and I usually end up cooking when I can't sleep in the morning. It was either cook or write, but hunger won out."

My grin deepens when I hear the irritation in her voice. She's still pissed about last night. Good. That makes two of us.

"It smells good." I fully enter the kitchen, my hunger growing when I see the prepared food on the center island. I always keep a stocked refrigerator.

"I didn't know what you were hungry for so I made a little of everything."

I stare down at her. The stirring in my pants tells me I'm hungry alright, but I'll have to settle for breakfast food.

"Thank you for cooking." I take a seat at the counter as she prepares a plate of waffles, eggs, and bacon and places in front of me.

"This looks delicious," I tell her as she sits down across from me with her own plate, wordlessly. I begin eating, savoring the flavors of chive and cream cheese she put in the eggs. I'm halfway through my meal when I finally look up to notice LaTasha staring at me, seemingly contemplating. I wipe my mouth, sensing she's pondering how to approach what happened last night.

"Love, when you have a question you need to ask it," I say before taking another bite of my waffles.

"Okay. What was last night about? Why did you stop and leave me there alone?"

The way she says *alone* tugs at something in my chest. I notice sadness in her eyes before she quickly masks it. Although I wonder what that look of sadness is about, I still refuse to let her off the hook. "You tell me."

Her brows crinkle in confusion. "What does that mean?"

"It means you should know by now what last night was about." I remain cryptic on purpose, wanting her to figure it out.

She squints, glaring at me. "Last night was a punishment," she finally says.

Slowly, I bring my last forkful of waffles to my mouth, nodding as I chew, but remaining quiet.

"What did I do?"

"You don't know?"

She sighs, clearly irritated. "No. I haven't done anything. At least I didn't do anything worthy of punishment."

"Are you sure? Think about the conversations we had yesterday."

"*Yesterday?*" She ponders for a moment. "We talked on the phone a bit, and then you came over to pick me up."

"Mmhm hum…" I agree. "And what happened while I was there?"

She rolls her eyes, trying to recall our previous conversations. "You waited in the living room. When I grabbed my bag you were…"

When she pauses, I fold my arms and hold my chin up, staring at her. I wait for her to continue. When she doesn't, I finish for her. "You lied to me. When I asked you why you would not attend the awards ceremony in New York, you lied."

"I didn't—"

She cuts herself off when I give her a hard look. "You think I don't know what the National Book Award nomination means? That's a *huge* honor. There's no way in hell you'd turn it down because Coral is having a baby. Does she even know you were nominated?"

"No, she doesn't." She shrugs, her eyes lowered to her plate.

"And you haven't decided not to attend because of the baby?"

Her shoulders slump a little as she uses her fork to push her food around her plate. "No, it's not the baby. I did lie about that."

"What's the real reason why you don't want to attend?"

She remains quiet for a few moments, and despite my natural inclination to push her, I remain silent also, knowing she's gearing to reveal something she doesn't want to admit.

"It's in *New York*," she finally says.

It's my turn to frown in confusion. "Aren't you from New York?"

"Yeah, that's the problem. I don't have many good memories of that city. I haven't been back since I was seventeen."

Hearing the deep sorrow and fear in her voice, I get up out of my chair, rounding the counter to come to stand in front of her. I pull her up to stand, wrapping one arm around her waist and gripping her chin with the other so she has nowhere to look but at me. "Don't ever lie to me. If there's something you don't want to tell me or don't want me to know, you say that, but do not lie. Are we clear?" I decide not to press her further on what specifically about New York that she's running from, but she still needs to know she can't lie to me.

She nods.

"Love."

"I mean yes." She half smiles. "I understand."

"Good." I lower my lips to her forehead intending to place a short kiss there, but my body has a mind of its own. Before I realize it I'm kissing a trail down to her plump lips, where she readily opens up for me. And just like any other time we've kissed, I completely lose myself in it...in *her*. I pull back to nip at her lower lip, causing her to moan. I quickly swallow her moan, covering her mouth with mine and letting my hands freely explore her lush body. I spin her so her back is to the counter and then break our connection, to pull her robe open. I growl when I see the grey boy shorts she is wearing underneath the robe.

"You don't wear underwear while in my home," I growl, roughly pushing them down her legs.

"What am I supposed to wear while I'm here then?" she asks breathlessly.

"Not a damn thing," I answer before possessing her lips again, biting her bottom lip and soothing it with my tongue. I lift her to sit on top of the counter and use my hip to nudge her knees apart. I step back, looking her up and down as she sits, legs splayed on my kitchen counter. I see her folds already glistening with her wetness. "Now this is my real breakfast." I bend down placing both her legs over my shoulders, forcing her to lean back on her elbows. I take a swipe of her with my tongue, savoring her flavor. Her entire body shivers.

"You could've woken up to this if you hadn't lied yesterday."

"Sorry, sir."

I growl again at her calling me that and immediately begin attacking her pussy—*my pussy* with my mouth. As great as the breakfast she prepared was, nothing compares to the taste of her juices on my tongue. I kiss and lick her labia, sucking on it as I move to enter her with one finger.

"Jere...Sir, that feels so good. Please don't stop!"

Even if I wanted to, there's no way I could stop at this point. Not until I see her to completion. I insert two fingers all the way to the knuckle, curling them to touch her G-spot at the same time I begin sucking on her engorged clitoris.

"Fuuuck," she groans as her head flops backwards.

"Keep your head up. Watch me pleasure you." I lift my head slightly to demand she watch me. Not until I see her looking down at me with that half-lidded gaze do I go back to work devouring her pussy. I pump my fingers at the same time sucking on her clit. I feel her juices covering my fingers. I know she's close to exploding when I feel her squeezing my fingers at the same time her thighs tighten around the sides of my head. Of course, this only spurs me on. Her taste, the moans and purrs coming from above me, and her tightening grip all encourage me. I'm greedy for the need to see her finish.

"Ahhhh, shit! I'm cumming, sir!"

I continue eating and fingering her through her orgasm, only stopping when her shivers and aftershocks downgrade and eventually stop. Feeling sated myself, I gently remove her legs from my shoulders, stepping back to look her over. Her appearance is that of a sexually satisfied woman. Despite my cock demanding its own release, I hold back. She's not ready for that level of connection yet. I keep my eyes on her freshly shaven vagina bearing my initials before taking a step back. "Come here, doll." I extend my hand to her.

On wobbly legs, she manages to climb off the counter and walk toward me. As soon as she's close enough, I pull her to me, owning her lips again. I allow her to taste herself on my tongue. She moans into my mouth when I bite her tongue.

"I wish I didn't have to leave tomorrow." I sigh and pull back, placing my forehead against hers.

She reaches up and rubs her palm against my cheek. "You'll be back soon, right?"

"Wild horses couldn't keep me away, doll." I place a quick kiss at the corner of her mouth. "Come on. I want to wash you up." I pick up the robe she had on, helping her into it. I tighten the belt around her waist before escorting her upstairs. Although I have no plans on taking her just yet, I still want my fill of looking at her and touching her before I leave.

CHAPTER 12

*T*asha
One month later...

Jeremy: Arrive at my suite at eight o'clock. Wear the dress and with the blindfold I sent you yesterday. Wear the Ben Wa balls. I want you on all fours, ass in the air on the bed as I enter the room.

My face flames as I read over the text message.

"Huh, Ms. Tasha?"

Oh shit. I fumble with my phone to darken the screen so Trudy doesn't see it. "I'm sorry, sweetie. What did you say?"

"I asked if we could also do the Harry Potter series as part of the book club." Those brown eyes staring up at me have so much behind them. She's only twelve, but I sense she's been through a lot. Still she's just a kid, and despite her attempts to seem aloof or uncaring at times, in moments like, this I still see the innocence of a twelve year old.

"Of course we can. I'll add it to the list and give it to Coral to order."

Trudy's eyes light up for a second before she gets a hold of herself. "Thanks." She shrugs before she runs off to play with a group of kids.

"She's come a long way. She never used to play with anyone else," Coral says rom behind me.

I turn to her as she observes Trudy with the group of kids. "Yeah, she's a good kid."

Coral nods. "They all are."

I notice her rubbing her side while her other hand rests on her ever-expanding belly. "You okay?"

She waves me off. "Fine."

"You sure? Shouldn't you be on maternity leave now anyway?"

She frowns. "This is my last week. I told you I'm fine. Butterball's just kicking my ribs. He's an active little guy."

"Well, considering who his parents are, I already know he's going to be a handful," I tease.

"Tell me about it. Li's already got all types of shit planned for this kid. Already planning the next Bennett business this kid will take over. He doesn't stand a chance."

"He'll probably end up being a spy like his mom."

"Over my dead body."

I raise my brows, surprised by her tone.

"That's not a life I want for any of my kids," she says, looking over at Laura who's reading with another one of the community center's counselors.

"Your children will be great. With you for a mom, they don't have a choice but to be great."

She tosses me a half smile. "Thanks, Tash. You've been very upbeat lately. And I know it's not just due to you breaking through your writer's block."

"You're right about that." I choose not to lie to my sister. I wait for her next question, but it never comes.

"I'm not going to question you about what you do in your private life. Just know I'm here if you want to talk about anything."

This damn near blows me away. "Really? No prying? No threatening Jeremy with castration in a secret dungeon out in the middle of the desert or wherever you spies have your secret hiding places?"

She looks at me skeptically. "You've been reading too much fantasy or spy novels."

I wait for it.

She shrugs. "Besides, Jeremy already knows where I stand on the issue."

I smirk at that. "And by knowing where you stand, I assume you mean that you've threatened him if he hurts me."

"I don't threaten. I merely warn," she says without a hint of humor.

"I love you, sis."

"Whatever. I'm going to play with my kid before we have to prepare lunches," she turns before heading toward Laura.

I watch her walk away and I grin again, wondering what that conversation between her and Jeremy was like. Eventually, my thoughts flow to just the man himself. It's been a week since I've seen him. He's been traveling a lot for work, leaving us to communicate mainly via Facetime. I grin harder, thinking about two nights ago when he woke me up at midnight to connect on Facetime. He demanded to watch me pleasure myself until I came, calling his name. That's become a regular event whenever we're apart. He constantly demands to watch me cum. I feel my body getting warm as I remember his text, and the dress that was unexpectedly delivered to me yesterday. It's black, leather, and form-fitting, that the skimpy thing barely covers my ass. I'll definitely have to wear a jacket over it. I'm tempted to pull out my phone and read the rest of his instructions, but I'll save that for later when I consider where I am.

The rest of my time at the community center I work to keep myself occupied so the thoughts of what will happen later on tonight don't intrude. It's a tough feat, but somehow, I manage through to the end of the day. I lag behind, cleaning up after the kids and helping the counselors put away the books. By the time I look up, the place is empty and it's well after two o'clock. I head into Coral's office to tell her I'm leaving. As I make my way out of the door and over toward my parking space, I notice Trudy still sitting out front of the center.

"Hey, Trudy. Are you still waiting on your ride?"

She gives me a half-hearted shrug without even looking up at me. "My mama will be here soon, I guess." The uncertainty of those last two words hits me hard in the chest. All the kids were picked up nearly an hour ago. Trudy looks as if she's been sitting out here about that long.

"How about I give you a ride home?" I offer.

Trudy's head snaps up and she stares at me with ghosted eyes. "No, Ms. Tasha. It's okay. I think she'll be here soon."

That answer isn't good enough for me. I can see it in Trudy's eyes that she doesn't even believe her own words. It's a hell of a thing to be twelve years old and not able to trust the adults who are responsible for taking care of you.

"It's no big deal. We can't have you waiting out here. I'm sure your mother just lost track of time or something," I reassure her. Of course it's bullshit. We both know it is. Her mother, like mine, doesn't care. But I do and I can't have this girl waiting out here by herself.

"I insist. We can talk more about planning for the book club. You know school starts in just a couple of weeks, so we need to get things organized."

When I mention the book club, it sparks her interest, and eventually her little shoulders sag as she finally relents. "Okay, Ms. Tasha. I did want to talk more about the book club anyway." She grins.

"Great! Let's go. My car is over here." I point in the direction of my car. Once inside, I ask Trudy for her address to put into my GPS. When she recites it, I immediately recognize it as one of the roughest areas in the city. That's not all I find surprising, considering many of the center's kids come from not-so-great neighborhoods. According to my GPS it'll take about twenty minutes to get to Trudy's home.

"So tell me about your ideas for the book club," I say as we exit the parking lot.

"Oh, I was thinking we could also do comic books. What do you think? I remember you saying you read comic books as a kid."

I listen attentively as Trudy continues talking about the idea of adding comic books to our reading list. She even comes up with the idea of having a movie night to watch one of the Marvel films. I thoroughly enjoy her enthusiasm and am drawn in by her excitement.

"Those ideas sound great, Trudy. We'll have to run those by Ms. Coral, of course or the interim director since Ms. Coral will be going on maternity leave soon. But I like that idea and I think comic books are a good way to shift gears between books." I finish my statement at the same time I pull up in front of the address Trudy has given me. I look over at the two-story house and notice the old beat-up car I've seen picking up Trudy a few times out front in the driveway. Trudy must notice as well as she looks at the car and frowns, likely drawing the same conclusion I have. Her mother is likely home and just forgot all about her.

As I begin to say goodbye to Trudy, she opens the passenger's door. The front door of the house crashes open, nearly falling off its hinges.

"Gary! What the hell you mean she's just a friend! That's the bitch you were with last night?!" Trudy's very irate mother is shouting at the man who'd identified himself to me as Trudy's stepfather at the center. His head is down, as he lazily makes his way down the front steps of the house in a pair of sagging jeans and a black T-shirt.

"Man, whatever. Gon' ahead with that bullshit, Lisa!" he yells back, waving her off.

Out of the corner of my eye, I watch Trudy cringe, embarrassed as she climbs out of the car. Not wanting her to enter this scene alone, I shut off the car and get out, planning to finally introduce myself to her mother despite the apparent fight she's currently involved in. I'm hoping her desire to save her daughter any further embarrassment will be enough for her to end this argument and focus on Trudy.

"Hi, Ms. Campbell, I'm Tasha one of the counselors at the community center," I say, extending my hand to the woman. As I get closer, I see how much Trudy resembles her mother. They have the same brown, almond-shaped eyes, nose, and round face. The only difference is that Trudy is about three shades darker than her mother. The woman standing before me is very pretty except the wild disdain in her eyes and twisted frown on her face right now would make anyone pause before approaching her.

"Who the hell are you?! Is this another one of the bitches you fucking?!" she yells at the man who is now in the driveway.

I look over my shoulder at the man.

He looks at me with a frown of his own. "I don't even know that chick!"

"No, Ms. Campbell. I'm a volunteer at the community center that Trudy attends. I gave her a ride home." *After you forgot all about her again.* Thankfully, I bite my tongue on those last thoughts but just barely.

"Ms. Campbell? Who the hell is that?!" She snarls.

"Oh, I apologize. I just thought that you and Trudy shared a last name."

"Psst… Nah, that's her *daddy's* last name. That fool had the nerve to ask me to give her his last name, but I ain't seen his triflin' ass since."

I nod at that, not knowing what to say. "Well, Trudy has been doing very well at the center. She's one of the smartest kids there. Just don't tell any of the other parents I said that." I attempt to joke in order to break up the obvious tension.

"Whatever. Trudy, go on and take your ass inside from all this sun. You know your black ass don't need any more sun," she says, acknowledging Trudy's presence for the first time.

My heart sinks at those words. I'd heard similar mean remarks too many times from my mother. "Well, there's nothing wrong with a little tan in the summer, right? After all, our skin does glow the darker it gets." I wink at Trudy, hoping I've taken some of the sting out of her mother's comments. "Just remember to use sunscreen, though. Our melanin may glow, but we're not immune to skin cancer."

I sigh a little in relief as Trudy gives me a big grin and begins heading up the stairs of the front porch. However, her grin changes when she looks over my shoulder to the driveway, staring at something. The look on her face causes a shiver to pass through me. I look over to see that she's glaring at *Gary* as he stares at her climbing the steps. He continues to stare until Trudy enters the house, disappearing from his line of vision. It was just a stare, but I shudder inside. I know that look all too well, but I don't want to believe what my intuition is telling me. As I continue watching, he finally climbs in the car.

"Gary! Gary! I know you not just gonna leave!" Lisa yells, hurrying over to the driveway, already losing interest in why I'm standing in her front yard.

Knowing I'll never get her attention right now, I reluctantly head back to my car. Driving home, I try to shake off the eerie feeling I got as I watched Gary stare at Trudy. I plan to carefully ask Trudy if he lives in the house with her. I hope against all hope that her answer to that question will be no. In the meantime, I remove my clothes from the day and take a shower to prep for my night with Jeremy.

* * *

Jeremy

"You know if you want to know more about your mother, you could maybe *ask* her."

I glare at the smart-ass smirk on Kyle's face. Kyle is the guy I call when I need to find out information quickly and quietly. I've had him do a number of jobs for me since we both left the U.S. Marines Corps. We were in the same battalion, having served in Iraq and Afghanistan. Right now, though, I'm about two seconds from forgetting all of our history together and knock his on his ass.

"Is that so? Just ask her, huh?" I retort, snatching the folder out of his hand. "Just give me the information you've collected on her."

Kyle chuckles. "I'm just fucking with you, Viper. I still can't get enough of pulling your chain."

"I'm usually the one yanking the chains these days instead of having mine pulled." That snide comment reminds me of the plans I have tonight. It's been days since I've seen LaTasha because I've been out of town for work. "Let's get this shit over with."

"Oh, hot date? Meeting one of your women tonight?"

I glare at him.

"Oh, we're not divulging secrets this time around, huh? Whatever. I'm sure I'll see you soon enough at the club."

I just grunt at his comment.

"Okay, okay. Well, from what I've found, your mother has been busy in the love department over the last twenty-five years. She's been married three times since leaving you. All of them were financially stable men...or so she thought. The first and third died of natural causes, but the second marriage was dissolved after only a few weeks. Looking at his bank records, he didn't have as much money as he'd pretended to have."

"That's probably why she left him. She loves money more than anything else in this world."

Kyle raises an eyebrow surprised at the bitterness in my words. "Yeah. Well, aside from picking wealthy husbands with a penchant for dying, your mother's been on the up and up."

"You sure those deaths were natural causes?"

His head jolts backwards, "You really think your mother—"

"She's *not* my mother. She's just the bitch who gave birth to me and left me."

"Whatever, man." He holds his hands up. "We've all got our own shit to deal with." He nods understandingly. "Anyway, they were deaths of natural causes. I combed through the medical records myself. Nothing fishy there. They were old a fuck. Unfortunately she also has a penchant for picking rich dudes with lots of kids. Kids they leave their money too. Turns out she's flat broke."

"Okay." I nod, knowing that last part already.

"You still got her at the hospice place?" he asks.

"Yup," I answer. I get daily updates on her condition, and I've visited a few times, but I never stay long.

"It's a pretty good place. It's upscale, but probably not her usual digs. But it'll do." Kyle nods.

"Thanks for the info." I don't care to respond to his latest statement. I want this conversation to be over. It's been a long week filled with meetings. The last person I want to discuss at length is that she-devil that abandoned me. I'm ready to relieve some stress and I have the perfectly planned evening to do just that.

"Alright, man. I see you're already thinking about other shit. I'm going out of town for a few weeks. I'll give you a ring when I get back.

Catch up on the scene and shit," he says, grinning and patting my shoulder before he heads out.

I grunt in response. Right now the only scene I'm interested in is the one that should be waiting for me in my hotel suite in about an hour. I double check, looking at my watch and note that it's close to seven. This gives me just enough time to finish up, use my office bathroom to shower, and head over to my hotel suite. For the first time that day I grin, remembering the specific instructions I sent via text to LaTasha this morning. I can just imagine the way she bit her bottom lip and blushed as she read over my words. A tight coil forms in my lower abdomen the more I picture her. I decide if I don't want to blow my load right here in the shower, I need to drop that image.

"Save it for tonight, Bennett," I grumble to myself, finishing my shower. I dress in more suitable clothing for the evening. As I slide my leather cuffs onto my wrist, I feel a shiver run through my body. The energy I need to release is beginning to burn me up and I move swiftly heading out the door. Tonight I plan to take LaTasha in ways she's never imagined.

CHAPTER 13

*T*asha

First, obtain the key from the front desk for suite 2023 at 8 o'clock sharp.

That was the first set of instructions Jeremy sent to my phone earlier today, detailing exactly when and where he wanted me to meet him. I remember the instructions to a T as I enter the hotel lobby and walk to the front desk.

"Hi. I'm LaTasha Collins. I need the key for suite 2023," I tell the smiling desk clerk.

Her smile grows. "Here you are," she announces politely, handing me the key. Then she directs me to the elevator that will lead directly to the suite. "Enjoy your stay." She winks at me.

I pause, contemplating for a second how many other women Jeremy has had come through this lobby to meet him in his hotel suite. My confidence falters for a little bit as I gaze around the lobby, wondering if anyone is thinking what I'm wearing underneath this damn trench coat. When I see a man across the room give me a smirk, I pick up the pace to the elevator, sagging against the side railing when it closes.

I remove my trench coat and hang it up on the wooden coat rack as indicated in the next set of instructions. I stare at myself in the full-length mirror. I observe how the very short black leather dress hugs every inch of my curves. The large teardrop-shaped cutout at my chest shows a considerable amount of cleavage, my breasts nearly spilling out of this thing. The lace trimming at the bottom barely reaches the middle of my thighs, which adds a nice touch. The four-inch heels definitely accentuate all of my legs' features, hiking my ass up in ways I'd never knew heels could. I finally look at my face in the mirror and smile at the image I see. I look damn good. Sexy even.

"Wow," I whisper. I manage to peel my eyes from the mirror, remembering the next set of directions.

Bring the silk scarf, nipple clamps, and ball gag I sent with you into the bedroom. There you will find more instructions.

Looking from side to side, I take in the modern décor inside the massive suite. I veer off to the left where the bedroom is, stepping inside to take in the huge bed. There's a note sitting on a sterling silver tray in the middle of the bed. Admiring Jeremy's attention to detail, I remove the note to read the instructions.

LaTasha,

Place the nipple clamps on the dresser at the side of the bed. Open the top drawer and remove the leather handcuffs. Get on the bed, fully dressed, heels included. Rest your body on all fours, facing the head of the bed. Tie the scarf around your head and then bind your wrists with the cuffs behind the center headboard post. Finally, lower the scarf over your eyes. I want your ass in the air and pussy on display when I walk in the room.

Holy shit. A shiver runs through my body and I feel the moisture between my legs, touching the tops of my thighs as I had strict instructions not to don underwear tonight. From the position he instructed me to assume and the shortness of the dress, my center would be on full display when he walked in the room. That level of exposure with my eyes covered both thrill and scare the hell out of me due to the vulnerability of the position. *Vulnerable.* Exactly how he wants me.

Taking a deep breath, I make quick work of getting into the position he has requested. The last step was covering my eyes with the scarf, leaving me totally in the dark. As soon as my eyes are covered, I feel my skin awaken. The coolness of the air hitting the sensitive folds of my core causes my heartbeat to increase with anticipation. I don't know how long I remain in this position alone, but I can feel Jeremy's presence the moment he enters the room. The goose bumps that sprout on my arms and legs tell me I'm no longer alone. The quickening of my heartbeat informs me that Jeremy is quietly observing every inch of my body as he often does. I want to squirm, move, to look at his face so I can know what he's thinking of me in this position. Does he like what he sees? I can hear his measured footsteps as he walks around the bed, seemingly to make sure I've followed his instructions. I want to reassure him that I had, but I remain quiet, following the rules of remaining silent until given permission to do so.

"Do you know how fucking long I've waited to have you in this position?" he growls low next to my ear. His voice is laced with something I've never heard before, and it makes me even wetter.

"You're so fucking beautiful."

I remain silent, swallowing the lump his compliment creates in my throat. I can hear the truth in his words. He means what he said. His words cause me to yearn for his touch, embrace, and his mouth on me. Anywhere. *Touch me, dammit!* I shout in my head, trying to silently convey my need to him. When I hear him chuckle, I become aware that he knows exactly what he's doing to me.

"We're not rushing this tonight, doll. I've waited too damn long to take you exactly how I've imagined in my dreams."

"Ohh," I purr when I feel a light touch start at my ankle and makes its way up and down my calf. It's soft and feather-like, but my already heightened state of arousal makes it feel much more content. He moves what I now realizes is his flogger made of rabbit fur to my other leg. He sweeps it up my thigh, achingly close to my pussy.

Please don't. Please don't. I silently beg him not to rub that flogger across my pussy knowing that I cannot take it without calling out, begging him to fuck me already.

"Tonight, you will have to ask my permission to cum. Is that clear?" He has the nerve to say that at the same time he runs the flogger across my core.

"Ahhh!" I groan.

"Do I make myself clear?"

"Y-yes, sir," I manage to stammer out. I have no idea how I'll be able to keep myself from cumming if he keeps this teasing up.

"Good."

I suddenly feel his withdrawal and miss the warmth of his body so close to mine. I hear a dresser drawer across the room open and close and try to listen for what he is going to do next. Of course I can't tell anything, leaving me only to wonder what lies ahead.

Swap!

"Oh shit!" I cry out as the sting from the flogger penetrates my senses.

"I don't recall granting you permission to speak!"

Swap!

"*Oh!*" I cry out again in response to another sting on my upper thigh.

"Love, if you speak again without permission I will use the ball gag. Do you want that?"

I shake my head, afraid to open my mouth.

"Okay then."

Swap! Another lash lands on my other thigh.

I manage to swallow my yell, but just barely. He keeps up with the flogger for a few more lashes, making sure to alternate where he hits me to avoid any real pain or injury. I'm panting by the time he stops. My pussy is quivering, begging for a release.

"Somebody liked my flogger." I hear the smile in his voice as I feel his finger touch my pussy, smearing my wetness around.

I feel both of his large hands pushing the bottom of my dress up, fully exposing my bare ass for his sight. He climbs fully between my legs, nudging my knees even further apart.

"It' time for my dinner," he growls a second before covering my core with his mouth.

Oh God! Oh God! I silently cry out, trying my best not to scream. I pant and squirm, but I can only move so much as my hands are still bound. Plus his arms have a very tight grip around my thighs. I can do nothing but take the pleasure he is giving me. He alternates between slow, sensual licks to my folds and clit, to sucking feverishly at my swollen nub. I feel the heat burning low in my belly, snaking around to my spine. My body involuntarily pushes back against his mouth, seeking its release. I need to cum.

"P-permission to cum, sir?!" I frantically pant out.

"No!" he growls against my pussy and goes right back to eating me as if he hasn't eaten in three days.

Fuck! I manage to swallow that curse down trying to think of anything besides what he is doing to my body. *"What the fuck?!* I think as I feel his tongue do the snake-like motion he does that always causes my pussy to gush even more. I try to think of something—anything—that will prevent me from cumming. I think of my latest book and which scenes I want to incorporate into the storyline. Finding that unhelpful, Danica's story seems to be no match for Jeremy's mouth. So I try to think about the latest television series I've been watching. Nothing helps. The man is relentless as he devours me. I'm so close to cumming, my legs are trembling. My total body is begging him for a release. Just when I think I can't hold out any longer, Jeremy stops. Moving so quickly behind me that I barely notice the retreat of his mouth, until his big body reaches over me, undoing the handcuffs and unbuttoning the back of my dress. With the speed of a leopard, he deftly flips me over and removes the scarf from my eyes.

"Open your eyes."

I blink a few times, adjusting to the light in the room. All the lights are on, allowing me to see every inch of his big frame as he towers above me on his knees between my spread legs.

"You're on the pill, right?"

Blinking again, I nod once I'm able to take in his words. I've been on the pill for a number of years due to irregular periods, which I'd told him about.

"I don't want anything between us." He reaches down and pinches my nipples and again I cry out, but I cut myself off, remembering his insistence on my silence.

"I'm going to use the nipple clamps as I take you for the first time tonight."

A shiver instantly runs down my spine at those words and I close my eyes, inhaling deeply. I've secretly been waiting for weeks to feel those damn clamps. I open my eyes and stare up into Jeremy's eyes. His irises have darkened to almost black. The promise of pure pleasure in them causes a flutter in my belly and lower. I try to urge him with my eyes to hurry up. He must know the anticipation is nearly killing me because he reaches achingly slow across the bed to the side dresser. Not once does he remove his eyes from mine, grinning mischievously. He knows exactly what he's doing to me.

Finally, he pulls the clamps out of the top drawer and they hold them above me, allowing me to see them. Two metal clamps are held together by a small chain and at the center hangs a lavender medallion.

"Do you remember your safe word?" His voice is laced with a barely controlled edge. He wants this as much as I do.

I nod.

"Tell me."

"Wolverine," I state, giving him the safe word I'd come up with weeks ago.

He nods, lowering the nipple clamps.

I gasp as the first clamp encloses around my pert nipple. Sensations of pain and then something else shoot through my body as he continues to clamp the other nipple.

"You are not to touch these no matter how it feels. If the pain becomes too much, use your safe word. Understood?"

"Yes," I manage to croak out, still reeling from the sensations of the clamps. "Ooohh!" I yelp when Jeremy slyly tugs on the chain between the clamps causing them to briefly tighten around my nipples even more. *Shit, he's going to kill me.* I yell inside my head, closing my eyes to try to regain control of my nerves.

"Eyes open!" he growls. "I want to see you."

My eyes pop open and I swallow deeply, inhaling to try and calm my erratic heartbeat.

"I've waited a long time to see these clamps on you." He's eyeing the clamps at the same time his hand reaches up to tweak my already squeezed nipples.

Oh God! My brain yells out at the same time my back arches off the bed, unable to remain still at the eroticism of his ministrations. This is pure torture as by now my pussy feels as wet as the Gulf of Mexico. I need him to do something—*anything.* I squirm, wiggling my hips, needing to get some kind of relief between my legs. I attempt to rub myself against his thigh that is in between my thighs.

"Uh-uh!" He shakes his head, glowering at me. He pulls back, moving off the bed entirely.

I growl out loud in frustration, pissed off at his refusal to provide my body with the relief it desperately needs. He merely chuckles, standing at the edge of the bed as he begins unbuttoning his shirt. When he allows it to fall to the floor, my breath hitches. It's not the first time I've seen his spectacular form, but I'll never be unimpressed by his perfectly sculpted physique embellished with an array of tattoos. I run my tongue along my bottom lip wishing it was the outline of that viper tattoo of his. I make a mental note to find out what he tastes like as soon as I'm unrestrained. I watch his eyes follow the movements of my tongue as his hands reach down to remove his pants. Slowly, I allow my eyes to trail down his hard chest and six-pack abs following the V-cut of his hips to the dark hairs on his lower abdomen. When he pushes his pants and briefs down, I gasp again at the monster that springs out.

I stare at his long, veiny shaft. Again my tongue sneaks out, swiping my lower lip. Moisture pools in my mouth as well as lower region. I swallow and inhale deeply, wondering how in the world all of him is going to fit inside me. Staring at his massive size, I know I'll do my best to try. I raise my eyes to look into his, again trying to implore him to take me. I open my legs wider, inviting him in. I silently beg him not to leave me hanging this time.

He stalks closer to the bed, eyes penetrating mine as he climbs on.

Like a panther stalking its prey. His movements are measured and precise. Inch by inch, he moves closer and up my body. Finally, he is seated right between my legs, his hand brushing against the short hairs above my pussy. I have to clamp my mouth closed to keep myself from crying out, begging him to take me. I have no doubt that as much as he wants this, he would make me wait even longer and use the ball gag to silence me if I were to break his rule.

"After tonight, you're officially mine," he growls at the same time he brushes his cock against my pussy lips.

My eyelids lower at the intoxicating sensation, but I manage to keep them open. I nod in agreement to his declaration, knowing that there's nobody else I'd rather belong to.

"You will take every inch of my cock. Understood?" He goads me as he begins pushing inside me.

Even if I were allowed to speak, there is no way I could with the feeling of being stuffed invading my body. I feel every vein and inch of him slowly pushing into me. I also feel the tension from his body. I know he is doing his best to restrain himself, but I don't want his restraint. I want it all. Deciding to silently convey I don't want him to be careful with me, I decide to contract my pussy muscles. The very muscles he's been training me to utilize in moments like this with the Ben Wa balls. His breath hitches as his gaze focuses on me.

"Fuck," he whispers right before he forcefully pushes all the way inside of me, causing my hips to raise completely off the bed.

"Holy shit!" I gasp unable to hold my tongue any longer.

"You're going to pay for that," he warns.

I don't know if he's referring to me squeezing him or my speaking out of turn, or both. And I don't have time to decide before he begins pounding into me relentlessly.

Yes! Yes! Yes! I say on a silent cry and I toss my head back to the pillow, my hands balling into tight fists at the headboard where my hands are still tied. I can feel his fingers digging into my hips as his hard rod plunges into the deepest parts of my body.

"Is this what you wanted?!" he yells, pumping his hips relentlessly.

Too turned on to even think of a coherent response, I continue thrashing my head on the pillow, giving in to the very pleasurable sensations he is giving me. I suddenly remember the clamps on my nipples as my breasts bounce up and down from the way Jeremy is drilling into me. With each of his downward thrusts, the clamps tighten and then release slightly. I somehow manage to keep my eyes open, remembering he wants to see all of my feelings. I look up at him, his lids lowered with passion and concentration, but staring directly into my eyes. I've never felt more connected to anyone than I feel in this moment. I begin to strain against the hand restraints, wanting more of a connection. I need to touch him to feel more of his body than just his cock and hands on me. And just as my frustration mounts at my inability to reach out to him, his lips come crashing down onto mine.

His kiss is as relentless as his thrusting cock, and I can't get enough of either. I open my mouth wide, allowing his tongue to sweep over mine, invading every inch of my mouth. I begin raising my hips up to meet his downward thrusts. This isn't gentle lovemaking. I knew it wouldn't be with him. This is forceful and the kind of sex that will leave bruises in the morning. I throw my head back onto the pillow, panting needing air. But Jeremy's lips soon find mine again, not allowing me much space apart from him. His hands move up from my waist up to my arms and then wrist, holding them down in place as his mouth invades mine. He tilts his hips and thrusts, his cock to making contact with my G-spot.

Oh God! I want to cry out, knowing I'm going to cum at any moment now, but I do my best to clamp down on that feeling. Without breaking our kiss, he takes one hand encircling both my wrists and reaches down to tug at the nipple clamps. "Cum for me!" he commands against my lips, as if I had a choice after that.

The squeezing of my nipples, his lips moving over mine, and his hand holding my hands down are pushing me closer to release. His stiffness pushing on my G-spot all is the primary source of pleasure. I am powerless to do anything but listen to his command and I release the tension, allowing myself to fall. Throwing my head back and arching my back to bringing my nipples in contact with his hard chest, I finally release. I wrap my legs around his lower back and squeeze my muscles around his still thrusting cock. I feel as if I am falling down a dark hole, but his grip on my wrists and whispered words in my ear keep me anchored to him where I feel safe. My body explodes. I hear a loud screeching noise only to realize seconds later that it's coming from me as my orgasm pushes me over the edge into pure bliss.

I don't know how long my orgasm lasts, but eventually, I come back to my body. My chest is heaving and my throat is raw from yelling as the aftershocks of my orgasm still ripple through my core. Jeremy hasn't stopped his piston-like movement in and out of me, stroking me through my orgasm and beyond. He lifts his head to look deeply into my eyes and then pulls out. I notice the veins in his neck strain, beads of sweat dripping down his neck and chest. He tugs on his cock once, twice, three times before white hot cum squirts out, spraying over my belly and breasts. I don't look away from him and his cum as it splatters over me, marking me as his. Seconds later, I feel his entire weight as he crashes down on top of me. I squirm, wanting to get closer to him. He reaches up, untying my wrists and I immediately wrap my arms around him. I stroke up and down his sweaty back as we allow our breathing to regulate. Once we take in adequate air, Jeremy anchors himself on his elbows and removes my nipple clamps. I moan at the sudden relief of pressure from my nipples. He quickly covers one nipple with his mouth, massaging it with his tongue, before moving to the other one, relieving the pain in both. That flame I thought was just extinguished in my core becomes ignited once again. Just as I push up to force more of my breast into his mouth, he pulls back and moves from over me, leaving me feeling cold from the loss of his body heat. My lips turn down into a frown, wanting more of his touch.

"Come on," he says, his voice strained as he picks me up as if I weigh nothing.

"Permission to speak?" I ask just above a whisper, still trying to find my voice because my throat is raw.

"Yes."

"Where are we going?" I ask as he continues to carry me as if we are walking over a threshold. *Wow! Where the hell did that thought come from?*

"Bath," he grunts, kicking the bathroom door open. Carefully, he lowers me to sit on the side of the wood paneled bath tub as he fills it with lavender scented Epsom salt, soap, and warm water. Once filled three-quarters of the way, he reaches for my hand, assisting me as I step in and sit. The feeling is heavenly, and I let out something between a sigh and a moan.

"Temperature okay?" he questions, kneeling at the side of the tub.

"It's perfect," I purr, smiling up at him.

"Good. Scoot up," he insists as he steps in behind me, straddling my back.

It feels like the most natural thing in the world as I ease back, allowing my body to rest against his. He begins lathering a loofah he's pulled from the side of the tub and rubs it up and down my arms. After dipping the loofah in the water, he begins massaging my tender breasts.

"How are you feeling? Was there anything you didn't like?"

I hear his murmured words in my ear, but I'm enjoying his hands and touch as he cleanses me far too much to respond.

"LaTasha, I need you to respond to me. Was there anything you didn't like? Was I too rough? I'm pretty sure you'll have some bruising in the morning."

I grin and turn to look at him. "It was perfect," I tell him as I reach up to cup his cheek, pressing my lips to the other side of his face. That's the honest truth. It was perfect...well, *almost*. I could tell he was holding back. I know he showed restraint. I decide not to mention it as I want to enjoy this time with him.

He nods, pressing a kiss to my temple before he resumes to cleaning me. "Okay," he says on a soft breath. He scrubs my back and I purr in response. The growing stiffness in his cock poking in my back tells me he is not immune to the sound emanating from me.

I feel his head press against the back of my head. "I was really trying not to take you for a second time tonight, but that's going to be impossible."

I giggle. "Don't hold back on my account," I encourage.

And just like that, bath time suddenly ends and within minutes, I find myself flat on my back with Jeremy's hard rod thrusting into me once again. My hands are bound above my head by his strong hands. For the rest of the evening, Jeremy shows me just how adept he is at bringing my body the pleasure I've craved for so long.

CHAPTER 14

*T*asha
I'm jolted awake by the phone ringing on the dresser. My eyes spring open, only to realize the phone is on the opposite side of the bed. I couldn't reach it even if I wanted to as there is a very large and heavy weight, entrapping me. I wiggle a little as the phone continues to ring, but Jeremy's arm tightens around me. He barely budges.

"Jeremy," I whisper with force behind my voice.

He merely grunts and shifts impossibly closer to me. As good as it feels to have his body wrapped around me; the damn phone is still ringing.

"Jeremy, the phone is ringing." I shift a little bit, managing to push his side. "Jeremy!" I call again.

"What?! Dammit!" he curses before his other arm reaches out widely, aiming for the phone's receiver. After a few misses, he finally grabs it. "What?!" he answers none too politely, his eyes still closed.

"Wait! What?" He suddenly sits up, fully awake. "Why the hell didn't you lead with that?! What hospital?" He pauses, waiting for a response.

I sit up upon hearing the word hospital.

"Okay, we're on the way." He hangs up, ripping the covers off of him and climbs out of bed.

"Jeremy, what happened?"

"We have to go to the hospital."

I'm on my feet now, searching for my clothes, my heartbeat racing. "Why? What happened? Is Coral or Liam hurt?"

"No. Coral had the baby."

I stop short, staring at him to see if he's serious. The look in his eyes tells me he's not joking. "Oh my God! But wait! He wasn't due until another four weeks. He's early. Is he okay? Is Coral okay? What hospital are they in?" I shoot off questions one after the other. A feeling of alarm begins to overtake me as I trip trying to find my clothes.

"Breathe, LaTasha. Coral's fine. The baby's fine. We just need to get to the hospital. Okay?"

I inhale deeply and close my eyes before releasing my breath. "Yeah, okay. I'm okay. Oh shit! I don't have any clothes."

"Top drawer on the right," he says before putting on the white shirt he'd had on earlier.

I make my way over to the dresser and pull the drawer open to find an array of women's clothing with the tags still on them. Every item is my size. I look over at Jeremy, grinning. I have no idea how he'd know I would need a change of clothes or how he knew my size, but that's one of the things that I love about him. He's always prepared and thinks three steps ahead. *Wait! Did I just say love?*

I bite my bottom lip at that thought as I pick out a pair of black skinny jeans and a black V-neck. The outfit is a little more form-fitting than my usual casual wear, but they are comfortable and fit perfectly. Minutes later, we are heading downstairs in Jeremy's private elevator where there is already a dark Town Car waiting for us out back. We're mostly silent on the way to the hospital, but Jeremy never lets my hand go. I'm comforted by his touch. I'm nervous, but in a good way. I can't wait to meet my new nephew and of course check on Coral.

"There's a new baby in the family!" I say, laughing.

Jeremy looks at me, his eyes mirroring the excitement in mine.

* * *

"About time you two showed up. I thought I was going to have to send out security to look for you," A smiling Liam greets us as we step off the elevator.

"Congratulations! I'm sorry, man. We were sleeping," Jeremy says, pulling Liam into a bear hug.

I duck my head, slightly embarrassed at his admission. I know Liam and Coral already knew what was going on between Jeremy and me, but to hear him say it out loud to Liam makes it even more real.

"Congratulations!" I greet Liam once Jeremy releases him. "Where is Coral? How is she? How's the baby? What did you decide to name him?" Again, I fire off questions as I launch myself into his embrace.

"She's fantastic!" He beams. "Room's right down here. She was in labor for all of four hours, and three pushes later, he was here. She gave birth right in our bedroom." He laughs.

My eyebrows nearly touch my hairline to the size of saucers. "Are you serious? In your bedroom?"

"Damn, baby is as impatient as his daddy, I see," Jeremy teases.

Liam laughs again, stopping at the hospital room. He knocks on the door before entering. Out of the corner of my eye, I see Mitch, Coral's ever-present bodyguard, standing next to the door. Liam and Jeremy give him a nod as we enter. The first thing I notice is Coral sitting up in bed, draped in a satin pastel pink robe. She cradles the sleeping baby in a light blue blanket. She looks up as we enter and the smile on her face could light up Times Square.

"About time you two showed up," she chides us just as her husband did a few minutes prior. "Tasha and Jeremy, meet Liam Junior." She grins, looking from the baby to Liam and then to Jeremy and me.

Everything becomes blurry as my eyes water with tears of joy. I sit down on the side of her bed, looking down at the sleeping bundle of joy in her arms. He's definitely a butterball as his plump cheeks show.

It's hard to tell who he looks like in this state, but his complexion is a couple of shades lighter than Coral's.

"Welcome to the world, Liam Junior," I whisper.

"Wanna hold him?" Coral asks.

My swallow deeply, nervous but nod my head vigorously. "Yes, I'd like nothing more."

Carefully, Coral hands me her pride and joy, making sure I keep his little head supported. "Hi, Liam Junior."

"LJ for short," Big Liam announces.

My grin grows. "Okay, then LJ. I'm your Aunt Tasha. We're going to get into lots of trouble together."

Coral and Liam laugh. I look up at Jeremy who is now giving me a look I can't figure out. His mouth has flattened, his eyes are guarded, and his body is stiff. I don't know what that means, but I look back to LJ as his little body begins to squirm. His tiny head bobs up and down as if he's searching for something. A small cry pierces the silence in the room.

"Someone's hungry." Coral grins, reaching for him. "Excuse us, guys."

I look up at Coral and realize she's asking us to leave the room so she can feed the baby in privacy. She begins to readjust her robe. "Oh!" I squeal. "We'll be right outside," I say and give Coral and LJ a kiss before I stand and exit.

"Where is Laura? Has she met LJ yet?" Jeremy asks Liam as we step into the hallway.

"No. Not yet. And she's going to be pissed that she missed his birth. She's spending the night with her grandparents. I talked to them last night and again once we arrived at the hospital. They're going to bring her here when she wakes up," he explains.

"Has Stacey been told yet?" I ask.

"Yup. I called her just a few minutes ago. Excuse me. I'm going to see if my wife needs help," Liam says before he steps back into the room.

Jeremy laughs at that. "I won't be the one to tell him that he doesn't actually have the equipment to help with nursing the baby."

I grin at his quip turning towards him and wrapping my arms around his waist. I stare up at his handsome face, feeling warm all over as he wraps his own arms around me. "She looks so happy." I sigh, remembering the look on Coral's face. I place my cheek against Jeremy's strong chest. His fingers begin stroking up and down the middle of my back, causing ripples of pleasure to move through me. "It's good to see her content." I sigh, feeling like I'm talking about both my sister and I.

Jeremy's lips brush against the crown of my head. We remain in this embrace for a few minutes, making small talk for a few minutes, pondering who LJ's going to look like when I hear a buzz come from Jeremy's pants' pocket. "Excuse me for a sec."

Reluctantly, I release my arms from his waist. Call me crazy but it seems as if he's just as reluctant to let me go.

I watch him stroll to the end of the hallway as he answers the phone. His movements slow and I frown his body stiffens at the end of the hall. His voice doesn't rise, but I can feel the tension coming from him as he engages in a conversation with an unknown person on the other end. I wonder if it's a problem with one of the hotels. He's had a few of those phone calls while we were together, and I can say I'm glad I was never the person delivering bad news to him. About a minute later, he returns with an unreadable expression on his face.

"Hey, I have to go visit someone in the ICU. I'll be back soon. Are you going to be alright?" he asks, looking distracted.

"Uh, yeah. Do you want me to come with you? Was it an employee?"

He shakes his head. "No. It's not work related. Just... It's a *long* story." He exhales.

The look in his eyes tells me this is more than he's saying. Without thinking, I grab his hand. "I'll go with you. ICU is only two floors up."

He pauses and looks at my hand in his. I hold my breath. Waiting for him to tell me to get lost or at least wait for him here. Instead, his face softens a bit and he squeezes my hand. I exhale, pulling him toward the elevator.

"What's the room number?" I question as the elevator doors close.

"Room 508," he responds.

Minutes later, we're striding down the hall, searching for the right room number. Jeremy pauses when he sees a woman standing outside the room as we approach.

"Ms. Watson," he greets her, clasping the older woman's hand. "Thank you for waiting here. H-how is she?"

My heads jerks back at the slight stutter I hear in his voice. I've never seen Jeremy anything less than totally confident and in control of his emotions. That small derailment from total control urges me to squeeze his hand again, silently conveying he's not alone. He looks back at me and nods.

"She experienced shortness of breath last night, but the doctors were able to stabilize her. They're letting her rest for a few hours before we transport her back to the hospice."

"Okay. So she's sleeping?"

"She's in and out of sleep. But she's been asking for you. I think it would be nice if you would go in and visit her," the petite, older woman goads. I get the feeling this is not the first time she's tried to convince Jeremy to see whoever the woman on the other side of the door is.

"I'm not so—"

"Jeremy," she says in a soft voice as she steps in and grips Jeremy's wrist. "I know it's asking a lot, but she really wants to see you. I just think it would be good for both of you."

"Fine," Jeremy relents pushing his free hand through his hair. He hesitates and takes a deep breath before turning the knob and entering.

I don't even realize he hasn't released my hand until we're both standing on the other side of the door and it closes behind me. Only then does he release my hand.

"I'll wait outside," I say, turning to leave.

His grip on my hand tightens. "Don't."

The strain in his voice tightens something in my chest.

The pleading in his voice stops me in place. Once he realizes I won't leave, he turns toward the woman in the bed. He takes a few timid steps in her direction. From where I stand, I can see her long dark hair spilling over the pillow. The lines on her face cause me to guess her age is somewhere in her fifties or sixties. Her eyes are closed and the steady rise and fall of her chest indicates she is indeed sleeping. Jeremy proceeds to the furthest side of her bed, staring out of the window. It's close to six in the morning, and the sun is just coming up, but it's still rather dark outside. With his hands in his pockets, he finally turns and looks down at the woman. He seems to be at a loss for words. I tamp down on the instinct to go to his side and comfort him. Before long, I hear stirring from the bed as the woman opens her eyes.

"Jer-Jer," a feather-light voice creaks. She clears her throat and removes the oxygen mask from her mouth and nose. "Jer-Jer, you came." The sides of her face crinkle as she smiles.

"Yes. How are you feeling?" His question is distant and cold.

"I'm fine, son," she returns the mask to pull in more air before removing it again.

I'm too shocked at the last word she said to notice how frail she looks. *Son?* This is Jeremy's mother?

"Ms. Watson said you had a little bit of a scare, but you're going to be alright. You just need to rest."

"Yes. But I wanted to see you." She pauses again, covering her face with the mask to assist her breathing before continuing. "I know I don't have much time left and I—"

"Let's not discuss that," Jeremy cuts her off rather abruptly. "Just focus on getting your rest so you can get out of here." With that, he takes the oxygen mask out of her hand and recovers her nose and mouth. He lightly pats her hand and looks over the room before he begins moving toward me and the door. He doesn't even look at me as we exit the hospital room. Quickly, he thanks Ms. Watson for her help and tells her to let him know when she is moved back to the hospice. Then he heads straight toward the elevator. I'm barely able to keep up with his long strides.

"I'll have the car drop you off at home before taking me back to the hotel," he says as we enter the elevator.

"Jeremy."

"I'll let Liam know we left so he doesn't worry," he says, ignoring my call for his attention.

The car ride is quiet and he doesn't even look at me once. I hate that he's closed himself off to me, especially after what we'd just shared last night. It was more than just sex to me at least. After seeing his mother, the very woman who had abandoned him, I want to know more.

"That was your mother." I say out loud as we reach the driveway to Coral and Liam's home.

When he remains silent I ask, "Can you come inside for a little bit?"

"I don't think that's a good idea."

"Please," I plead, tugging his hand.

Finally, he nod. As soon as we enter the front door Jeremy heads to the couch, collapsing on it and covering his face with his hand. I go into the kitchen to grab two bottles of water. I return to the living room and perch myself on the coffee table directly across from him. After unscrewing both bottles of water, I set them aside on coasters and then bend down. I lift one of his legs. Carefully, I remove his loafers and then massage one foot and then the other. I move my hands up his legs to his thighs. I feel the tension in his body relax little by little until I feel it turn into something else. Making my way up his thighs, I press firmly into his strong muscles, silently encouraging him to release. He removes his hand from his face, his eyes piercing me. I see the worn look on his face and want nothing more than to take it away.

I move up to his belt buckle and undo it along with the button and zipper of his pants.

"LaTasha," he whispers, hoarsely.

Goosebumps spring up all over my body as I move closer, coming to my knees in front of him. After some maneuvering, I'm able to pull his pants and boxers down far enough that his semi-erect penis is exposed. Tentatively, I extend my tongue, licking the entire underside of his shaft. The reaction is immediate, as it stiffens in my hand.

I smile at the power I feel because I'm able to turn him on in this way.

"You're not the only one who knows how to relieve tension," I state saucily right before I cover his entire cock with my warm mouth.

The gasp and groan of pleasure he releases causes me to feel a sense of power I've rarely felt before. Up and down I bob my head, setting a slow pace to moisten him. Releasing him, I twirl my tongue at his tip, savoring the taste of his precum before I take him all the way in. I lower my head down, pausing to adjust to the sheer girth of him. I close my eyes trying to pull it together. This is my first blowjob.

"Relax your jaw. Breathe out through your nose," he coaxes from above me.

I feel his hand cover the back of my head, urging me to go deeper. I do as instructed and soon I'm able to take him all the way in. He's in so deep that he's hitting the back of my throat. I pause, trying to stave off my gag reflex. When he tightens his grip on the back of my head, I begin moving up and down, sucking and slurping. Once comfortable, I use my tongue to stroke the vein at the underside of him while hollowing my cheeks as I move up and down. I can feel him grow incredibly hard as I continue sucking him. The pressure at the back of my head grows also, telling me he is enjoying this. I'm even surprised to realize that I'm feeling wetness between my thighs from this. My knowledge of this actually encourages me to move quicker, and before I know it, I'm using my hands to reach the parts of his shaft that won't fit in my mouth.

"Shit! I'm going to cum. Swallow it!" he barks, and I brace myself for his eruption.

Seconds later, I feel the first squirt of his warm liquid on my tongue as he thrusts his hips into my face, yelling out. I try to take every drop but his essence spills out of my mouth. Still, I wait for him to completely empty and his body to go still before I release him. I hearing a popping sound as he exits my mouth. I sit back on my heels, looking up at him between my lashes, wiping my mouth.

"That's the first time I've ever done that," I admit.

His head pops up from the back of the couch and a half-cocked smile emerges. He stuffs himself back in his pants before pulling me onto his lap. "You're shitting me." He chuckles.

I shake my head. "Can I tell you something?"

"Right now you can tell me anything, doll."

"I've been watching how-to videos of doing that."

"How-to videos to give a blow job? Doll, you know I'd give you all the practice you need." He chuckles.

"I know but I wanted my first time with you to be...special, not instructional." I give him a one shoulder shrug, my eyes lowered to the floor.

He bends over, using his finger to tip my chin up to look at him. "I appreciate your effort. Best blow job ever," he states, before taking my lips with his, and pulling me up to his lap.

I snuggle into his embrace, laying my head on his shoulder. "That woman was your mother?" I ask after a few moments of silence. At first, I regret the question, feeling his body go rigid underneath me. But I won't take it back. I want to know more about him and this woman who obviously has an effect on him. I caress his jaw, trailing down to his neck, shoulder, and arm. I massage it to release the tension again. Slowly, his body relaxes and he sighs.

"Yes. That was her."

"She's sick."

"Lung cancer, courtesy of her two-pack-a-day, thirty-year habit."

"How long does she have to live?"

"Doctors said six months." He sighs. "That was three months ago."

"When's the last time you saw her?"

"A few weeks ago. The first time I saw her in more than twenty years was the night of our second date when I had to leave early. That was the day she stormed into my office to tell me she was broke and dying. I set her up in a hospice and I talk to Ms. Watson a few times a week to check up on her condition."

"But you don't visit her regularly." It was a statement, not a question or condemnation of guilt.

"No."

I let his answer hang in the air for a while. "My mom left me too," I admit. His grip around my waist tightens. "She'd never really wanted me. She didn't say as much, but I could tell. She only paid me a little bit attention to whenever my father came around, she would dress me up like a little doll to try and please him. It never worked. He didn't want me either. Aside from that, she only cared for me enough to chastise me about being too dark or too fat or not enough of this or that. My grandmother shielded me from the worst of it, but when she died when I was ten, there was no one to shield me. We moved from New York to Virginia a few months later. My mother's new boyfriend got her mixed up with drugs or maybe she started doing drugs before then. I'm not really sure. She'd leave for days at a time until one day she never came back. I was almost twelve and alone," I recall those scary and lonely days. Blinking to hold back unshed tears, I let out a deep sigh. "Anyway, I never saw her after that. It wasn't until I was eighteen that I learned that she'd died of a drug overdose back in New York. She'd been buried in an unmarked grave. I never got to say goodbye or ask her why she hated me so much."

I sit up and look at Jeremy. I frame his face between my palms. "She's your mother. She was obviously terrible at it, but at least you have a chance to talk to her. Ask her why she threw you away."

"I wouldn't even know where to begin." I can tell that admission is hard for him.

"You'll find the words. I never thought I'd be able to forgive my mother either. It took a while, but I no longer hate her. You can start by simply making time to visit her."

He sighs, pulling me in even closer. "I'll think about it. Right now," he says, sitting up, and pulling me with him. "I need to take a nap. It's been a long night."

I gasp as he raises us both and carries me effortlessly to the bedroom. Soon enough we're both cloaked in the weariness of the past twelve hours, surrendering to the sleep we both desire.

CHAPTER 15

Tasha

Standing over the stove, I relish the aroma wafting in the air. It's Friday evening and I'm at Jeremy's cooking chicken marsala with risotto. He gave me a key to his house a few weeks ago and told me to use it whenever I wanted to. Since then, there have been a couple of times since then that I've received a text message in the middle of the day, demanding I meet him in his playroom dressed in a pair of handcuffs and blindfolded. Those times resulted in me emitting ear-splitting screams from orgasms. I see my reflection in the mirrored finish of the stove and blush at the heated look on my face. I seem to have that look whenever Jeremy crosses my mind, which happens to be a hell of a lot these days.

Returning to the present moment, I hear the front door open and close. Butterflies immediately start fluttering in my belly. That happens whenever he's near. I hear him making his way to the kitchen. I take out a spoon from the drawer, wanting him to taste a sample of tonight's dinner before he goes up to take a shower and get out of his work clothes. However, as soon as I look up from the stove and into those dark green eyes, I know he is not thinking about dinner; at least not the dinner on the stove. He leans his long, solid body against the edge of the doorjamb, staring at me. I know that look.

"Hi." My voice is already breathless.

"Hello," he returns, looking me up and down. He pauses to take in the outline of my ass in the long skirt I'm wearing. I know he's assessing whether or not I have on panties or not, which would be breaking one of his rules. No *panties while in my home.* His words echo in my mind. Realizing I'm *panytless* indeed under the skirt, he raises his gaze to look me in the eye at the same time his hands reach for his shirt collar. Deftly, he removes his dark blue silk tie. That move alone causes my insides to hum in anticipation, but I try to keep it under control.

"How was your day?" I play coy, pretending not to realize what type of mood he's in. Something has triggered his need to release some extra energy. And that knowledge alone makes my pussy pulsate in anticipation.

"Hands behind your back." He gets straight to the point.

I smirk, turn off the stove, and cover the pots. "No answer to my question?"

He stalks toward me with narrowed eyes and growls lowly in his throat. "Love," he scolds.

"I just want to know how your day was."

"Mine is about to get a lot better. *Yours* may worsen if I have to repeat myself."

Biting my lower lip to keep from grinning, I slowly move my hands to my lower back. Quickly, I feel Jeremy's strong hands take hold of mine, twining the silk tie around my wrists securely. But it's not tight enough to cut off my circulation or cause pain. He begins to gather my skirt at my waist, groaning when he makes contact with the skin of my backside.

"No panties." I hear the satisfaction in his voice. "Spread your legs," he orders, but in his impatience doesn't wait for me to do so. He uses his foot to separate my legs. "You want to know how my day was?" he whispers in my ear while his fingers outline my pussy lips.

I moan at the intimate touch.

"Quiet!" he growls, smacking my ass for emphasis.

That move prompts me to poke my ass out for more, which is exactly what he wanted. Gripping a handful of my hair, he pushes me down on the countertop and separates my legs even more, leaving me completely exposed to him to do whatever he wishes. That thought sends even more liquid to my already wet pussy.

"My day was shit!" he grunts, pushing his way into me forcefully.

I gasp at the sudden fullness, but do my best to keep quiet. Without warning, Jeremy starts pounding into me, angling his hips to penetrate me as deeply as possible in this position. One hand remains on my hair while the other grips my ass, squeezing painfully. His strokes are relentless as he tunnels into me for dear life. When he eases up for a second, I think he's going to pull out, but instead I hear one of the kitchen stools scraping across the floor until it's right next to me.

"Leg up," he commands, lifting my right leg, placing it onto the stool. This allows him even deeper penetration, which I was sure was impossible before now.

Ohhhh Goood! My brain screams over and over as he pushes my head down onto the counter and takes what he wants. I feel wetness sliding down from my pussy to my upper thighs. The slapping of my ass against his hard body mixed with his grunts are all that can be heard. But it's enough to arouse me even more and soon my pussy is fluttering. I need to cum.

"Sir, can I please cum," I manage to ask, my voice hoarse.

"No!"

I want to whine and turn around and smack him at the same time for denying my orgasm. I decide to punish him as he is punishing me. I continue to take his unwavering strokes, gripping my pussy muscles on each of his down strokes. When I hear him gasp and smack my ass, I grin, knowing I'm able to make him lose control too. He picks up the pace of his strokes, hammering into me, moving his hand around to my front to stroke my clit. My toes curl from the pleasure coursing through my body mixed with the pain from the way he continues to grip my hair. Soon, I can't take it anymore. My body can't possibly get any higher on this cloud of pleasure. I need a release.

"Cum with me!" he yells, his voice hoarse.

Thank you, God, I think right before my body takes over and my orgasm crests, causing every inch of my body to feel suspended off the ground. I strain and shake uncontrollably until the last moments of pleasure leave my body. When I come back to reality, my throat is dry and hurting from the screams I emitted and I feel Jeremy's heavy body folded over me on the counter. I love the way he lays on top of me, protectively after he cums. It's as if he's protecting me from the gravity of what we've just shared. He's letting me know he's all in it with me. These are the moments I feel the safest I've ever felt in my life. Much too soon, I feel his weight let up and he pulls himself from me. The feeling of loss is quickly replaced when he pulls me up from the counter, releases the tie, and then tugs me down to sit down on the kitchen floor with him. Still panting, we remain quiet for some time as we come down from our high. Jeremy continues to absent-mindedly rub my wrists, massaging any hurt away. I don't bother to tell him that he doesn't need to do that since he didn't hurt me. He wouldn't stop anyway. I smile at that knowledge, snuggling even closer to him.

"You know most people would say doing that in the kitchen is inappropriate."

He grunts. "It's *my* house. I do what the fuck I want," he retorts.

"You want to talk about it?" I feel his chest rise as he inhales deeply. He releases but remains quiet. For a while I think he's not going to answer my question.

"I went to see her today," he finally answers. Without him saying I know who *she* is.

"How is she?"

"She's dying," he states, not bothering to sugarcoat the situation.

I remain quiet, stroking his back. I decide not to push him. Jeremy will open up in his own time and I'll sit right here until he's ready.

"I asked her why she came to me only once she knew she was dying. She said it was because she had nowhere else to go." He snorts. "Imagine giving a child up and then only contacting them when you're dying because you've lived such a fruitless life that no one else cares about you."

I pull him in tighter, wanting somehow to shield him from the jarring pain of rejection. I know that pain all too well.

"Maybe," I say.

"Maybe what? She didn't mean it? Nope, she meant exactly what the fuck she said," he spits bitterly.

"I'm sorry." That's all I know to say right now.

"For what? Did you abandon me and come back in my life twenty years later sick and dying of lung cancer?"

I don't take issue or get defensive at the tone in his voice. I know it's not me he's angry with.

He sighs heavily. "Then after saying all that, she apologizes."

My hand pauses.

"I know, right? She's a regular Dr. Jekyll and Ms. Hyde."

"What did she say? Her exact words."

"She said, 'I'm sorry for leaving you like that.' It probably was her pain meds talking anyway." He shrugs.

"When are you going to see her again?"

"I'm not."

"What?" I sit up to look him in the eye.

"I went and saw her. It's over." His face hardens, but I see the flicker of vulnerability in his eyes.

"You *have* to go see her again," I insist.

Jeremy gives me a hard stare, but I refuse to back down. "I don't *have—*"

"Yes, you do!" I say exasperated although I know I'm breaking one of his rules. But I don't care. "You need this. And you will never forgive yourself if you don't. I know it."

He just glares at me for a full minute before lowering his lashes and then looking back at me with an impish grin. "Fine. If I *have* to see her again, then you *have* to go to the National Book Awards dinner."

My face tightens. It's been months since he found out about and weeks since we even talked about that stupid dinner. I thought he'd forgotten all about it, but I should've known better. Jeremy forgets nothing and he's always two steps ahead of me. I roll my eyes and wiggle, trying to get off his lap, but he holds me in place.

"That's different," I huff, sounding like a school child.

"How so? Seems to me like you're running from something the same way I—"

I smile at his slip up and pounce. "See! You *are* running from it. You can't—"

"Nice try," he says, cutting me off. "But right now we're discussing *you*." He points his index finger toward my chest.

I fold my arms over my breasts, narrowing my eyes giving him my best 'don't mess with me' look, but this big bully remains unfazed.

"If I go to see her again, you'll go to the awards dinner. In fact, I'll go with you."

Those last two words loosen something in my chest, making the impossible seem possible. New York City is a big scary place with some ugly memories for me, but it seems less so when I realize I don't have to take it on alone.

"You'll come with me to New York and I'll go with you to visit your mom."

Something in his chest must soften too because he releases a breath I didn't realize he was holding, and squeezes my thigh, reassuringly. Silently, we agree to be each other's strength.

* * *

"WHEN IS MS. CORAL COMING BACK?" Trudy asks me as we continue to clean up the community center. We've just finished one of our after-school book club meetings and most of the children have been picked up by their parents or guardians. Trudy, as usual, is one of the last children here. I don't mind her company at all. Contrarily, I relish our little talks and listening to her theories on Danica or whatever book we've chosen for the month. She's become an avid reader, often bringing new books she's picked up from the library to my attention. According to the academic counselors here, she's one of the top in her seventh grade class and her teachers think she has a real chance at attending one of the top high schools in the city if she keeps up.

"Well, she had little LJ about five weeks ago and I think she's going to take about six months off. So she has a little under five months left." Considering it was already October, it likely would be spring before Coral returned full-time to the community center. She wanted to spend time adjusting and enjoying parenthood before returning to work. I think if Liam could have it his way, she'd *never* return. But that was neither here nor there.

"Wow! That's a long time."

"It'll go by quickly. And when she comes back, we can tell her about all of the different books the club has read."

Trudy nods. "That'll be cool. She looked really happy when she came for a visit last week with the baby. I bet she's a really good mom." Her voice was filled with sadness on that last sentence.

I look up from the chair I'd just turned upside down on one of the desks. I notice Trudy's head lowered. My heart breaks a little for her. I remember the day she's referring to. Coral had come in for an hour last Tuesday. She brought LJ and Liam with her. I'm sure it's because Liam didn't want either one of them out of his sight. Coral was practically glowing as the staff oohed and ahhed over the baby and congratulated her and Liam. The way she looked at LJ, anyone could see how much he meant to her.

"Yeah, she's a really good mom," I comment, remembering how protective my big sis has always been over me. "Now, tell me about this math test you aced in school the other day," I encourage, changing the subject.

"It wasn't a big deal." She shrugs.

I stop abruptly. "Trudy." I pause, waiting for her to look up at me. I want her to see the seriousness in my eyes. "Don't ever short change yourself, okay?" I wait for her to nod before continuing. "There will be enough people in this world trying to bring you down and those who think you should humble yourself. Those people are *wrong*. Don't let anyone, not even *you* downplay your accomplishments."

Trudy's eyes widen a bit and I see the uncertainty in them. But I

165

remain steadfast. When she sighs and nods I break our stare off. "Okay, so now, tell me about the math test you aced."

For the next fifteen minutes Trudy retells how she barely even prepared for the math test, but she'd paid attention in class and remembered the strategies for solving the algebraic equations. "You know, I love reading, but I *really* like math and science too. I checked out a book from the library a few weeks ago about careers in engineering."

My eyebrows spike up.

"You think I could-"

"Trudy! Let's go girl!" The yell from across the parking lot grabs our attention.

I turn to see a male figure sitting inside the beat-up car that usually comes to pick up Trudy. My body stiffens as I realize it's Trudy's mother's boyfriend. I've barely met this man, but everything in me is telling me not to trust him.

"Hey, Trudy, have I ever given you my cell number?" I ask, still staring at the vehicle.

She looks up at me confused. She shakes her head.

Quickly, I take out my bag and pull out a Post-it note and scribble my cell and home phone numbers on it. "Use this whenever you need to. Alright?" I say, handing her the sheet of paper.

"Come on, girl!" he yells.

"A'ight. Thanks, Ms. Tasha. See ya next week." She waves before hurrying off.

The unease in my stomach refuses to die down, but all I can do is pray she'll be okay and that she'll use my numbers if she ever needs them.

CHAPTER 16

*T*asha

"You said it's her mom's boyfriend?" Jeremy asks, entering the bedroom after just brushing his teeth in the bathroom.

I look up to answer and I swear my brain short circuits. He's completely bare from the waist up. I watch every ripple of his abdominal muscles as he walks toward the bed. The way the pajama bottoms sit low on his hips, showing off that V-cut causes me to run my tongue along my lower lip.

"LaTasha, focus," he demands, but I hear the laughter in his voice.

"How am I supposed to focus with you looking like that?!" I wave my hand, gesturing up and down his body.

"Easy." He grins and my pussy muscles instantly clench at that mischievous look. "If you focus right now, I'll reward you later on," he says before he leans down and takes my mouth with his. He reaches underneath me to grab a handful of my ass.

"Mmm...Promise?" I groan when he pulls back.

"Have I ever lied to you?"

"No." I shake my head. "No, you never have." That admission warms my chest just as much as his lips on mine. Blowing out a breath, I sit back against the headboard as he climbs into bed. "What was I saying? Oh yeah! I think it's her mother's boyfriend. I doubt they're married." I had opened up to Jeremy about my misgivings concerning Trudy's home life. I don't know why I'd brought it up at dinner, but it had been on my mind since I'd left the community center earlier today.

"And you don't like him? Has he said anything to you?"

I smirk at the hard look Jeremy gives me at that question. I know if I say yes, Jeremy wouldn't hesitate to find this guy. "No, he's never said anything to me besides a few passing words. But it's not what he says to me. It's not even his rudeness with Trudy. It's this look he gives her. I..." I pause. I know that look, but I don't want to tell Jeremy how I know it. I'm not ready to share that part of my story yet.

Being as perceptive as he is, Jeremy sits up, examining me. Sometimes, like right now, I hate how exposed I feel with this man. *A look?*

"Yes. I know it sounds stupid."

"No, it doesn't. It's called *instincts*. We all have them, but some of us are just more attuned to them than others. And whatever you've been through that you still refuse to share with me has helped hone your instincts."

See, what I mean? He has absolutely no qualms about calling me out when I hold back. He's not shaming or guilt tripping me for not opening up. He's just calling it what it is.

"How can you be so sure of that?"

The faint lines around his eyes deepen as his eyes crinkle from his smile. "I'm a marine."

I throw my head back and laugh.

"No, but seriously, my service and even my life before joining the marines honed my instincts. Living in five foster homes in a year and a half will teach you about you can and cannot trust real quick. I'm bettering it's similar to the way your instincts were honed." He pauses as if waiting for me to interject, either confirm or deny his suspicions. I remain silent, again not ready to go into the full detail of my history.

He continues. "If a look this guy is giving off bothers you, I don't trust him either. Watch out for him. I can have a guy I know look into him if you want."

I wave him off. "No, that's not necessary. I'm sure it's nothing."

"Don't be so sure. Promise me you'll never be alone with this guy and if anything happens, you'll let me know *first*." His fingers grip my chin, so I'm forced to look directly in his eyes. I realize that he won't let this go until I've said what he wants.

"I promise," I finally say, thinking it wouldn't ever come to that. I'm sure I'm overreacting.

"Good. Now, how's the writing going?"

I grin at the swift change in subject matter. I moan. "I've entered the editing stage. This is that part of the writing phase where I rethink my entire career as an author and think that maybe going into something like... I don't know. Maybe real estate would be a better option."

Jeremy's chest expands as he lets out a laugh. "*Real estate*, doll?"

I quickly nod. "Yeah. I mean, who doesn't like real estate. Everyone needs a place to live or run their business, right?" I joke.

"I know a thing or two about real estate."

"Oh right. I forgot I was talking to the hotel magnet."

"Apparently," he quips. "Trust me. You don't want any parts of this business. Besides, I need to know what happens to Danica, and you're the only person who can tell me. And considering where we're headed in a few days, you're pretty good at this writing thing."

I groan. Just when I'd forgotten for a little while, he brings it up. The Awards dinner is in three days.

"Speaking of *that*, I don't know why you want to leave so early. The ceremony isn't for another three days." Although the dinner is still three days away Jeremy has us scheduled to leave tomorrow.

"Because, doll. We're not going to New York first."

That surprises me. "Where're we going then?"

"It's a surprise."

"I don't like surprises."

"Oh no?"

I don't even get the chance to register his questions before I'm squealing as I'm flipped over onto my belly and my waist is being pulled up. Then a pillow is placed under me.

"Mmm..." I moan as his fingers make contact with my bare pussy.

"It seems your pussy likes surprises." He merely laughs when I wiggle, kick my leg, back, but miss him. "Now, now, doll. I was just about to reward you for focusing earlier, but I can make this into a punishment if you want," he warns.

I squeeze my eyes shut against the feeling of his fingers still massaging my labia and the memory of his last punishment. I was forced to wear those damn Ben-Wa balls all day as I ran errands. That night I was so wet I swore I could've cum from just one look, but he fucked me until I could hardly walk, refusing to let me cum. I refused to talk to him for half of the next day. It was all because I had forgotten to eat lunch and dinner the day before. It's not my fault I was in the zone writing.

"Ah, so you do remember your last punishment," he says against my whimpers. "No punishment tonight," he growls as he slowly pushes his way into me. I feel the usual sensations of ecstasy of having him inside me. The pleasure short circuits my brain and the previous conversation is all but forgotten as he takes me to the skies.

* * *

"When can I take this dang thing off?" I question anxiously, resisting the urge to pull the blindfold off. After a very short plane ride, Jeremy insisted I put a blindfold on before we stepped off the plane. He still won't tell me where we are. I have my suspicions. I could feel the heat of the sun beating down on us as soon as we stepped off the plane.

"Patience, doll," he croons low in my ear.

I choose to ignore the shiver that runs down my spine. I feel his hand at my lower back.

"We're taking a twenty minute ride to our final destination. You think you'll be okay with this blindfold for another twenty minutes?"

I can hear the smirk in his voice. He knows I can last more than twenty minutes. "I don't know. You tell me."

"Watch it, love," he growls low so only I can hear him.

I hear voices in the background and realize we're not alone. I hear more scuffling and I assume whoever is with us is putting our suitcases into a vehicle. "I'll be fine for twenty minutes," I say as Jeremy grips my fingers, leading me to what I assume is an waiting vehicle. When I hear the door open and he directs me to duck my head and step up to get in, I know I'm correct. I feel the coolness of the leather seats against my bare legs and Jeremy's presence behind me, urging me to scoot over. Once seated, I hear doors shutting, and minutes later, we're pulling off. Jeremy is in the backseat next to me. Typically, this type of thing would be freaking me out. But I've come to trust Jeremy implicitly in such a short period of time. His grip on my hand tightens, tugging me closer to his side. He leans away from me for a second, raising his arm to wrap around my shoulders, pulling me into his chest. I inhale deeply, taking in his favorite cologne and his natural scent. I recline into his embrace, sigh, and relax. I'm still not all that excited about heading to New York in two days, and in fact, I had difficulty sleeping the previous night. I tossed and turned so much that Jeremy woke me up with his head between my thighs. He gave me not one but *two* incredible orgasms in such quick succession that I could do nothing but fall into a deep sleep afterwards. I guess that was his way of letting us both get some rest before leaving early this morning.

"We're here," A voice that sounds far away announces.

I feel my shoulder being massaged as I come to. "I fell asleep?" I ask wearily, looking around, only to remember I'm still blindfolded.

"Yup. You're a lousy road trip partner," he teases, chuckling at his own joke.

I snort and sit up straight, blinking a few times although my eyes are still covered by the blindfold.

"Just a few more minutes," he says as his fingers adjust the blindfold around my head.

"A few more minutes? I thought we were here," I protest.

"We are, but you still have to wait."

I feel the weight of the car shift as he exits and then pulls me toward the door to assist me a I get out. Again, I feel the warmth of the sun and dry air. My suspicion heightens as Jeremy helps me up what I assume is a walkway. He pauses for a moment before I hear a door open. He guides me over a threshold where we are immediately surrounded by the cool air from an air conditioner.

"Put those in the bedroom please," he instructs someone.

Impatiently, I begin to tap my foot, hating how anxious I feel in this moment.

"Okay, doll. I know the suspense is killing you. Let us take care of that." He releases the blindfold, finally allowing it to fall from my face.

I open my eyes and immediately shut them again against the brightness of the sun shining through the huge floor-to-ceiling windows. But the small glimpse of my surroundings intrigues me and I struggle to make my eyes cooperate. I blink continuously until they finally adjust to the brightness. I gasp at the scene before me. We're standing in the middle of a huge living room in front of glass doors and windows that lead to the most majestic view of desert mountains.

"Arizona?" I question, still drinking in the sight before me.

"The spa I've been working on for the past year. You, doll, are our first guest before it officially opens next month."

My eyes scan the view before me. There's a fireplace along the far right stone wall. There are low sitting, tan loveseats forming a U in front of the fireplace. To my left is a huge kitchen and dining area. All of the colors coordinate with the desert theme in light tans and earth tones. But my eyes are immediately pulled back to the view of the mountains.

"Later we'll take a horseback ride up that way to give you a much better view of the desert," Jeremy says, gripping my fingers. He pulls me. "Let me show you the rest of the villa."

"We're staying in a villa?" My head whips around, still looking at the surrounding scene.

He laughs. "Of course." We continue down a hallway. "To the right is the bathroom with the garden tub with spa features. There's a separate shower with a waterfall showerhead." He grins mischievously. I blush slightly, knowing that he's referring to how in love I am with his waterfall shower at his home.

Next, we venture into the massive bedroom with a king size canopy bed, another fireplace, and a few chairs set on the sides of the bed. There are more huge windows, which give us another great view of the mountains.

"It's still early, so the staff will be delivering our breakfast soon. After that we have a ten o'clock appointment to do a two-hour horseback ride along one of the trails. I knew you wouldn't be able to take your eyes off the mountains, so that was one of the first things I thought would be fun to—"

I take his face between my hands and bring his mouth down to mine with a passionate kiss, cutting him off. I pull back. "I usually hate surprises, but this one was perfect. Thank you."

"Oh, don't worry. You're going to thank me properly later on," he says, squeezing my ass.

Even as I giggle, the warmth low in my belly causes me to feel flushed. I look up into his eyes and become warmer than I was as we'd stood out in the Arizona sun. Just as he begins to lean down to take my lips again, there's a knock on the door.

"That's breakfast."

I nod, disappointed as my hunger for something else is extinguished. We return to the living room where Jeremy lets the room service attendant in to deliver our breakfast. The table is soon covered with an assortment of breakfast foods. There's steaming hot sausages, eggs, Belgian waffles, three flavors of syrup, a delicious-looking fruit salad, and bacon. There are also three different types of toasted bread, scones, and muffins.

"I may have gone a little overboard with ordering all your fave breakfast foods." He grins.

"I'm not complaining," I respond, my stomach growling as the delicious aromas intermingle and float to my nostrils.

As we eat, Jeremy fills me in on the details of the spa. His company bought it about a year ago after its previous owners wanted to retire. The spa had been going downhill for years because the owners were getting too old to properly take care of and promote it. Jeremy's Bennett Industries purchased the company and took the last year to revamp and remodel the estate, update all the facilities, and get the necessary licensing to operate the different services.

"It has taken a little over a year to get everything completed, but she's just about ready. The grand opening is a month from now, but we're having a soft opening next week. I want to bring you back for the grand opening," he says, grabbing my hand as I attempt to do the dishes in the sink after our breakfast. "Don't worry about those. Will you be up for coming back?" he questions.

"If you make it worth my while," I tease as he escorts me outside. He looks back at me with a steamy look, silently conveying he intends to make it worth it. I look over and am surprised to see three horses and a man standing beside them. "Horseback riding!"

"It's the best way to see the entire spa grounds before the temperature becomes too hot. There's a manmade lake on the grounds, we can take a swim later before lunch," he announces, guiding me toward the horses. "This is Edward. He'll be our tour guide."

"Just call me the horse guy," Edward says. His weathered, tanned cheeks crease as he gives me a warm smile.

I instantly feel at ease around Edward. It could just be because Jeremy obviously trusts him, and I've come to trust Jeremy with my life. Either way, I'm excited for the tour.

"Thank you." I nod as Edward introduces me to my horse, Betsy. She's the smallest of the three, animals. She's light grey with a white patch on her back. I pet her jaw, making nice before I mount her. Back at Haven House, one of the therapists incorporated horses into her outdoor sessions. So when Betsy nays and bobs her head, obviously enjoying my petting, I grin and let out a breath. Horses can be temperamental creatures, but Betsy doesn't seem like she'll give me any trouble. Edward starts to help me mount her, but Jeremy stops him. He deftly, lowers his hand to hoist me up and over Betsy's wide back. He even secures my feet in the straps once I'm seated. I notice the grin Edward gives Jeremy and duck my head. I turn and watch as Jeremy mounts his horse. His is larger than Betsy and its coat is a beautiful coal black. At first glance, he looks mean, but Jeremy bends over and says something low in his ear. The horse dips his head and nays, taking on a deferential pose toward the man on his back. A warm sensation courses through my chest after that little exchange.

When Jeremy looks up directly into my eyes, winks, and flashes a panty-wetting grin, that warmth moves down to my core. *God, I love him!*

We spent the entire morning and early afternoon exploring the spa grounds and hiking a few of the trails. I never knew the desert could be so beautiful. The backdrop of the mountains provided the perfect scenery. Jeremy proudly pointed out the spa's gym, which will offer all types of low and high impact cardio classes and will house an assortment of state-of-the-art fitness equipment. We then explored the industrial size kitchen filled with all modern appliances and gadgets where healthy cooking classes will be offered to patrons. We got to see the rest of the horses under Edward's care. I was introduced to the instructors who will teach meditation sessions, art classes, photography, and more. The best part of all was the absolute pride in Jeremy's eyes and body language as he showed off the entirety of the resort and spa.

"You've done well here, Mr. Bennett," I say as he helps me off the horse at a little canopy that's been set up just off one of the trails. There's another smorgasbord of food set up under the canopy, but I'm still full from breakfast.

"I'm sure you're still stuffed from breakfast, so let's go for a swim before we eat."

I nod, wondering how he already knows what I'm thinking before I say anything. With anyone else, I would normally hate that, but with *him*, everything is different. "That sounds wonderful."

He had instructed me to wear a bathing suit underneath my clothes before we'd left the villa this morning. I notice him removing his T-shirt and jeans, so I do the same. I strip out of my black shorts and lavender T-shirt, revealing my purple one-piece suit. I walk over to the manmade lake and see Jeremy already in. Sticking my toe in the water, I notice how warm the water feels. It's not uncomfortably hot definitely a relief from the hot sun. But it's not nearly as cool as I'd imagined.

"What are you waiting for?" he teases from the midway point in the water.

I inhale deeply and trudge in before I finally submerge my entire body underwater. I hold my breath until my lungs begin screaming at me for air. When my head breaks the surface, I wipe my eyes and catch my breath. I blink a few times and look for Jeremy. I don't see or hear him for a few moments.

"Ahh!" rushes from my lungs when I feel a splash of water behind me.

My scream is followed by his deep belly laugh that warms my core. Turning towards him I see those green eyes glinting with mischievousness as he splashes me again. I return the favor and I get lost in our little splash fest. We swim around each other and laughing like school children. I'm sure to an outsider we look like two crazy-ass people who somehow sneaked onto this private resort. No one would ever suspect the owner of such a place to be so carefree. That's just one of the things I love about Jeremy. With most people he's his reserved, albeit charming self, but he allows *me* to see his carefree self.

If the purpose of this short trip was meant to break up my underlying tension surrounding the Awards dinner, he's certainly done his job. I haven't felt this relaxed in quite some time.

* * *

"WHAT DO YOU THINK?" he asks as we lounge around after stuffing ourselves with the delicious lunch spread. He's relaxed a reclining chair with me tucked between his legs. I'm lying back against his stomach and chest. His fingers are stroking through my tangled curls and coils. I'm sure I look quite the sight, but he doesn't seem to mind. The canopy provides just enough shade and coolness to protect us from the afternoon heat.

I turn and face him. "I think this place is like a slice of heaven on earth."

The stroking of my hair and I look up to see his eyes darken with some emotion I can't quite identify. Seconds later, his grip on my arms is pulling me up to his face. Our position is now awkward, but I'm within kissing range of his lips.

"You'll come back with me next month?"

"Um, I—"

He captures my lips in an urgent kiss, robbing me of my next words. There is something extraordinary about this kiss, but I'm too caught up in the passion to decipher the hidden message.

"Come on, there's more I want you to see before we settle in tonight. I've got big plans for our evening."

The promise in his tone makes my belly quiver. Now *that* meaning I'm all too familiar with. I can't wait to see what he has in store for this evening.

* * *

"You're so fucking beautiful," he whispers against my lips as we dance in front of the fireplace to music playing in the background.

I swallow down the lump in my throat caused by the sincerity in his voice. I've been told I was beautiful before, but never with this type of emotion behind it. With Jeremy I don't have to question if he's telling me the truth or what he thinks I want to hear. With him, what you see is what you get. "Th-thank you."

"Don't thank me for telling you the truth. I can't wait to watch you win that award. You deserve it."

His words remind me of that damn awards ceremony. I bite my lower lip, ducking my head between his shoulder and neck. I feel like I want to hide again. Of course he refuses to let me. He pulls back and brings his hand underneath my chin, raising my head up so my eyes meet his. His eyes are searching mine, and although everything inside of me is telling me to look away, I can't. Here in this dim living room with only and the fireplace illuminating us, once again, I feel completely exposed to this man. When I think he's going to finally ask me why I've worked so hard to avoid my birth city and why this dinner is such a big deal, he doesn't. Instead, he lowers his head and nips my bottom lip with his teeth before he uses his tongue to slowly outline my lips. The slow sensuous glide of his tongue causes me to gasp, parting my lips and making way for him to plunder my mouth full force.

"Mmm," I moan into his mouth as he takes mine.

He starts off slowly, exploring, and teasing, but then turns into the take-no-prisoners Dom he is. His hand moves to the back of my head, trapping me against his mouth, not allowing for me to move. Soon I realize he is moving us to the floor where he'd removed the coffee table earlier. He lays us down on the plush carpet in front of the fireplace and sits back on his haunches, staring down at me. He remains quiet but still in complete control of the situation. I can see the look in his eyes. He's in full Dom mode.

"You will feel my diamond encrusted nipple clamps tonight with weight added," he says as he runs a finger from my chest over my abdomen and down one leg. Even though I'm still fully dressed, that light touch sears my skin. This isn't the first time he'll be using those particular nipple clamps on me, but it will be the first time with the weights added. My nipples begin tingling in anticipation, and I can already feel the moistness dampening my thong.

"No restraints tonight, though," he adds. "Just my hands." His grin tells me the only restraints he needs are his two hands. They can be just as effective as any belt or scarf he has. Meticulously, he begins undoing the buttons of my dress, exposing more skin with each flick of his fingers. Once completely undone, he spreads each side of the dress, revealing my lace bra and panty set; another item he insisted I bring along on this trip. His low grunt of approval encourages a smile on my lips. He helps me sit up to completely remove the dress and places a pillow down to support my head. He begins to reach for my bra, but I stop him with a hand on his.

"I want to undress you," I say out of nowhere. I've never undressed him before, but I want the chance to revel in this process.

He pauses, pondering for a moment before nodding. I sit up on my heels and begin unbuttoning the white shirt he'd worn to dinner. Each undone button reveals more of his colorful chest. When I reach the last bottom, I remove his shirt, leaving his top half completely bare. Without thinking, I use my tongue to outline the viper tattoo that snakes around from his belly all the way up to his neck. He's told me that was his nickname in his marine battalion. The viper is one of the deadliest snakes alive.

"Love, that feels good, but you did not ask permission," he scolds.

I close my eyes, wondering how he is able to maintain such control in this moment. I can feel his heartbeat thundering under the prodding of my lips and yet, his voice sounds like he's in total control. I just want to touch him all over. Reluctantly, I pull back, but not until I swipe my tongue across his nipple one last time. The hitch of his breath alerts me that he is not as unaffected as he'd like me to believe. "I need you to stand so I can take off your pants," I remind him.

"I'll do that. Sit back, plant your legs, and rest on your elbows." He doesn't even wait for me to move. Instead, he helps me into the requested position. He quickly releases the front clasp of my bra and removes it. His hands are on my breasts squeezing and massaging them. My head falls back as my nipples harden even more; no doubt his intention. My eyes tightly shut as I feel him move between my legs before his warm mouth surrounds one nipple. I cry out at the pleasure his tongue provides my nipple. He next moves to my other breast causes the same reaction. When he pulls back, I shiver with need to feel him again. Instead, he shifts and opens a bag. He pulls out the nipple clamps. I see the glint of light reflecting off the diamond as he moves it in front of me before taking one nipple and placing the clamp on. Again, I cry out from the immediate pressure of the clamp around my nipple and then again when I feel the second clamp engage. I bite my lower lip to keep from crying out again. Slowly, as usual, the pain subsides and a familiar pleasure emerges, moving straight to my core. I continue to bite my lip to keep from moaning this time. Just as the pleasure subsides slightly, I intake another sharp breath as the pressure increases and I realize Jeremy has added a weight to the middle chain of the clamp, causing the clamps to tighten around my nipples.

"Jer-Jeremy!" I moan.

"What did you call me?"

I hear the warning in his voice and my eyes pop open. "S-Sir," I manage to say.

"Better." He moves back from me, stands, and begins unbuckling his belt and pants. When he pushes his clothes down and his fully erect cock springs, out I bite my lower lip so hard I think I may draw blood. Every ounce of my body is inflamed and ready for him to take me anyway he wants. But I know him by now. He will drag this out as long as possible. He kneels down between my legs and kisses me between my breasts, using his tongue to lick my soft mounds, but avoids my nipples. Still the feel of his tongue that close to my clamped nipples reignites the fire, and the pool between my legs expands. My legs widen on their own accord, silently begging him to take me already. I almost cry out in relief when I feel his hands at my waist, gripping the edge of my panties. He moves his mouth to mine and our tongues begin to duel. His kiss becomes so forceful until it pushes my head back against the pillow and I encircle his neck with my arms, remembering I'm free to do so. Suddenly I feel a pressure on my waist and then a tearing noise and I realize he's just ripped my lace panties from my body.

"Much better," he says, grinning against my lips.

His finger rubs my labia before he pushes his way inside of me. I moan against his mouth at his intrusion. He answers by adding a second finger.

"J-jer...Sir," I moan breathlessly as he continues to breach me.

"You're going to win that award," he says out of nowhere.

I open my eyes and I'm met with such an intense look that I have to reclose them.

"Look at me," he growls, his fingers still working their magic on my pussy.

I open my eyes again.

"You're amazing in every way possible," he reiterates before crushing his lips to mine again. He removes his fingers and within seconds, I feel his massive cock pushing into me. I inhale sharply at the contrast between his fingers and his cock, but widen my legs to make room for his big body between my thighs. "You're going to win and I'm going to be the proudest man in the room," he groans as his cock pushes into me.

I blink, trying to keep the tears in my eyes from spilling over. Jeremy refuses to let up. He buries his head in crook of my neck, continuing to whisper words of encouragement. He tells me how deserving I am and how proud he is of me. Those words along with his thrusting cock and the nipple clamps all work together to send me higher and higher to a place I've never reached before. I close my eyes, trying to push back against the onslaught of emotions swirling around inside me, but it's no use.

"Cum for me," he demands right before biting my shoulder as his cock pushes against my G-spot and I fly completely apart.

I arch my back completely off the floor. I part my lips on a silent yell that the orgasm rips through me with more force than I've ever felt before. I pant uncontrollably and somehow realize I'm crying at the same time. The tears I'd tried to keep from spilling are gushing like a tidal wave now. I continue to pant, sob, and climax all at the same time. Jeremy just holds me through it all, still whispering his encouraging words, which cause me to cry even harder. But now I feel less afraid. I have no idea how long this goes on for. Maybe five minutes or five hours, but when I finally come back to myself, I'm completely drained.

Carefully, Jeremy pulls out of me and removes the nipples clamps, causing me to flinch. He stands up, but I can't move. He pads over to the kitchen and I hear the refrigerator open and close. Moments later, he brings me back an opened bottle of water. He lies beside me, handing me the water, and pulls me to him. "Drink," he commands, holding the bottle to my lips. The water is a balm to my dry and scratchy throat. I must've done more yelling than I thought.

"Better?"

Silently, I nod and turn to curl against his chest, needing his strength right now. He wraps his arm around me, pulling a blanket over to cover our naked bodies.

"Thank you," I whisper. I feel his lips brush across my forehead and I close my eyes again after more tears flow. We lay quiet and still for a long while. The only movement is my forefinger making tiny circles across Jeremy's chest.

I decide to break the silence. "You know my therapist used to say kids who experience trauma, often become adults who are emotionally stunted at the age of their trauma." I don't look up at Jeremy to see his reaction to my words. I can't. "Danica is twelve, almost thirteen. I never realized that until later on." I pause, sighing heavily before the next words spill from my mouth. "I was almost thirteen when I was forced to turn my first trick." I feel Jeremy's entire body stiffen next to me, but I continue, needing to say these words out loud for some reason. "My mother moved us to Virginia with her boyfriend and then got hooked on drugs. She eventually left one day and never returned, choosing drugs over me. For a while her boyfriend allowed me to stay, saying he'd take care of me. Then one day a few months later, he told me it was time I started to earn my keep. He used to bring home this guy who was in his forties. He claimed the guy just wanted to *talk* to me privately. That wasn't true, though. When he took me in the bedroom, h-he..." I stop and take a shuttering breath, but I refuse to stop telling my whole story. "He assaulted me." I snorted. "That's the professional term for it. *Assault.* Over the next two years I was forced to service whomever he brought home. I was defiant, though. I never gave oral sex and whenever he took me to the store, I stole packs of condoms, forcing the Johns to wear them. He used to beat the shit out of me for that, but I never stopped. He locked me in the bedroom and tried to keep me high on drugs to keep me out of it. But I started making myself vomit the pills up that he was giving me. I had to remain aware of my surroundings. I don't know how I knew, but I knew I'd someday have the chance to escape. And the day before I turned fifteen, he fell asleep and left my door unlocked. I saw it and didn't even think twice. I went in his wallet I saw lying on the table and took as much money as I could and left with nothing else. I found the closest Greyhound bus station and made my way back to New York. For about a year, I slept wherever I could. I went to homeless shelters, the backs of train stations, or wherever." I stop to wipe a tear that had managed to escape.

"What happened then?" Jeremy asked in a low voice from behind me. He'd been so quiet and still until I'd almost forgotten he was there.

But now I feel his fingertips grazing my shoulder, stroking and comforting me. That encourages me to continue. "One day I got desperate. I was hungry and had no money so..." I sigh, ashamed most about this. "I decided to go back to what I knew. I began tricking to make money. I only lasted a few weeks before I was arrested. I thought I was going to jail for a long time, but even that scared me less than the idea of having to go back to the street and do what I was doing. I was young with no discernable skills and no family. The guards in jail weren't much better than the tricks on the street, though. Most of them were grown men who would prostitute the girls they were supposed to be supervising. I saw everyone from prison guards to police officers involved in it. Thank God, I never was never in there long enough to be recruited for that, but it was happening. I even knew a few of the girls involved. The guards threatened anyone who dare to tell. And who the hell would believe juvenile delinquents over prison guards anyway, right?" I snort and shrug, a part of me still feeling like that helpless seventeen-year-old.

"How'd you get released?" His voice is laced in a tone I've never heard before.

Is he disgusted by me?

"About a month after my arrest, a guard appeared and told me to come with him. I was scared as shit. I just knew he was going to try to pimp me out. I was ready to run. Instead, he escorted me to the front of the jail where I was given my meager belongings and told I was free to go. It scared the hell out of me too until I looked up and saw Coral standing there, ripping into a prison official for not trying to contact someone about me. It was the first time I had seen her in years."

"She came for you."

I close my eyes as more tears fall and nod. "She did," I say in a shaky voice. "That was the first time I met Liam too. He was with her. She had taken time out of her leave from war to find me. S-she...she... is my sister. Stacey...too," I stutter. "We have the same father. He cheated on their mother with mine although Stacey didn't know until recently. Coral has known since we were kids. When we were still young she promised to always look out for me, even though we weren't supposed to know we were sisters. My father barely acknowledged my existence. Even after she moved away and went to college, Coral still kept in contact with me until my mother dragged us to Virginia. Coral got me into a program up in Central Massachusetts that provided me with counseling, GED classes, and a place to live and heal. I stayed there for nearly three years until I felt stable enough to move out on my own. I got a job working as a legal secretary and lived just outside Boston for a few years. I took some community college courses in creative writing and decided to finish a story I'd started when I was thirteen years old and locked up in a dingy bedroom in Virginia. That would become my first published book. When I realized I could live off the money I made as an author, I quit my job and moved to Vermont for the peace and quiet. I rarely dated. The idea of sex repulsed me for so long because of what I'd been through. Eventually, it got better and I dated someone for awhile. He was okay, and our relationship was...nice. But we weren't on the same page sexually. I'd shut down and just lay there until he was finished. That was my last relationship. It's also why I hate New York and why I refuse to do public appearances for my books. The fear of being recognized by someone or the world finding out my sordid past." I tremble at that thought. "Anyway, when Coral moved to Dallas and asked me to come with her to be closer, I agreed, happy to live so close to my sister again. Then I met you and all of a sudden, I wanted *more*," I admit finally, looking up at him.

His eyes were dark, something lurking behind them. They remained on me, searching for something. We stared at one another for a long time before he pulled me in, kissed my forehead, and pulled the blanket completely over us. He gently lowered me down, silently encouraging to me to go to sleep. Without protest, I did. I was tired and mentally drained after all I had just revealed; my secret shame. My eyelids fluttered before finally closing as I drifted off to a deep sleep.

CHAPTER 17

*J*eremy

"Okay, what do you think of this one?" LaTasha asks, holding up an electric blue dress against her body. It's sexy and stops right above her knees. With the pair of high heels I'd purchased her for this event, I'm sure she'd look great in it.

"It's perfect," I say half-heartedly. I try hard not to display what I'm feeling, but after what she'd revealed last night it's hard. The anguish in her voice as she recalled what that bastard had made her do as a child, fucked with me. It made me want to tear the entire state of Virginia up looking for him. And if Coral hadn't assured me that he'd been taken care of long ago, I would do just that. I got up in the wee hours of the morning to call Coral just to double check that everyone involved in LaTasha's horrific past had paid a price. She'd assured me they all had. Everyone from her mother's boyfriend who had pimped her, his friend who was her first John, and even the prison guards that were involved in the prostitution ring at the juvenile detention center —they all had been handled. And Coral had even forwarded me copies of their obituaries and gravesites to prove it. I didn't think anger oozing through my veins hadn't subsided. In fact, it felt worse. The fact that I wanted to hurt those bastards but I was unable to because they'd already been handled, bothered me.

"Is everything okay?" LaTasha asks.

I peer up at her, from my position on the bed. I can see fear clouding her pretty eyes.

"You've been distant most of today, and I completely understand after what I told you last night. I realize it's a lot to deal with and if you want to back out or..." She hesitates, looking everywhere but in my eyes. "Or if you don't want to be involved with me—"

"Come here," I say, extending my hand to her. When she reaches for my hand, I pull her onto my lap and nuzzles her neck with my nose. "There's *nothing* you could tell me to make me want to end things with you," I say, realizing for the first time the truth of my words. "Nothing. Because I've already fallen in love with you."

She gasps and pulls back peering down at me.

I continue. "The truth is I *hate* what those bastards did to you and if I didn't already have assurances that they'd been taken care of, I would've had my investigator on the phone in the middle of the night to hunt them all down." I hear the danger in my own voice and wonder if I'm scaring her.

"What do you mean they've already taken care of?"

I shut my eyes, briefly debating on what to tell her...*if* I should tell her anything. "Coral," I simply say.

"She did something to them?" she queries, her voice disbelieving.

"She eliminated them," I say with little remorse.

"*Eliminated?* You mean..."

The look I give her is unflinching. "Yes. They're dead. Your mother's boyfriend, his friend, and the prison guards were all eliminated a long time ago. And if Coral hadn't offed them with Liam's help of course, *I* certainly would have."

LaTasha's stares at me in disbelief.

"Coral and I are cut from the same cloth," I continue. "She's a natural protector. There's no way someone can hurt the people we love to the extent you were hurt and be allowed to continue walking this earth. No way." I shake my head at the mere thought of it. "I'll just needed some time to get past my anger of not being the one who put the nail in their coffins. I hate that I couldn't do that for you." I press a palm to her warm cheek and stroke it with my thumb.

I notice LaTasha's watery eyes sparkle with something as a tender smile touches her lips. "You love me?"

I nod. "Yes." I don't even have to think about that answer.

"Me too," she admits above a whisper.

"You too what?" I want to hear the words.

"Love you. I love you too."

The muscle in my chest squeezes from her declaration.

"This shit is crazy," I say before sighing and rubbing my hand through my hair. I never thought I'd be one much for love, yet here the hell I am, chest deep into the shit with the woman in my arms.

"My very own Wolverine."

That makes me laugh out loud for the first time that day. "And you're my real-life Storm," I return.

"Tuh," she mocked. "I don't think so. Ororo is fierce—"

"And a survivor with a vulnerable side just like you. She has the power to turn a stormy and cloudy day into sunshine within minutes. That's exactly what you do for me. Jesus, when the fuck did I start sounding so Goddamn lame?!" I question out loud, causing LaTasha to chuckle as she pulls me in for a huge.

"You're a regular sap, Mr. Bennett."

"Only for you, doll." I mean those words with every fiber of my being. I pull back enough to see her wiping tears from her eyes. Her dark skin peeking out from the edges of the white plush hotel robe she's wearing, is begging to be touched. Never one to be able to deny myself of this woman for too long, I oblige, pushing the top part of the robe down over she bare shoulders. Her smooth skin greets me like a present on Christmas morning, and I push the robe down further until one of her naked breasts is exposed from underneath. Her nipple is already pert, asking to be licked. I lower my head, stick out my tongue, and twirl it around her areola, teasing her. My cock begins to stiffen when I hear her hiss at my tongue's contact.

"Jeremy," she whispers breathlessly.

187

The hairs on the back of my neck stand up, something that happens anytime she says my name. Right now, I'm not Sir. I'm Jeremy Bennett. Not a Dom, but a man who is fully intent on making love to his woman. I groan with anticipation as I lay her back against the bed, managing to pull open her robe. I hold her arms above her head and stare down at the woman beneath me. She's so strong yet so pliable underneath me. Her huge honey eyes never leave my face, begging me to touch her. I lower my head to kiss one corner of her mouth. Then I kiss the other one, the top of her nose, forehead, chest and on and on until I reach the valley between her legs. She easily opens her legs, keeping her hands perched above her head even though my hands are now wrapped around her thighs. She's surrendering to me just the way I love. I gladly spend the rest of the night devouring her body. The screams she emits as I take her alerts anyone within earshot that this woman belongs to *me*.

CHAPTER 18

Tasha

    "Surprise!" Stacey screams and pulls me into a tight hug.

"Oh my God!" I say stunned as I look over Stacey's shoulder to see a smiling Coral.

Coral, Stacey, and their husbands have just surprised Jeremy and me as we entered the National Book Awards dinner.

"What're you doing here? How did you know about it?" As soon as those questions fly from my mouth, I turn to look over at Jeremy's smiling eyes. "You planned this?"

"I thought your sisters would want to watch you win this award."

I remain mute, unable to say anything past the huge lump that has just formed in my throat. I blink rapidly to keep the tears from falling.

"Don't get all teary-eyed now. You still have yet to explain why you neglected to invite us," Coral insists, angrily.

Despite her attitude, I admire how gorgeous she looks in her dark blue dress that hugs her new hips thanks to LJ. The hemline flares out at the bottom. Stacey is dressed in a pastel pink dress that stops a few inches below her knee. Both of their husbands are dressed in black colored tuxedos that have been tailored to fit their bodies perfectly. The almost look as good as my man.

"Congratulations, Tasha and welcome to the family," Andre greets me and pulls me into a hug. He places a soft kiss on my cheek too.

I hear Jeremy clear his throat behind me. I look over my shoulder to see him frowning at Andre's closeness.

"Calm the hell down, Bennett. No one's making moves on your woman, especially not with my wife standing right here," Andre retorts, causing everyone to laugh except Jeremy.

"Anyway, you still haven't answered my question." Coral's face remains trained on me.

I sigh and look at Jeremy for help, but he offers none. "*Traitor*," I mouth to him. "I…uh…wasn't planning to attend, but *someone* convinced me that I should, but it was kind of last minute."

"Coral, leave our sister alone. It's not like she neglected to invite us to her wedding," Stacey retorts, causing everyone to laugh.

Coral and Liam's first wedding was a private ceremony in Hawaii and Stacey has yet to let our big sister live it down.

"Leave my wife alone," Liam defends pulling Coral into his side. "Anyway, we should probably find our seats."

With that, Jeremy sticks out his arm for me to wrap my hand around. He escorts me into the dining hall, the rest of our family in tow.

SOMETIME LATER, the boisterous conversation at the table helps to drown out the pounding of my heartbeat—*almost*. It helps to have all my family here with me. Their confidence in me winning tonight makes me almost believe I will too. I try to convince myself that even if I don't win, having everyone I love right now with me is still worth it. But I really want to win. I can finally admit that to myself now. I begin to tap my leg as a result of nervous energy coursing through my body. A large hand squeezes it, halting my movement. I turn to my left to see a devilish smirk and a pair of sparkling green eyes staring at me. He's silently telling me how proud he already is of me and, that I have nothing to be nervous or ashamed about. I'm not even sure how

I can tell he's communicating all of that, but I know. I notice the beating of my heart relaxes and the anxious knot in my belly subsides slightly. It's still there, but much less ferocious. Jeremy leans down and presses his lips to my cheek.

"Eat. You don't want to make your thank you speech on an empty stomach," he says, before pressing his lips to my cheek again and pulls back.

"What will you do if I don't?" I ask, feeling bold all of a sudden. Even with all my nerves and the anxiousness of this night, I get off on teasing him.

"You already know the answer to that," he growls low in my ear, squeezing my thigh again.

The flutter in my belly is no longer due to nervousness about the award, but now it's all about the man sitting beside me. I grin as I pick up my fork and knife to cut into the chicken breast.

"He's a keeper," a feminine voice to my right sings.

I look over at a smirking Camille, my book agent. She's the only non-family member at this table.

"What are you talking about?"

Her bright brown eyes glint with a familiar mischievousness as her full, pink tinted lips quirk into a knowing smile. "Don't act coy with me. I've been watching you two since you arrived tonight," she says just above a whisper. "And he had your people fly in just to celebrate you," she says, nodding to everyone at the table. "But I'll mind my business for now. Your category is next."

My brows crinkle in confusion as I watch her turn her attention to the front of the room. I too, swivel my head in that direction and realize the speaker is now talking about my literary category. This is confirmed when I look behind the speaker and see a copy of my book's cover along with three other young adult book covers, belonging to my fellow nominees. The butterflies in my stomach begin again and I can barely make out what the speaker is saying. All I can see is my book cover that features a young girl with skin the color of cedar wood, wearing an afro puff and her golden retriever, Side-kick, poised to take on the world. It's a vision that first took over my imagination at the tender age of thirteen when I was in a very dark place. Years later, it's being embraced by some of the most renowned figures in literature. Who would have thought? The image before me blurs as my eyes water and all sounds drift to the background.

"That's you, doll," Jeremy says excitedly.

I hear his deep whisper in my ear. Blinking a few times, I look over at the shit-eating grin on his face as he claps. "Wh-what?"

"You won!"

My eyes bulge as his words sink in. I look around the table and see Coral, Stacey, Liam, and Andre on their feet, applauding. All eyes are on me. Before I can fully comprehend the situation, Camille is standing to my right and Jeremy is up on his feet, helping me out of my chair. I take a deep breath to calm my scattered nerves at the precise moment Jeremy squeezes my arm and plants a kiss on my cheek. It's quick, but gives me the bolster of reassurance I need in this moment to go up and accept my award. On wobbly legs, I make my way to the podium and accept the heavy crystal stauette with my pen name and title of my book engraved on the sterling silver name plate. I stare at it for a few seconds, allowing this moment sink in before I turn to the audience to begin my speech. I place the award on top of the podium, I pull out the note cards I jotted down some acknowl-edgements in case I won, but now those notes seem lacking. I look out onto the sea of expectant eyes and feel the usual nervousness that creeps in whenever I'm around a crowd of people I don't know. Scan-ning the audience, I recognize a number of literary heavyweights and begin to feel out of place. That is, until my eyes collide with *his*. They're glistening with pride mixed with a hint cockiness that tells me he knew I would win. Even from where I'm standing, his presence is enough to center me. I take another deep breath.

"You know, if the literary world liked my books so much why on earth would they punish me by making me give a speech? I'm a writer, not a public speaker." I grin as the audience laughs at my nervous quip. "But in all seriousness, I, ah, I began writing stories at the age of nine. My love of reading spurned my own desire to create a world where I felt less weak, less vulnerable, and more like I belonged. The real world around me wasn't very welcoming to a girl from one of the poorest neighborhoods in this very city who loved reading science fiction. But even in those stories, it was often difficult to see someone who looked like me until I picked up my first comic book with an image of Storm on the cover. I remember that feeling of finding a story with a character who looked like me, save for the white hair." I grin and the audience laughs again. "I first thought of Danica's story well over a decade ago at a very, very dark place in my life." I pause, looking toward Jeremy for reassurance. Sure enough, his eyes are planted on me, encouraging me. I shift my gaze to see Coral who has tears in her eyes and before I know it, I have to quickly wipe away tears that escape my own eyes. Clearing my throat, I continue. "There were many days I wasn't sure if I'd live to see the next one or if I even wanted to. No thirteen-year-old should ever feel that way. I know that now, but back then all I had were my made-up stories. I truly believe it was the possibility of being able to get this story out on paper one day that kept me going. That faith and perseverance is what I wanted to give to little girls through publishing Danica's Travels. They needed to know that you can survive and make the world around you a better place. I wouldn't be here if it wasn't for Danica and thankfully, for an older sister who never gave up on me when I needed her the most." Now I pause to see Coral actually crying. "I want to thank my sister, Coral and my other sister, Stacey, for accepting me." I toss Stacey a wink and she also has tears in her eyes. "Thank you to the counselors and workers at Helping Hands who helped me rebuild my life after tragedy and my bad-ass agent, Camille, whose belief and commitment to making room for diverse books in the literary world may be even stronger than mine." I grin, looking at Camille who is beaming. "I'll never forget how adamant and hard you worked to get Danica's story into the readers' hands, or how you refused to let any aspect of her be changed to appeal to mainstream audiences," I say looking directly at her. "And to the man I came here with tonight..." I pause and inhale deeply, looking at Jeremy. Once again, my vision blurs. "In the short time I've known you, you have made me a better writer, a better friend, and a better person. I don't know what the future has in store for us, but I will thank God for every day I've have been blessed to have you in my life." I quickly wipe more tears from my eyes.

"One final thing." I look back over the rest of the crowd. "Never in my wildest dreams did I imagine I'd ever be up at this podium receiving such a prestigious award for doing what comes to me naturally—writing. But I know that I have been given a gift so that I can give back. And for this reason, I have decided to use the proceeds of this award and a portion of my book royalties to open a Helping Hands charity right here in New York. Unfortunately, recent news of young Black and Hispanic girls being kidnapped or going missing in the Bronx has been widely overlooked. It is highly suspected that these girls are being trafficked and no one outside of these communities is doing much about it. This must end, and I aim to use my voice, my money, and the resources I have available to aid in bringing these girls home and seeing that our communities remain safe places for children to grow up. Thank you for this," I say, holding up the award and stepping back from the podium.

My breath catches when I see my whole table standing and applauding wildly, without caring what anyone else thinks. Then one by one more audience members rise to their feet and applaud. Overcome with emotion, I finally let a few more tears fall freely as I cradle the award in my arms. Once again, on shaky legs I step down off of the main stage and I'm greeted by strong arms. I have no idea how he made it from the table over to the stage in that short amount of time, but I'm grateful that he did.

Jeremy pulls back, cupping my chin. He looks deeply into my eyes. "You did good, doll."

That causes more tears to fall and I let them, welcoming a feeling I only have whenever I'm in his arms wash over me.

* * *

Jeremy

"THAT WAS ONE HELL OF A SPEECH." The words are said to my back, but I know the owner of that voice.

"Senator Nathaniel Roberts, how nice of you to join us this evening." I smugly turn to greet the senator.

He's standing a few feet away from me, at the exact, same height. His eyes are shooting daggers at me. He's lucky Coral and Liam left just moments ago, needing to get back to the hotel for LJ's next feeding. I scan over the crowd to see Andre is schmoozing with some other business associates.

"I'm just waiting for my date to finish speaking with her agent and sister. How can I help you, Senator?" I barely pay him a glance as I look down at the time on my watch. LaTasha is in the restroom with Camille and Stacey, which means she may be in there for a while. That agent of hers can talk a mile a minute.

"Coral's sister?" Nate's eyebrow lifts high.

I shrug not without saying a word.

"Don't think I forgot what you did," he says low enough so passersby don't hear him.

"What I did? What exactly was that?" I know what he's referring to, but I want him to say it.

"Don't play dumb. Setting up *my* woman with that cousin of yours."

At that I scoff. "Nate, you know damn well Coral was never yours."

"I was working on it," he shoots back.

"No. You were *losing*. You were *always* going to lose that battle for two reasons." I pause and wait for him to ask.

"What might those two reasons be?"

"One, Coral has always belonged to Liam. That's a fact of life whether they were with together or not, they would've made their way back to one another with or without my help. And two," I say, moving closer to him. "Coral could never give you what you need. You know it and I do too."

His eyes narrow on me. "What's *that* supposed to mean?"

"You know damn well what it means. Coral's nobody's sub. You could try to suppress it all you want, but you need someone who'll submit to you. It's your nature to be a Dom the same way it's in me." I continue to stare him down the same way he glares at me. Senator Nathaniel Roberts may be the all-American, articulate, well-groomed guy from the picture perfect family, but behind closed doors, he's anything but. We both have been in this life for a long time. He's even deeper in than I am.

"Hey, Nate, what are you doing here? Don't you have some business in D.C. to tend to?" Camille sounds off behind me, alerting us of the women's arrival.

I step back at the same time Nate does as well, his face morphing into a friendlier one as he sets his sights behind me. "I just wanted to congratulate the woman of the evening and my favorite cousin." He steps around me to press a kiss to Camille's cheek before grabbing LaTasha's hand and pressing his lips to it. "A pleasure, Ms. Jones and congratulations," he says, calling LaTasha by her pen name. "And you must be Stacey," he greets. "Your sister speaks highly of you."

Stacey's brows crinkle in confusion, looking toward LaTasha.

Tasha quickly shakes her head.

"Oh! You mean, *Coral*." Stacey concludes. "How do you know my sister, Senator?"

"We served together," he answers swiftly.

LaTasha looks to me, knowingly. I had a feeling she knew about Nate and Coral's little fling.

"Camille, I didn't know Senator Roberts was your cousin," LaTasha states.

"Ugh..." Camille waves her hand dismissively. "I try to keep it under wraps. Do you know how many women would hound me if they knew I was related to this man? They would drive me crazy trying to get hooked up. No, thank you!" Camille teases and we laugh.

"We'll have to discuss how you've been cock blocking a brother later, cousin. Right now, I have a ride to catch to our nation's capital. Ladies, it was a pleasure. Bennett," he says my name with a tinge of scorn in his voice, resulting in my cocky grin.

I know he's still pissed because he thinks I came between him and Coral. But the truth is the truth. She was never his to begin with, and it would have never worked between them. Neither one of them was what the other needed.

"I'm going to go grab my husband and head back to the hotel. Celebratory brunch tomorrow, right?" Stacey asks, looking at LaTasha and me.

"Eleven o'clock sharp," I confirm.

"Great. I'm so proud of you! Congratulations again," Stacey gushes and pulls LaTasha into a hug before sauntering off.

"What was that about?" LaTasha asks once Camille and Stacey depart.

"What was *what* about?" I play dumb.

LaTasha stops short in front of me, folding her arms causing her breasts to poke out even more. I grin, licking my bottom lip, imagining the taste of her soft skin. "Jeremy, the senator… He seemed mad at you for some reason."

"Nothing important," I say, reaching out a finger to caress the silky skin on her neck and chest. "I can think of about a hundred other things I'd like to do with you besides talk about Nate Roberts."

"Only a hundred?" The way she bats her long lashes at me causes stiffening in my groin area.

"You're in so much damn trouble tonight," I growl, pulling her close to my side to make our way out to the waiting vehicle. I've got plans that will not be denied tonight.

CHAPTER 19

*J*eremy
"You ready for this?"

I angle my head to look down at the woman next to me. The concern in her eyes warms me from the inside out. I feel her squeeze my hand and as she cups it in both of hers, steadying me.

"How could I not be ready with you next to me?" Where the hell did those words come from? Sure, they're the truth, but that's not what I originally meant to say when I opened my mouth. I bring one of her hands to my lips. "I'm ready," I assure her as we enter the hospice doors.

It's been three days since we've returned from New York, and LaTasha has not left my side since. Or maybe I should say I haven't allowed her to leave my side. The only time she's been back to her place was to get fresh clothes and spend some time with Coral and the baby. It feels unnatural to have her sleep anywhere besides my bed at night. Today she's finally convinced me to come in and speak with my mother again after receiving a call from the night nurse the previous evening on her worsening condition. Doctors are saying she may have only have a month or two left to live, and LaTasha is insistent that I spend as much time with her as possible. Ordinarily, I wouldn't let anyone boss me around or tell me what to do with my damn time, but shit is different when she says it. So here I am.

"Oh, Jeremy, I didn't know you were coming in today," Ms. Watson, the director who happens to be at the front desk greets me with a smile.

"Hello, Ms. Watson, you're looking quite lovely today," I reply. "This is my girlfriend, LaTasha," I say, ignoring the way her head snaps up in shock at the word *girlfriend*. It's the first time I've ever introduced her as such, but again, it just feels natural.

"Well, it's nice to meet you, LaTasha."

"Please, call me Tasha. Nice to meet as well."

"We came for a visit. How is she this morning?"

"She's much better this morning than she was last night. There was a little bit of a scare, but she's improved now that she's rested a bit. I think she just overdid it a little yesterday, trying to go for a walk during the day."

I nod.

"I'll walk you two back."

I squeeze Tasha's hand as we turn to follow Ms. Watson around the receptionist's desk and down the long hallway toward my mother's room. Along the way, we pass a large room with televisions mounted on the wall. A few residents are sitting inside the room with what I presume are their visitors. The look of sorrow on one woman's face hits me in the gut as she looks down at an elderly man in a wheelchair, trying to feed him applesauce. My stomach twists uncomfortably with the knowledge of what this building holds. Not just the sick, but the *dying*. Most residents who come in here do not leave alive. I shake my head and turn my attention to the hallway ahead. We finally reach my mother's room after making a right from the main hallway. Ms. Watson opens the door.

"Look who's up this morning," she greets cheerily. "You have a visitor this morning."

"Who is it?" a paper thin voice asks, and for some reason it pains me to know that voice belongs to my mother.

"Jeremy," Ms. Watson responds. "Oh, don't worry about fixing your hair. You look fine," she fusses. "Come on in, Jeremy and LaTasha."

"Oh no. I—"

I pull LaTasha in the door behind me, cutting of her refusal. I have zero intention of leaving her out of this.

"Hi, Mar..um...Mo...Mar... Hello," I greet, feeling too wound up to find the name that I feel more comfortable calling her. "This is LaTasha," I introduce. "LaTasha, this is Marilyn, my mother."

"Good morning, Mrs. Bennett."

"*Mrs. Bennett?*" my mother repeats confused. "I was *never* a Bennett. Just call me Marilyn."

"Sure thing, Marilyn."

"I'll leave you all to visit. My shift is about to end. I'll be back in tomorrow night. Alright, Marilyn? Enjoy your son and his girlfriend."

I wait until Ms. Watson leaves the room and shuts the door behind her before I speak. "How are you feeling?"

"I'm no worse for the wear." She shrugs a pair of thin shoulders.

I take in her appearance, seeing that her normally shiny hair has lost its luster, turning into a dull grayish-black color. Her skin is pale as well, and she has definitely lost even more weight since the last time I saw her, which was only a few weeks ago.

"Have you been eating?"

"You two sit down. It hurts my neck to have to look up at you standing there at the foot of the bed all stiff like that," she says, ignoring my question.

LaTasha looks around the room before opting to leave me the chair closest to my mother's bed. She takes the chair near the window.

I sit in the seat beside my mother' bed. "Have you been eating?" I ask again.

She waves a bony hand, dismissing the question. "The food here is *terrible*. They feed me this bland crap all steamed or baked and taste-less," she scoffs.

I know that's not the full truth. This place has one of the best repu-tations in the state as far as hospices are concerned. They do serve mostly lightly seasoned food because many of the residents can't stomach a highly seasoned diet.

"You need to eat. How else are you going to keep your strength up?"

She shrugs again, but its cut off when she begins coughing. LaTasha's immediately at her side, bringing the oxygen mask to her face. It must have been on the side of the bed. My chest hurts and expands at the sight of LaTasha, consolingly my mother and rubbing her back as she patiently holds the oxygen mask to her face. A few minutes later her cough quieted down and she lays back against her pillows, looking exhausted.

"Maybe we should let you rest," I say, standing.

"No!" she attempt to yells. "I mean…uh…*please* don't leave."

The pleading note in her tone forces me to retake my seat.

"We're not going anywhere," LaTasha announces from the other side of the room, and I'm grateful for it.

"Are you my son's *girlfriend?*" My mother suddenly asks, eyeing LaTasha.

I stiffen at that question, ready to cut this little interrogation short if I feel my mother is about to get out of control or rude. Even in her weakened state, I still remember her curtness and dismissal of those she deems less than her; even me, her own son.

"Y-yes," LaTasha answers smiling across the room at me. "Apparently, I am."

That garners a laugh from me. Truth is, she's much more than my girlfriend or my sub, but that's a different discussion.

"Good. He needs a good woman in his life. Lord knows I wasn't the mother he needed." She sighs.

That little moment of self-awareness leaves me stunned.

"Facing death has a way of making one reevaluate their life." She covers her mouth as she yawns, which turns into coughing. She quickly holds up her hand, halting LaTasha, who's reaching for the oxygen mask. "I-It's okay." She soon quiets down, as this coughing fit wasn't as bad.

"You need your rest," I say. Feeling the need to do something, I stand and pull the covers up over her. "We'll be here when you wake up." That comment seems to settle her and she finally gives up the fight against sleep and closes her eyes. I continue to watch her silently for a few minutes until the steady rise and fall of her chest tells me she's asleep.

"Do you mind?"

"Not at all," LaTasha answers.

I can't leave her yet.

"I was thinking," LaTasha's says just above a whisper as she stands by me at the bed. "You have a number of guest bedrooms in your home."

I clench my jaw and close my eyes, wondering where she's going with this.

"Maybe you should bring her home."

I inhale deeply.

"I'm sure hiring twenty-four hour care would be just as much or even less than the cost of keeping her here." She gestures around the room. "And I'll help," she commits, grabbing my hand.

"I wouldn't ask you to do that. She's *my* mother," I insist.

"I know you wouldn't ask, but as your girlfriend, I want to do this for you." She grins and bats her long lashes.

"When you put it like that," I say, running my hand through my hair. I let out a huge breath, thinking of exactly what I'm taking on by having my mother in my house, living with me, and sleeping under my roof in her last few days of life. I've hated this woman for years. I wished I could have been born to anyone but her. I told myself for years I wouldn't give her a second thought if I ever saw her again, but now here she is. Not only is she back in my life, but the woman I adore beyond measure is asking me to take her into the comfort of my home.

"It's the last thing you'd think of doing. Believe me, I know the anger one carries around at a mother who's wronged you in every way," she continues as if she's reading my thoughts. "But this isn't just about her. I saw the way you looked around this place as we entered.

You felt the coldness of it just as I did. And I don't think you'd be able to live with yourself if you let her die here *alone.*"

I sigh and look down at the frail woman in the bed, sleeping comfortably. Rubbing my hand along my chin contemplatively, I try to muster up the anger and hatred I felt for her for so many years. To my surprise, it's no longer there. Sure, the pain of being left never really goes away, but the flame of anger that used to burn deep in my gut just isn't there. Angling my head to look down at Tasha who is gripping my hand, I gaze into those light brown pools and know that it's her presence that has doused that fire. Slowly, I nod. "Okay," I say. "Okay."

CHAPTER 20

*T*asha

"Okay, Trudy. I'll remember. I promise I will be there this Thursday." My frown grows as I hear the pleading nature in her voice. "Are you sure you're okay?" I ask for the second time.

"Yeah, I'm good," she responds, but even over the phone I can sense the hesitation in her voice.

"Trudy, don't tell me what I want to hear," I insist, feeling a bit worried, but peeking over my shoulder at the woman resting in the bed. "Are you sure you're okay? Do you need me to do anything for you?" I may be watching Jeremy's mother right now, but I would call the night nurse in early if Trudy needed me.

"I'm fine, Ms. Tasha. I just, I missed you this week. That's all. The book club ain't the same without you."

There's a tug at my heartstrings as I smile. "I missed you too. I promise I'll be there this Thursday and you can call me anytime you need something okay?"

"Yeah, I remember."

"I have to go, but don't forget what I said."

"A'ight, bye."

When I hang up I place my phone on the dresser in the bedroom and step back over to the bed. I think Jeremy's mom is sleeping until she begins to talk.

"You're good for him."

My brows shoot up, wondering if what I heard was correct since it was slightly mumbled. "I'm sorry?"

"For my son... He's tough. He's had to be. Lord knows he didn't have a real mother." She snorts. "I know I wasn't the mother he deserved. And I know how that type of shit can mess up a person, especially when it comes to relationships. Hell, my own life is proof of that."

By now she's looking directly at me, her brown eyes glittering with intensity I've never seen before in the few weeks I've known her.

"Neither of my parents gave a damn. I didn't know how to be anyone's mom. Giving Jeremy up was the second best thing I ever did. Finally, telling his daddy about him was the *best* thing I ever did. He didn't give a damn about me, but the man loved that boy to death. He did right by him too," she says, her eyes darting around the room.

I remain silent, not wanting to interrupt her. Somehow, I can tell this has been weighing on her for a long time. I wonder if this is the real reason why she came back into Jeremy's life once she knew her health situation was terminal. I know she hasn't said any of this to Jeremy yet. She's been here for about two weeks now, and most days when one of the nurses isn't here, I'm here with her, making sure she has what she needs. Jeremy comes home in the evenings from work, pops in on her for a few minutes to ask how she's doing, and drags me out to spend the rest of the night with him. Don't get me wrong, I *love* every second of my time with him, but I think he may be avoiding a very necessary conversation with his mother.

"I won't burden you anymore with my random musings about my sorry state of motherhood. Tell me where you're up to in your story."

I release a breath, relieved by the change in conversation. For the past few weeks, I've been working on my writing and edits here at Jeremy's and when she found out I was an author, she asked me about my books. Since then I've been reading her excerpts from my published books and the one I'm currently working on. We spend the next thirty minutes talking about my stories until I hear the alarm go off, alerting me that Jeremy has entered the front door downstairs. I try to hide my grin as goose bumps appear on my arms.

A minute later, he knocks on the door and opens at the same time. His green eyes bounce around the room until he zeroes in on his mother first. I see sadness clearly present in his gaze. He lingers on her for a few moments and then turns his gaze onto me. Something in his eyes changes. The usual warmth spreads over me as he takes in every part of my face. Despite his welcoming gaze, the deepened lines around his eyes and the sheer intensity of his gaze tells me his need before he opens his mouth to speak.

"Good evening." He nods toward his mother. "How're you feeling today?" His tone is polite but distant, which is normal whenever he speaks directly to her.

"As well as can be expected." She nods.

"I'll let you two talk for a few," I interject, attempting to exit to give them some privacy. As usual, Jeremy grabs my wrist as I try to pass and holds me in place. He looks down at me silently, conveying I'm not to go anywhere. My protest dies on my lips as usual and I nod slowly.

"Have you eaten dinner?" he asks his mother.

"Yes. Tasha made the most delicious chicken noodle soup. I could only eat some of the vegetables and the broth, but it was delicious." She smile faintly.

Jeremy's grip tightens around my wrist. He squeezes me, but it's not uncomfortable for me. I sense it's reflexively as he too noticed again for the umpteenth time the sickly state of his mother.

"Alright, we'll be back in a little while to check on you. Get some rest," he suggests, stepping toward the door as he pulls me along him.

Once outside the room, Jeremy releases my wrist to allow me to turn and quietly shut the door. Before it's even fully shut, I feel him pressed against my back, his arms wrapped tightly around my waist. His grasp is so secure that I can't even turn around.

"I need you," he whispers in my ear.

My eyelids flutter shut only to fly open as I feel his teeth sink into my shoulder.

"Now."

My entire body trembles with the same need for him as his begins licking the spot he just bit, soothing the pain into a euphoric pleasure. I allow my body to melt into his embrace as he turns us toward the stairs. Although his bedroom is only a few doors down, out of respect for his mother we've temporarily taken over the playroom as our bedroom. Jeremy has assured me she can't hear us from down there, but I'm still not sure if I completely believe him. Thankfully, if she has heard us, she hasn't mentioned anything about it. I'm not sure I could handle that level of embarrassment.

"Are you okay?" I ask him what has obviously become a theme for the day—me worrying about the people in my life.

"Are you wearing them?" he asks, ignoring my question. His fingers are already unbuttoning my blouse.

"Wearing what?"

"The Ben Wa balls," he says as if *I'm* the crazy one for not knowing what he's talking about.

"Jeremy!" I clap back, sharply. "How do you expect me to wear them while I'm taking care of your *mother*? Are you insane?" I ask at the same time he practically rips my shirt off, leaving me in just my bra on my top half.

He frowns, unperturbed. "Probably," he has the nerve to answer. "My sub not following directions doesn't help my sanity. Are you not supposed to wear them every other day this week?" he scolds.

"Yes, but—"

"Yes, what?"

I close my eyes and inhale in a deep breath. *This crazy man...* "Yes, sir," I answer and open my eyes. "But I've been busy with your moth—"

"That's the same excuse you had two days ago." His tone is unforgiving, as he begins pushing my leggings down my hips and dragging my panties with them.

"Jer-Sir," I try to reason only to be stopped by another bite on the shoulder.

"You don't have permission to speak, love," he growls.

I close my eyes and inhale again, trying to regain control over all of the feelings coursing through my body. I could tell when he first walked in the room upstairs he was in a mood, and now, my failure to wear the Ben Wa balls has given him all the ammunition he needs to punish me. My nipples harden as the range of possible punishments flow through my mind. I open my eyes and stare at Jeremy who is now giving me a cold look. I attempt to shut them again, but I'm quickly flipped over onto all fours on the bed. A gasp escapes my throat and I have to quickly clamp down on the urge to scream. *What the hell?!* Jeremy's big body is behind me, kneeing my legs even further apart, exposing all of me to him. My insides begin to tremble with that feeling of vulnerability this man causes in me. Even in the darkest period of my life, I've never felt as vulnerable and exposed as I do with him in these moments. But unlike those times, I also feel safe, knowing somehow that he'd never go too far with me or that I couldn't handle whatever punishment he'll inflict.

Suddenly, my head is yanked back, causing my back to arch even more in this position.

"Don't move. Stay just like this," he orders and then moves from the bed.

I tighten my eyelids as I hear him rummaging through the closet that houses his many floggers. *Oh shit!* I tighten my grip on the sheets, wondering which flogger he'll choose for this occasion. I hear his footsteps returning from the closet and continue to hold my eyelids shut, but trying to listen carefully as he approaches. I anticipate his next move.

"Didn't I tell you, you're to wear the Ben Wa balls every other day this week?" A slashing sound fills the room and I instantly feel a sharp pain on my right ass.

Holy shit! My grip tightens even more on the sheets, my only course of reprieve from the intense feeling on my rear end.

"I asked you a question!"

I feel another sting, but this time it's on the left side. "Y-yes, sir." My voice is already trembling.

"Then why...." *whap!* "...when I come..." *whap!* "...in from work..." *whap!* "...I discover my sub..." *whap!* "...is not following..." *whap!* "...my directions!" *Whap! Whap!*

There's no way he expects me to answer that question, right? I can't even think at the moment as the stinging pain from the flogger invades my entire body, slowly dissolving into an ache that somehow manages to turn into a throbbing need. My pussy muscles are aching to be taken, even though up until now he has managed to avoid making contact with that area. My buttocks and the backs of my thighs are on fire from his repeated lashes.

"I'm waiting for an answer." His breathless voice reaches my ears, coldly.

"I-I didn't think it was appropriate considering..." I trail off, unable to speak anymore. My entire body is still vibrating, and he wants to have an honest-to-God conversation.

"Considering what, love?"

I squeeze my eyelids tighter in frustration. I'm frustrated that the answer should be obvious. He *knows* I'd feel uncomfortable as hell wearing those things as I care for his mother. Of course he knows, but clearly does not give a fuck.

"Considering what!?"

"I'm caring for your mother!" I yell.

Whap!

"Dammit!" I yell as my back arches even more from the sting of the flogger.

"So, your discomfort around my mother is more important than your obligation to me?"

My eyes fly open. *What?* "No!" I snap forcefully. "I just—"

"Just what!?" *Whap!*

God dammit! I'm not sure how much more of that damn flogger I can take.

Whap! "We can do this all night!" he growls before striking me yet again.

Even though I can hear the anger in his voice, I also hear his vulnerability. I know this is more about the stupid balls. He's testing me to see how committed I am to him as my Dom and my lover.

I let out a shuddering breath. "I-I'm sorry. I'll wear them," I finally declare. As soon as the words leave my lips, I hear the flogger hit the hardwood floor and feel the bed compress as Jeremy climbs on.

"Mmmm…" I moan as I feel his hard rod sink into my wetness, but I quickly cut myself off.

"Let me hear you!" he growls, granting me permission to be as loud and vocal as I choose.

I sigh in relief. The tenderness in my nether region from his whippings has incredibly sensitized me. Each of his strokes feel like he is hitting my womb. He knees my legs even further apart for better access, which I didn't even think was possible until he starts digging into me even deeper. Jesus! This man is going to kill me. I'm sure of it in this moment.

"Nooo!" I scream as he pulls out.

His only response is a deep chuckle. His hands are on me, turning me over to lie on my back. "I want your legs on my shoulders so I can see you when I finally let you cum."

Somehow his words make my pussy become even wetter than before. With him I don't even question how turned on I can get anymore. This is the man who gave me my first orgasm. My legs are perched high on his strong shoulders and I feel him lift my ass even higher. He places a pillow underneath it to angle my pussy even higher.

"Oh shit! Je-Sir!" I yell as his stroke hits my G-spot. I reach for his arms that are now anchored on each side of my waist. I need something to hold onto as I feel my body losing its touch with reality and gravity. His grip on my waist tightens to the point of bruising, but all I can feel is the incredible pleasure he is delivering.

"You're mine!" That's a declaration he's made many times before. The fact that I'm his has never been in question since the first time I laid eyes on him. But his words cause the usual coil inside my body and I can't put it off much longer.

"P-per-mission to cum, sir?!" I beg.

"No!"

Anger permeates every part of my body just as much as the pleasure, and it only serves to heighten my need to climax.

"P-please!" I ask again.

"No!" he says as he pulls back, halting his relentless strokes for a moment to adjust my legs. Placing his hands underneath my thighs, he pushes them all the way back to meet my chest. Instinctively, I reach above my head, grabbing the bars of the headboard for leverage as Jeremy starts pounding me again with my legs pressed against my chest. I didn't think it was possible to be this damn turned on. Every part of my body is sensitized, needing to release. My eyes roll to the back of my head and I try desperately to think of anything besides the way he is making my body feel.

"*Fuuck!*" I hear him growl and I know he is close to cumming having prolonged his own orgasm in order to deny me mine. Mutual sacrifice is what he calls it.

"S-sir!" I beg one last time.

"Cum!" he yells as I feel his hot seed gushing into me.

"Thank God!" I yell as shutters overtake my entire body.

My grip tightens on the headboard. Somehow Jeremy continues to stroke through our orgasms. I shake and yell until I see stars before my eyes. Then everything finally goes black. I don't know how long it takes me to come to. This isn't the first time I've passed out after one of our encounters in this room. Every single time I do, I awake to a semi-worried Jeremy stroking my side as if he is comforting me out of a deep sleep. I grin as I look up into those green eyes, darkened by concern, lust, and something else. Wordlessly, he presses his lips to my forehead and pulls me in even closer.

"How long was I out this time?"

"Not long," he simply says as he moves from the bed. I know he's just going to get a damp cloth to wipe me down but I hate the sense of loss I feel.

Seconds later, he returns and begins his usual process of inspecting my body to either ogle the marks he's caused or make sure none are too deep or painful. I can't begin to describe how comforting it is to know he takes that kind of consideration of me. Finally satisfied that I'm okay, he climbs back onto the bed, pulling me to him. Wanting to look at his handsome face, I turn so we are facing one another. I use my finger to trace his nose, lips, chin, down to his neck and the outline of the viper tattoo. I don't know which I enjoy more, the actual memorizing contours of his body with my fingers or the fact that he lets me as he patiently watches me as I commit every inch and angle of his body to memory. I use this time to garner the courage to address something that's been on my mind for two weeks.

"You need to talk to your mother," I say.

Jeremy's eyes that had been half-closed bulge in surprise and then something else. "I talk to her every day," he says, emotionless.

"No, you don't. You ask her how she's feeling and if she's eaten every day," I remind him. "That's *not* the same as talking to her."

"I don't want to talk about this. It's been a long day at work and—"

"Too bad," I insist. "She has things she wants to say to you. She makes comments to me. I think she's afraid she won't get a chance to say them to you so she talks to me, probably hoping that I'll tell you for her."

"Things like what? What does she say?"

I shake my head even before the question is fully out. "No. I won't be the middle man here. You need to talk to *her.*"

I can sense his growing frustration as his body stiffens. "Love, I said I don't want to talk about this."

"And *I* said too bad. You *need* to hear what your mother has to say and you probably have some things to say to her." I grasp his face in between my hands, waiting until his eyes lock on mine. "Say them to *her.*" I don't release his face, so he knows how serious I am about this.

His stern countenance eventually changes, his eyelids, fluttering showing his concession. With that, I release his face and reach up to place a kiss on his forehead. Unable to help myself, I leave a trail of kisses down his face until I reach his neck. Then I use my tongue to outline the end of the tattoo where it widens on his chest. Feeling his body relax, I push at his shoulder until he relaxes on his back. I sit up and allow the sheet to fall from me.

"Permission to ride you, sir." I question, my voice dropping to a seductive tone.

The left side of his mouth kicks up into lecherous grin. "Permission granted," he says as he places his hands behind his head and angles himself to watch me.

I doubt that position will last for long as I climb on top of him, hovering above his already hardened cock. I bend over, kissing and licking his tattoos before I pull back to slowly lower myself onto his hardness. Teasingly, I swivel my hips as I grind down lower and lower onto his shaft, already creating the bubbling tension in my lower abdomen. Once fully seated on him, I take a few moments to allow my body to adjust to his length and girth at this angle. Slowly, I rise again, almost to the point of completely lifting myself off of him. I pause with just the tip of him inside me. I squeeze my pelvic muscles and grin as I hear Jeremy emit something halfway between a groan and a growl. I manage to hide my smirk as I feel the growing tension in the hard body underneath me. Just as slowly, I begin lowering myself onto his cock, rocking back and forth. Without warning, Jeremy's hands shoot from underneath his head and grip my waist like a steel band, pulling me forcefully down onto him as his hips rise to meet mine.

"Ahhh!" I moan and throw my head back at the sudden onslaught of sensations. I bite my lower lip and find Jeremy's forearms with my hands to hold on as he takes over control from beneath me. Up and down, he jerks my waist, causing me to rise and fall on his shaft over and over again. My nipples begin tingling all over again, needing to be touched. He sets a rhythmic pace, as he lowers his hips at the same time, he raises mine, and then back again, causing our bodies to slam into one another repeatedly. One big hand snakes its way up my side to cup one breast and then pinch my nipple before the other hand joins in on the other nipple. Never breaking his pace at his waist, he pinches my nipples and strokes me from below and I'm left to hang on as he takes me for a ride. Minutes later, the feelings between his stroking thickness and his unrelenting fingers on my nipples causes the usual coiling sensation in my pussy.

"Perm—"

"Cum!" he demands before I fully ask. And just as if his words have a direct line to my pussy, my muscles clench tightly as my orgasm begins; starting at my core and moving its way up my spine wave after wave of ripples of pleasure wash over me. When it's finally over, I collapse onto Jeremy's sweaty chest, wrapping my arms underneath his back and around his shoulders to get as close to him as possible. I always need the comfort of his embrace after I cum to slowly bring me back down to reality; to ground me.

He angles his head to kiss my forehead and rolls over until I am on my back and he is hovering above me. We're still connected below the waist as we struggle to catch our breaths. Once we do, Jeremy finally pulls back and out of me. I groan at his sudden absence only to be met by his deep chuckle. The last thing I remember is the feel of a warm, wet cloth swiping against my lower half as I drift off into a deep sleep.

* * *

Jeremy

I CLOSE my eyes and pull in a big breath before perching the tray against my hip with one hand and lightly knocking on the door with the other. After LaTasha fell asleep, I got up and showered, wanting to wash the scent of sex off me before I went into have a long overdue talk with my mother. It's only about eight-thirty and the night nurse doesn't come in until ten. So, I figured now would be as good a time as any to have this conversation I'd wordlessly promised LaTasha I would.

"I'm awake," a weak voice sounds off on the other end of the door.

After turning the knob and pushing the door open, I step inside. Just before I turn to close it, I see her eyes open in apparent surprise. Normally, it's LaTasha who checks in on her at the end of the night, bringing her nightly medications. A wave of guilt moves through my belly at that reminder. LaTasha's been here for two weeks, helping to take care of *my* mother between nurses and still working on her writing. I should be doing this shit. I shake my head, disappointed in myself.

"LaTasha's resting, so I brought your medication and some water and juice. Is cranapple still your favorite?" My voice is even and calm despite my underlying tension. It doesn't surprise me. I've spent many of my formative years in foster homes where showing any emotion besides gratitude garnered you a beating. The act of hiding my emotions worked in my favor in the military, in business, and even as a Dom.

"Yes, thank you." She looks as if she wants to say more, but only opens and closes her mouth a few times before finally opting to remain silent as if more words from her will cause me to disappear or something.

I place the tray on the hospital table and push it directly in front of her. Unscrewing the water bottle, I hold it up to her lips, so she can take her two pain pills. She eagerly sips the juice, and for a moment, a memory resurfaces. I must have been about six years old and had to be brought home from school by a classmate's parents as my mother had forgotten about me again. Having my own key, I let myself inside the two-bedroom house we were living in at the time. I made my way to her bedroom, finding my mother dressed in a pair of jeans and button up shirt, looking as if she'd slept in those clothes. I briefly remembered her wearing the same clothes the day before. The dazed look on her face told me she'd just awaken.

"Jer-Jer," she smiled and slurred. "Good, you're home. Here," she thrust a hand with waded up cash in it. "Go to the store and get me a bottle of cranapple juice."

The store was a few blocks away. At the time it felt normal, but now, as an adult, I realize it was much too far to send a six-year-old boy by himself.

"I wasn't a very good mother to you." Her words penetrate my memory.

"No. You weren't." I don't see a need to lie to make her feel better.

215

"I could make a thousand excuses. My daddy was terrible. I never had real parents myself. I was young when I had you." She waves her hand in the air. "All true, but the real deal is I had no business being anyone's mama."

Some honesty. I can respect that. I know it to be true and I'd come to that conclusion long ago. When I finally went to a Ms. Janice's foster home, I learned what a real mother was supposed to be like. No, my biological mother wasn't it. Ms. Janice and my father were the two best people in my young life. I finally sit in the chair next to bed and pull it closer.

"Not everyone's meant to be a parent." That was said without any malice.

She nods. "Your father, though…" She trailed off.

I crinkle my brows, confused at the lightness I heard in her voice as she mentioned my father. Was that admiration?

"What about him?"

"He loved you from the moment he found out about you." She lowers her head and looks down at her hands in her lap and bites her lip.

Her words punch me in the gut. It isn't anything he hadn't told me himself when I first went to live with him up until the day he died twelve years later. But hearing her say it still affects me although I don't react outwardly.

"How did he find out about me?" I ask, wanting to hear her version of how it went down. I already knew my father's side of the story.

"I saw him again at a party or some type of banquet about four years after—"

"You dumped me in foster care." The accusation in my voice causes my mother to flinch. Shamefully, seeing that reaction causes a feeling of satisfaction in my gut.

"Yes." She nods. "I was there with someone else," she continues.

Her first husband, as my father had told me this story already.

"I saw your father there with another woman and well, I was jealous." She shrugs. "I started drinking and when I saw him go into the bathroom, I cornered him when he came out. He tried to act like I was nothing; telling me what we had was over and I needed to get over it. He was right, of course, but that only angered me. So, I spat out that his son said hello." Continuing to look down at her hands, she shakes her head.

Sitting back in my chair, I simply observe her, beginning to feel sorry for her. Once I move past my own anger, I begin to see this woman for who she is.

"He was completely thrown off, but I just laughed and told him everything. I was pregnant when he broke things off with me. I raised his bastard son until he was ten and then dumped him in foster care so I could live my life. He was livid. He told me I was lying, but that just made me laugh louder. I told him the children's home I'd taken you to four and a half years earlier. And..." She shrugs.

"And a few months later he found me and brought me home," I finish her story.

"After he found you, he came and found me again, forcing me to sign my parental rights over. He told me to never contact you again and if I did he'd make me pay."

I didn't know about that part, but I couldn't blame my father for that. Since the day I met him, he'd done everything in his power to protect me. Even if that meant keeping the woman who'd given me life away.

"He did send me pictures of you," she says, turning toward the drawer next to her, but she begins coughing at the exertion.

I hand her the oxygen mask, but she insists on me getting what's in the top dresser drawer. Opening it, I pull out her wallet. Once she settles down from coughing, she opens the wallet with shaky fingers and pulls out a small stack of photos and hands them to me. The top photo is of me when I was about fifteen on my first hunting trip with my father. The next is my high school graduation. I'm holding up my acceptance letter to Columbia. I snort at that photo. My father had insisted I take that damn picture. He was so pissed when I opted to skip college and join the marines. That's the next photo. It's my swearing-in ceremony. Next, there's a bunch of photos I'd sent my father when I was stationed in Iraq and other locations abroad.

"He was so proud of you. He didn't want me anywhere around you for good reasons." She snorted. "But he couldn't help showing you off."

The slight smile on her face and reverence in her voice are clear. They're not for me. It's all for *him*.

"You loved him." A revelation. I'd always assumed she was too selfish to love anyone; not even the son she'd birthed.

"Donald Bennett was a good man, but he was a complicated man. He was hard when he needed to be and pliant when he wanted to be. Yes, I loved him. But he loved his wife." Still twining her fingers, she lifts her head to stare out the darkened window. It's then I see the sheen of tears in her eyes. The ones she's refusing to let fall. My stomach churns in knots. It's taken thirty-five years to see my mother this vulnerable. To acknowledge her as more than the woman who birthed me, barely raised me, and then abandoned me. But as a woman who didn't know how to love or admit that she didn't know. "So, I did the only thing I knew how to do when he left me."

"Hurt him by keeping his son from him," I clarify.

She nods slightly. "His wife couldn't get pregnant, which was her only downfall in his eyes," she admits, mournfully.

My father's wife had died the year before he found out about me. He'd told me once he wished she could have been my mother.

"And you kept me to hurt him, using me to throw up in his face once you finally saw him again." My voice remained calm, steady, and detached.

She lets out a big sigh. "If I had it to do over..." She trails off, but I don't need to hear the rest. What's in the past is in the past. Truthfully, I know if she had it to do over again, she'd do the exact same thing. It wasn't in her to think of anyone else besides herself. Her wants. Her needs. She kept me not out of love but to hold on to my father.

"Yes," she says just above a whisper, making me realize I'd said that last realization out loud.

I close my eyes, replaying what's just been said over again in my mind. I inhale and exhale, scanning my body for areas of tension where uncomfortable feelings reside. A few seconds later, I realize the burning anger in my belly that usually happens whenever I think of my mother isn't there. The hot coals of regret, pain, and sorrow that usually spur my anger just aren't there. What is there is *acceptance*. I slowly open my eyes, angling my head to look out the window first and then back to her. Her pale skin and sunken cheeks, small frame done in by the ravages of cancer are all I see. Not the woman who forgot to pick me up from school or left me at a children's home without a backwards glance. The anger and hurt have dissipated into acceptance and gratitude. Grateful for my life, no matter the circumstances that made it possible. I'm glad to be alive and to have what little family I do, my business, and most importantly, the woman sleeping downstairs.

A long silence stretches out between us. Finally, I speak, "It's okay." That's all I can summon as I pat her leg lightly. "It's okay," I tell her without telling her I forgive her. Even if she doesn't want my forgiveness, she has it. I refuse to carry anymore of her burden into the next phase of my life. A lightness I'd never felt settles over me. A world has been lifted off my shoulders—a world I hadn't known was sitting on them.

And that new lightness and acceptance has allowed me to cater to my mother unlike before. Every evening after work, I would check on her, relieving LaTasha or whatever nurse was present, spending around thirty minutes feeding her or talking with her about the latest project I was working on. I kept it up for the next three weeks. Up until the time she took her final breath as I sat by her bedside. And with that breath any hold she or my past had over me was released.

CHAPTER 21

Tasha
"Fancy meeting you here. To what do we owe the pleasure?"

I giggle, shaking my head and turn from the stove to face my sister. She grins and looks damn near angelic, holding LJ. She's dressed in a simple black T-shirt and skinny jeans.

"Whatever, smartass."

"Watch your mouth in front of the baby," Liam interjects, coming into the kitchen.

I frown at Coral. "He does know he's barely four months, right?"

She shrugs and laughs, rolling her eyes. "What are you making?"

I turn back to the stove, lifting a few lids and opening the oven to pull out the pancakes I'd placed in there to keep warm. "Pancakes, eggs, bacon and there's sliced fruit over there." I incline my head towards the counter.

"I've missed you in the mornings." My sister sighs and hums, reaching for a piece of cantaloupe.

"Me too. It's not like this one cooks and Ms. Mary's had off the last two weeks." Liam frowns.

Coral turns and eyes at her husband. "The only things I'm serving these days are breast milk and takeout."

"How's Jeremy doing?" Liam asks, chewing on a piece of bacon.

I chew my bottom lip, contemplating that question. Jeremy's away on a business trip and he's supposed to return early this afternoon. That's the main reason I'm here this morning. It's been about three weeks since his mother passed. He held a small ceremony for her. Liam and Coral were the only ones who attended besides Jeremy and me. He'd had her cremated and her ashes scattered in the Gulf per her request. He took a few days off after that and we'd gone back to Tucson for the grand opening of the resort. When he came back he'd had the room his mother was sleeping in cleaned out and restored to its usual guestroom appearance. Overall, he was the same. At times, I've noticed a faraway look of sadness in his eyes, and he's definitely been more hands-on with me lately. I bow my head, smiling to myself just thinking of exactly how hands-on he's been the last few weeks.

"*Daaamn!*" Coral whistles under her breath. "I know that look," she says out loud, giving Liam a smirk. He gives her a knowing wink and presses a kiss to her lips. Then he kisses the squirming baby in her arms.

"Whatever." I wave her off. "He's okay. I think he's made peace with it." I shrug.

Liam gives me a satisfied look before taking LJ in his arms and leaving the kitchen, but not before he gives Coral one last kiss.

"And how are *you?*"

I look at my sister and shrug. I pull out two plates from the cabinet and fill them with breakfast. "I know you don't typically eat much in the mornings, but you're breastfeeding now so you've gotta eat to keep up your supply." I nudge a full plate toward her.

"I asked you a question."

I sigh, sitting across from her at the counter. "I'm-I don't know. I was worried about Jeremy after his mom died not knowing how he'd take it. But he's been okay throughout and he hasn't pulled back or shut down on me as I'd expected. And although he's been gone less than forty-eight hours, I know it's exactly four hours and thirty-eight minutes until his plane lands back in Dallas. And I've already got out the nipple clamps I want him to use on me—"

"Whoa! Whoa! Time the fuck out! I do *not* need to know all that," Coral protests, holding her hands over her ears.

A giggle rises up through my throat, turning into a full-on belly laugh. I bend over, holding my stomach at the disgusted look on my sister's face.

"That shit's not funny, Tash. You're gonna have me kick his ass just thinking about it." She shakes her head sternly trying to rid herself of the vision of what I'd just revealed.

"Okay, okay," I manage to get out between laughs. Sobering up, I take a sip of my orange juice. "I'll spare you the details of what I plan on doing to him or rather letting him do to me once he gets back." I sigh dreamily just thinking about it.

"Tash." The warning in Coral's voice evident.

I hold my hand up in surrender. "But really, it's good." I shrug. "Great actually. And not just the physical. I felt safe enough to open up with him in ways I'd never imagined." I pause, looking my sister in her eye, allowing my revelation to sink in. When her eyebrows arch high, I know she's picked up on my meaning.

"You told him *everything?*"

I nod, biting my lower lip. "Everything," I repeat. "And he didn't run screaming. Not that a man of Jeremy's caliber would, but I mean, he didn't pull back or dump me to go find someone with a less seedy past."

Coral snorts at that. "I'm sure you know by now his past wasn't all smiles and roses."

"I know. It's kinda what makes our connection deeper." I leave it at that, not wanting to share more. I opt to keep the deeper, emotional details of my relationship with Jeremy to myself. Coral seemed to understand because after staring at me, trying to read my face for evidence of lies or lack of confidence in my own words, she bows her head, and drops any further inquiry.

"Stacey's coming out this weekend."

I smile. "I know. She told me." Stacey and I talk at least three times a week. Getting to know her from her own mouth instead of through Coral has been great. She still didn't know everything about me or my past but the shame I'd felt about it for so long even after years of therapy has begun to fade. I know that has to do with Jeremy.

"She'll be happy to see you in person again. She's already trying to arrange a trip to the ballet out here," Coral added, bringing me back to the discussion. Stacey is a former ballet dancer who'd suffered a career-ending injury. Things got kinda bad for her after that, but eventually she managed to get back on track, go to school, and became a social worker. Not to mention she married a very handsome and successful business mogul in Atlanta.

"I'm looking forward to it."

* * *

CORAL and I spend the next hour eating breakfast and talking before I headed back to the guesthouse. Coral revealed to me that she wasn't going back to work for at least another three months, wanting to spend as much quality time with both kids.

"They're just so young and I've spent so much time moving from one place to another; not really being settled anywhere for long. I want to give them the stability we never had as kids. Plus Li finally convinced me to sign the adoption papers for Princess." She shrugs in an uncommonly bashful moment. "After having LJ, I couldn't imagine not knowing what or who would be there to take care of him if something happened to Li and me. I felt the exact same way about Princess. If something were to happen to Li, I'd have no legal rights to her. So after discussing it with her maternal grandparents, we all agreed that me adopting her was the best thing," she told me after I'd asked what made her finally make a decision.

I smiled, remembering that earlier conversation, as I sat down at the desk in my bedroom, preparing to go another round with these edits. Looking at the clock, I see it's only a little after noon. I'd spent the last hour or so cleaning up as the place had gotten a little sloppy since the only time I'd come here was to drop off old clothes and pick up new clothing over the last few weeks. But even that became few and far in between as I'd wake up some days and Jeremy would have bags and boxes of clothes delivered to me so I wouldn't have to drive across town to get more stuff. It was almost as if he didn't want me to leave. I'd just received a text from him not too long ago reminding me his flight lands in less than an hour. He'd moved up his flight time, he said to be back and well rested for a meeting he had Monday morning. Deep down, I knew it was because it was as difficult for him to be away as it was for me to have him away.

Smiling at that, I sit to read over the edits and changes my editor has suggested, making adjustments here and there when necessary in my manuscript. I'd gotten so into it, hoping I could finish these edits this weekend, I didn't hear my phone vibrating across the room until the call finally ended. Figuring it was my agent who'd called earlier in the day, wanting an update on the edits, I decided I'd give her a call when I finished. However, only a few minutes later I hear my phone vibrating again. My agent can be an impatient ass, but she rarely calls back to back on weekends. Feeling curious, I venture over to my bed and pick up the phone to see a number I don't recognize. Figuring it's either the wrong number or some type of promotional call, I nearly decide to not answer. But something tells me to pick it up. When I do, I hear heavy breathing on the other end.

"Hello?" I answer, my voice mixed with curiosity and a tinge of impatience.

"M-Ms. Tasha," a weak voice, just above a whisper comes through the line.

I barely recognize it. But something tells me...

"Ms. Tasha, it's Trudy," she whispers.

My stomach drops and my entire body stiffens as I brace myself. I can hear fear in her voice and I picture her lips shivering as she tries to push the words out her mouth.

"Trudy what's wrong?" Because I know something's wrong. I can feel it.

"H-he brought...I'm scared."

Those words finally kick me into gear, as I start looking for my discarded tennis shoes around my bed. Finding them, I push my feet inside them, throw on a long sleeve T-shirt over the camisole I had on and head to the kitchen for my car keys.

"Where are you?" I do my best to remain calm, not wanting to frighten her anymore than she already is.

"Home."

"Can you tell me what's happened?" I ask, shutting the door behind me and making my way to my car parked in the driveway. It's just me here as Liam and Coral have taken the kids to a local museum and then out to eat. I pause, wondering if I should leave a note, but I don't want to stop. Right now my sole objective is to make sure Trudy is okay.

"Th-they tried to touch me."

My stomach plummets as I hear Trudy try desperately to hold onto the sob that wants to burst from her lips. Now, I know there's no time for me to stop and write a note. I decide to text Coral to let her know what's happening once I'm in the car. I wonder if I should call the police, but I remember Trudy's neighborhood isn't too fond of police intervention. Hell, I grew up in a similar neighborhood. And truth be told, I still have a distrust of cops after seeing more than a few involved in the shady sex trafficking ring I was a victim of as an adolescent.

"Trudy, where are you in the house?" Finally in the car I have to move my phone from my ear and hear her low voice come through the speakers.

"The closet in the back bedroom."

"Okay. Listen to me very carefully. Do not come out of that closet for anyone besides me. I'm on my way over there. I'll find you. Do not open the door, do not make any noise. I want you to keep the phone close to you. I'm not going to hang up so you can hear me the whole time. Okay?"

"Okay, Ms. Tash—"

And just like that, the line goes dead. *Oh God!* I do my absolute best not to panic and give into the worst fears running through my head. I hope the phone Trudy was calling from just went dead instead of

whoever she was afraid of finding her. I have a feeling this has something to do with her mother's boyfriend. Looking down at the GPS on
my phone, I see I'm only about ten minutes away from Trudy's house.
I pray that she's okay when I get there. I try to push the sick feeling
that threatens to cripple me by just imagining all the sick things that
bastard could be doing to Trudy. Truth is, I didn't have to imagine. I
knew first hand just what sick pedophiles like him do to girls who
barely look old enough to wear a training bra. My fists tighten around
the steering wheel to the point of pain. An anger I'd never felt before
bubbles up in my core just as I pulled up in front of Trudy's home. I
don't see any cars out front, making the place look empty. At the last
second, before getting out of my car, I decide to send a quick text to
Jeremy instead of Coral.

I cut my car off, climb out, and carefully looking for signs of life
inside the house. Curtains cover most of the windows, making
viewing inside the house difficult. But I do spot a shadow behind the
curtain. Looking from one side of the house to the other, I look over
toward the house on the right and notice it's abandoned. On the left,
the house looks as if someone lives there, but it's unoccupied at the
moment. Finally, I reach the top of the rickety steps and then knock
loudly on the door. A few seconds later, I hear someone shuffling
toward the front door.

"Aye, Brandon, man I told..." He pauses when sees me standing at
the opened door. He's dressed in what I've come to think is his usual
white T-shirt, sagging, faded jeans, and a pair of old Jordans. The
scowl on his face is aimed directly at me. His present frown deepens,
surely not expecting to see me.

Despite my actual feelings, I manage to plaster a smile on my face
while tightening my grip on my keys in my hand. "Hi! Remember me?
I work at the community center that Trudy attends. There was an
assignment one of her instructors there wanted to give her, so I
decided to bring it over today. Can I see her?"

"Nah, she ain't here." He snorts, moving to shut the door in my
face. His face tightens when his movement is halted by my foot in the
door frame.

"Are you sure? I spoke with her earlier and told her I was coming over." My voice is dripping with fake niceness.

His eyes slant, assessing the truth of my words. He scans me from head to toe. I see his eyes shift the moment he makes some decision. Without rhyme or reason, he steps back, widening the door a bit. "A'ight." He nods.

I step just inside the door, but instead of moving further inside, I take a step to the right, moving further away from him, but keeping him in my peripheral. I look around the living room to see it's empty save for an old couch, loveseat, small wooden table, and a chair off to the side. I can also see it's a mess. There are old newspapers and clothing strewn about and a lamp on the side table has been knocked over. All signs of some type of struggle. My heartbeat quickens as worry seeps through me for Trudy.

"Where's Trudy?" I turn to look directly at him.

"I'on't know." He shrugs. "Maybe you can tell me." Something in his tone causes goose bumps to rise on my skin. "How about you sit and wait for her for a minute?" The eeriness of his invite makes me want to head straight for the door and never look back. But I won't leave here without Trudy. I don't know all the details yet, but I know something bad is happening here.

"Sure, can-uh, can you direct me to the bathroom first? I forgot to go before I left the community center." I smile, playing innocent.

"Y-yeah. It's down the hall to the left." He points and I hear the click of the lock of the front door. My stomach jumps. Everything in my body tells me it's well past time to go. But Trudy... I take a tentative step in the direction he pointed and then another until I make it to the hallway. I turn left to walk down. I don't hear footsteps behind me so I know he isn't following me *for now*. I turn and peer over my shoulder just to be sure and see him making his way to the couch in the living room. I relax slightly, as I look to each side of me. I spot the bathroom on the left as he said and see another door across the hall. Thinking that must be the bedroom Trudy was referring, to my fingers itch to try the knob when I hear a creak behind me. Turning I see he's standing at the other end of the hallway now watching me.

"You find it?"

"Y-yup. To the left at the end of the hallway just as you said." I try to give a half-smile but sure it comes out as a grimace. I enter the bathroom and shut the door behind me. Leaning over the rusty sink, I try to control my breathing and pulse. I remove my phone from my bag to see a text from Jeremy.

WHERE THE HELL ARE YOU???

I can feel his anxiousness through the phone.

Trudy's house.

That's all I type before I put the phone back in my bag. I look around the bathroom for any signs of a struggle even though Trudy said she was in a bedroom. I make sure to pull back the shower curtain, checking the bathtub and then the closet to make sure she isn't hiding in here. Flushing the toilet and then turning on the sink to try and throw off any suspicion, I close my eyes and gather my courage for what I'm going to have to do. This house is too tiny to go looking around without arousing suspicion. Gripping my keys tightly in my left hand, I turn the nozzle on the head of my small bottle of mace that's attached to the keychain, unlocking it. I shut the water off and turn to the doorknob. I take in another deep breath of resolve. Opening the door, I almost jump out of my skin as he's standing right there, a lecherous look in his eye. Without hesitation I lift my left hand up, pressing the button to release a stream of mace directly in his face.

"Aggghhh shit!" he yells, covering his face with both hands. He stumbles and falls into the hallway, making room for me to run out. I don't attempt to spray him again. My sole focus in this moment is to get to the door across the hall. I leap out the bathroom door, landing right in front of the other door, twisting the knob and sighing in relief when it immediately opens. Shutting the door behind me, I look erratically around me, hoping to find a closet somewhere in here. I spot the closet door just inches from the bedroom door along the same wall.

"Trudy!" I yell. "Trudy! It's Ms. Tasha. Are you in here?" I yell, knocking on the door. I jump back when the opposite door slides mere inches from my fingers, almost pinching them.

"I'm here," she whispers, eyes wide with relief and fear.

"Sweetie," I go to her, kneeling in front of her, cupping her cheeks in my hands. "What happened? Did he hurt you?"

By the way Trudy's eyes begin to water, I already know the answer to that question. I swallow back my own tears, needing to remain composed for the both of us.

"Where's your mother?"

Trudy shrugs. "I don't know. She ain't been home in a few days."

Déjà vu, I think, remembering how my own mother had abandoned me, leaving me with a sick fuck like Trudy's mother. "What happened today?" I ask, turning toward the door to see if I hear anyone coming. I can faintly make out grunts and stumbling around in the hallway.

"Gary's friend came over and he s-said I had t-to be good to h-him," she stutters. "He took me upstairs and started touching me, but I ain't want to be touched like that by him too. So I bit his hand and ran downstairs and out the front door, hiding in the abandoned house next door. I could see out the side window, they both ran out calling my name. When I saw them get in his friend's car, I came back to the house, grabbed my mom's cell phone she left behind and hid in the closet and called you. The phone died, but I stayed hidden like you said. I heard the front door open just a few minutes before you came." She was panting by the end of her story. I pulled her to me to calm her down. Her little body was shaking with fear and the memory of what these bastards had tried to do to her.

"You're so brave. You know that? You did the right thing." I try to comfort her, looking around the room for a window to try and climb out of. I curse in my head when I see there aren't any. We're going to have to go out the door I came through. I'm sure that mace is still working on Gary, but just in case, I grip the handle in my hand tighter and push Trudy behind me.

"Stay behind me. If I tell you to run, then you run no matter what.

Understand?" I say as sternly as possible, wanting Trudy to know under no uncertain terms is she to remain with me if I tell her to run.

She nods, but her facial expression remains unsure, her big brown eyes imploring me to help her out of this situation.

"Come on," I urge, inching toward the door. Before opening it, I lean the side of my head on the door to see if I can hear any movement outside. When I don't, I say a quick prayer and slowly pull the door open. When I look down the hallway I see it's empty. I grip Trudy to me with so much force I fear I may leave scratches, but making sure she gets out of this alive is more important at the moment. I turn and motion with my hand in front of my lips for her to be as quiet as possible. She clings closer to me and we make our way into the hallway. Halfway down, I hear pounding on the door and pause. A set of footsteps comes down the steps and seconds later I hear the door creak open. I'm surprised I can hear anything over my erratic heartbeat.

"You find that lil' bitch yet?" an unfamiliar, gritty male voice sounds off.

Though I don't recognize it, Trudy clearly does the way her fingers dig into the skin on my arm. Her body begins to shake even harder.

"That's him," she whispers when I look down at her.

I gasp in alarm and I gesture again for her to remain quiet.

"What the fuck happened to you?" a second man snarls.

"That bitch sprayed me with mace!" Gary yells.

"The lil' bitch? She's here?"

"No, her fucking teacher or some shit. But Trudy's here. I know her little ass is. I'ma light that other bitch up on sight too!"

I hear the unmistakable click-clack of a gun being cocked. My knees wobble, but I remain erect, needing to be strong for Trudy. Quickly, I say another prayer and slowly retreat backwards at the same time the door slams shut. Moving quickly, I turn and push Trudy toward the bathroom. There was a little window I saw when I was in there. I probably won't be able to fit through it, but Trudy should be able to.

"Aye! There them bitches is!" Gary yells.

"Shit!" I yell at the same time we make it to the bathroom. I slam the door shut, locking it. I know my mace is no match from the nine millimeter in his hand. I see an old wooden dresser next to the sink and move to slide it in front of the door.

"Trudy, I'm going to help lift you and push you out the window, okay?"

The pounding on the door startles both of us. I turn my back to the door to open the window, but it's stuck. "Dammit!"

"We can't fit Ms. Tasha!" she yells, her eyes shifting between me, the door, and the window.

"Trudy! Oh God!" I yell when I hear the first shot at the door. He's trying to shoot the knob off. That door and dresser are not going to hold against the powerful weapon. Sure enough, within seconds, the knob is dangling off the door and they are pushing their way through. The dresser can only hold them off so much longer.

"Trudy, you have to move now!" I shriek, struggling with the window, but it's too late. Not even a full three minutes, Gary and his accomplice are able to push the door open, causing the dresser to tip over. I turn, pushing Trudy behind me to stare into the face of two very angry men.

"G-Gary, listen. Just let me take Trudy out of here. I won't call the police or tell anyone," I try to reason. Our situation is looking bleak and I doubt either one of us are going to make it out of this house or even this room alive. The looks in these men's eyes tell me they don't give one iota of a fuck about Trudy's safety or mine.

"Bitch, you ain't gonna have the chance to call no fucking police!" he snarls, spittle flying from his mouth. His eyes are still noticeably swollen and red from the mace.

Boom!

The loud noise causes all four of us to jump. I pull Trudy closer to me and Gary and his friend shift toward the hallway.

"Who the fuck—"the friend starts to yell, but he's cut off when a bullet pierces his skull, immediately and thoroughly ending his life.

"Aaahhh!" Trudy screams upon witnessing the blood that spurts from his wound.

"Aww shit!" Gary yells, holding up his gun, preparing to fire. He doesn't even to get it halfway to his chest because a bullet splatters his hand. "Fuck!" he yells, dropping his gun.

All I see after that is a pair of strong hands reaching for Gary, pulling him out of the bathroom and into the hallway. I can't even get a full grasp of what is happening before I see blow after blow raining down on Gary. His screams are full of agony as he realizes fighting back is useless. I will my feet to move, bringing Jeremy's full body into my view. He's perched over Gary beating him savagely. I only catch a glimpse of his eyes, but there's a look I've never seen before and I damn sure never want to see again. Just as that thought passes through my mind, Trudy's shrill screams bring me back to what is happening in front of us.

"Jeremy! Stop!" I call out. Truth is, I don't want him to stop. I'd rather Gary have his life ended right here, but there is a twelve-year-old girl who's already been traumatized enough witnessing this.

"JEREMY!!" I scream to no avail.

I even notice Liam behind Jeremy trying to pull him off Gary, but he's having little effect as well. On instinct, I yell, *"WOLVERINE!!!"* I belt the one word at the top of my lungs.

Our safe word.

And just like that, fist in mid-air, Jeremy halts, breathing heavily. His eyes finally move upward to meet mine. The look in those sea green orbs sends a cold shiver down my spine. He stares at me and then glances behind me, finally noticing Trudy. Then he looks back at me.

"Take them outside," he says never, removing his gaze from me, but he's obviously speaking to Liam.

A heartbeat later, I feel Liam's hands pulling me and Trudy down the hallway toward the door. "Let's go," he urges, his voice as stern as Jeremy's glare.

Wrapping my arms around Trudy's shoulders, I shift her body so mine is between her and Jeremy, Gary, and the dead body. Once outside, I feel like I can breathe again. I close my eyes and inhale deeply. It's not until I open my eyes again that I realize Trudy's arms are tightly wrapped around my waist. She's shaking as she cries against my stomach. Wrapping her up in my arms, I hold her tightly, whispering soft words in her ear. I look up and finally notice that they aren't alone and it wasn't just Liam. His whole team of security is out front, running in and out of the house. Another one reaches for Trudy and me, ushering us to a black SUV with tinted windows. I go willingly, feeling safe.

"We're going to take you to the hospital to have you checked out," Liam informs me.

I stop at the opened door of the SUV. "Wait. Jer—"

"He's going to follow us."

I hesitate, looking toward the house to see if he's emerged yet.

"Trust me. He's not letting you out of his sight anytime soon," Liam reassures.

"Alright." I nod, knowing that Trudy needs to be checked out. I hope to God she hasn't experienced the worse of what my imagination thinks she has.

CHAPTER 22

*J*eremy
    The anger flows through my veins just as assuredly as my blood does. My grip is so tight on the steering wheel my already sore knuckles, beg for relief.

"You can't tell Coral."

That makes my eyes squint even tighter. "What?"

"You can't tell Coral that I turned my back to Gary. She taught me better and she'll be pissed to find out I did," she explains.

I cut my eyes at her, fighting the instinct to pull the car over and show her exactly who she needs to be afraid of in this moment. "You think *Coral* is who you need to be afraid of right now?" I see her visibly swallow and then bite her lower lip at that. *Yeah, you should be nervous.*

It was now well after nine o'clock. We'd been at the hospital for hours. Our security team at the house had disposed of the two bodies before we got to the hospital. As soon as Tasha left out the house with Trudy in tow, I commenced to beating that fucker's ass until he took his last breath. My knuckles bared the evidence of that. And even with the pain shooting through my hands, my anger overrode it. A doctor that I paid to keep our visit off the books gave Tasha and me clearance. I had no fingers or knuckles broken. They were just bruised to hell. Tasha had a few scratches mainly from Trudy clutching at her arms. Trudy didn't have any scratches or bruising, but she'd had to have a gynecological exam. Just thinking about that makes me sick to my stomach and stirs my anger again. Too bad you can't kill someone twice. We still couldn't find Trudy's mother and after all the hoopla, Liam had agreed to take the girl to his place for the night and figure out how to handle the situation in the morning. Right now, I had to tend to the woman next to me.

* * *

Tasha

"ARGH," I groan as I roll over to my side from my ass. I reach beneath the cool sheets, rubbing my butt. I close my eyes, sighing just thinking of the punishing my body took last night from Jeremy. The worst part, though, is rolling over to the empty side of the bed. After an ass paddling, intensified by nipple clamps and then Jeremy's refusal to let me cum as he took me from behind, he'd sent me upstairs to sleep in his bedroom while he remained downstairs in a guest bedroom. I frown more from missing him than from the soreness of my body. I squeeze my eyes shut as I sit up and think back to the night before. Jeremy's anger in the car had been palpable. I knew he would be angry, but not nearly as much as he was. But there was no way I couldn't answer to Trudy when she called. Still the worry that was so clearly etched on Jeremy's face the previous night made me feel guilty. Thinking about it, I could have gone about helping Trudy differently. I had ended the night, screaming my apologies to Jeremy as he took me over and over. I really meant it. I promised to call him here on out if anything like that arises again.

Standing, I recall the bruises on Jeremy's hand. I throw on a pair of shorts and T-shirt and make my way to the kitchen first, grabbing an ice pack and a dish towel before heading to the guest bedroom where Jeremy slept. I listen to the door for any noises or stirring on the other side. When I don't hear anything, I knock lightly and open the door. Those eyes are the first things I see, wide, alert and a hint of the anger they were filled with the previous night.

Is he still mad? I hesitate for a second. I wonder if it was a good idea to come down here, but I push forward anyway. Stepping inside, I push the door closed behind me and make my way to the opposite side of the bed. I climb under the warm blanket that now is filled with the scent of him. Without looking at him, I pull his hands over to me, lightly placing the ice pack across his knuckles that are now swollen and marred in purple and blue.

"I thought you could use this." I finally take the opportunity to peek up at him to find his half smirk on me.

"My knuckles are fine," he insists, trying to pull away only to be trapped by my hands on his wrist.

"Just sit with the ice pack for a few minutes." Something in his eyes changes and his body relaxes as he realizes this is my way of continuing to apologize.

"I don't need the ice pack. Come here." His arms move quickly, pulling me to his side and moving the ice pack to the dresser.

"I missed you last night," I confess, laying my cheek to rest against his chest.

"Good. You deserved to."

I frown. "I apologized."

"You're gonna be apologizing all day, doll." He grins, his hand grabbing one of my ass cheeks and squeezing.

My whole body tenses as I hiss from the pain.

"Still sore?" he asks as if he doesn't already know the answer to that damn question.

I frown at him. "What do you think?"

"I think your ass can take it." He pushes me back onto the mattress and rests over me. He grins, squeezing my butt again and lowering his lips to meet mine. "You know what I couldn't take?"

I look up at him, questioningly. "What?"

"Losing you."

My heart flutters.

"That's why I can't have you running into dangerous situations like you did yesterday. You're mine, doll. And I protect mine. I told you when we started this I wasn't a soft, romantic type. I'm still not so much, but I do love the hell out of you and if feeling my paddle is what's going to keep your ass out of trouble then so be it." His voice is hard, stern and uncompromising.

I should feel fearful, but all I feel is safe, cared for and loved. I shift, raising my head to meet his lips because I'm at a loss for words. When I lower my head I feel an uncomfortable lump underneath the pillow. I frown. "What's that?"

"Take a look."

I stare, noticing the hard expression he wore just a few moments ago has changed to one of anticipation. I allow my gaze to linger on his as I reach back behind me with one arm feeling around under the pillow until I feel a hard box. I bring it to my face and I see it's a ring box. My eyes fly back to Jeremy's whose gaze is now completely serious.

"I hated sleeping without you last night too," he says as if that answers the question my shocked face is asking. "And every other night of my life before I met you."

"I-is this…" I can't even finish my question.

"Open the box."

With shaky fingers, I open the ring box and gasp. Inside is what looks like at least fourteen karat diamond sitting atop a white gold infinity band also adorned with diamonds.

"*Jeremy…*"

"Read the inscription."

Looking from the ring to him and back to the ring, I pull it out to read inside the band. *My Storm…*

"I made a stop in New York on my last business trip." He plucks the ring from my hand, examining it and then reading the inscription. Nodding his head in approval, he grabs my left hand and slides it on my ring finger. "Perfect."

I pause, waiting for words that never come. "Um, don't you have a question to ask me?"

"No." He shakes his head. "What is there to ask?" He looks genuinely confused, as he rolls us both over so now I am on top of him.

My mouth hangs open. "Are you serious?!" I screech.

The rumble from his laughter starts in his chest, moving up his throat and finally spills out of his mouth.

"What's so damn funny?" I pout.

"You," he quickly answers. "You think I'm going to *ask* you to marry me and give you even the *slightest* chance to say no?" He chuckles some more. "Unh unh, doll. That's not how this works. I've already poured my damn heart out to you. You're mine. Probably from the first dance we shared back at Liam and Coral's wedding. I love you and I damn sure know you love me." His grin widens. "This ring just makes it official to outsiders, but you're already mine, especially after the shit you put me through yesterday." He frowns, his hands coming around to clasp both sides of my ass in his firm grip. He pushes down my shorts to touch the skin on my ass. I have to keep from moaning when he begins massaging my butt, relieving any lingering soreness.

My heart rate quickens, but I try to ignore it. "So I don't get that whole getting down on one knee thing?" I try to frown to hide the smile threatening to erupt on my face.

"As I recall I had you on your knees last night." He looks pensive as if trying to remember.

I lower my head into his chest, grinning.

"I'll leave the date and location up to you. The honeymoon will be my secret, though," he says as if it's a foregone conclusion.

I hold out my hand, displaying my gorgeous ring.

"Doll, the ring is pretty and all but I'd rather you focus on what I'm trying to do right now."

At that moment, I feel him sliding my shorts all the way down my legs.

"Sit on me." His voice causes goose bumps to rise up on my skin. "Take that damn shirt off. I don't want you wearing anything but my ring."

I do as instructed, tossing my T-shirt to the side. I raise my hips to slowly lower myself onto his stiff cock. "Mmmm," I moan as Jeremy raises his hips to meet mine. Head thrown back in pure pleasure, I shout out "I love you too. Yesss!" agreeing to be his wife, although the question wasn't asked.

My fiancé pulls me down, crushing my lips to his. "Damn right!" he grunts and we fall into a wonderful rhythm, getting lost in one another.

EPILOGUE

Six Months Later

"Crawl to me," he orders, his voice deep, full of love, and demanding.

I bend over on all fours and crawl to my husband at the other side of our cabin suite. We arrived in Tucson earlier today for a five-day honeymoon. It'll be short, but Jeremy has promised we'll take a longer one once Trudy is out of school for the summer. Despite my current position, I smile, thinking about Trudy. It took days to locate her mother after what happened with Gary. As it turns out, she'd been arrested for possession of drugs. Since it was her third strike, she's going to be locked up for at least another fifteen years. I went to see her in the local country prison. She'd had the decency to ask if I wanted to take Trudy on to raise. Her mother explained that Trudy's father wanted no parts of her and there were no close relatives in the picture. Trudy's aunt who'd she spoken of before, turned out to be a family friend who had no interest in taking on another child. So, after consulting my fiancé I readily agreed to be Trudy's guardian. Jeremy and I had to break the news to Trudy. She appeared to be relieved. I've gotten to see a side of Jeremy that many don't see when he's with Trudy. He's comforting and so loving with her. We've already begun the adoption process. It should be finalized in the next few months.

In addition to getting Trudy settled, we'd been planning the wedding and redecorating Jeremy's home. Jeremy decided to move everything out of the playroom and set it up again in the hotel suite. Now, anytime we have playtime, we do it far away from the home Trudy sleeps in. At Jeremy's insistence, of course.

"Look at me, doll."

The seriousness in his tone catches my attention. My eyes rove up his long legs, bent as he sits in the plush leather chair. I stop just at his knees, sitting back on my heels.

"It's time we really make this official."

My eyebrows raise, questioningly. We just got married twenty-four hours ago. I'd say that's pretty damn official.

"This," he begins, grabbing my hand and kissing the white gold wedding band and engagement ring. "This is you becoming mine legally." When his lips part giving the most seductive smile I've ever seen, the seat of my silk negligee becomes soaked. "But this," he leans over pulling something out from behind him.

I gasp when I realize what it is. A leather collar with his initials made also of white gold hanging from it.

"It's so you know just how much you belong to me." He sits forward to wrap the collar around my neck. The fit is snug, but not too tight. "Perfect." His voice is hoarse.

"Thank you, sir," I say through a wobbly voice and a sheen of tears.

He nods. "Thank me properly."

I give him my most lascivious grin. "Yes, sir." I reach for the button of his pants. Reaching in, I grab his stiffness and lower my head and begin to show my husband and Dom just how grateful I am for my new gift and life.

THANK you for reading Tasha and Jeremy's story! I hope you enjoyed their journey to love.

If you're looking for more stories by Tiffany, keep in contact by subscribing to her Newsletter here.

CPSIA information can be obtained
at www.ICGtesting.com
Printed in the USA
BVHW010248240522
637868BV00023B/156